LIGHT WORKER

Anna DeBey

Dedicated to All Humans

Table of Contents

Chapter 1

'Can you believe this? They are calling us gods! Angels?! Even Saint Mary?! Jesus!? Can you believe this? Why don't they call us what we truly are - light workers?'

'I am sure they would have called us by our real names if they were on a conscious and spiritual level to understand who we are. They need time to evolve, as we did. Do you remember when we were considered lower beings? Do you remember what we used to call our brothers and sisters? How were we once afraid of them?'

'Oh, yes, I remember very well. But I am over these feelings now. I am happy to be where I am now. It took us a long time to reach this level, and now I would like to enjoy myself like you are doing at the moment. I hear the sound of gurgling water where you are.'

'Yes, I am exactly by my favourite creek. I will stay here for a while. Enjoy staying on Earth.'

'Oh, I will. They are so funny, like little children.'

Urruh continued to gaze at the running water, its crystal clear flow surrounded by grey stones and green moss. She loved sitting in this place, surrounded by the vivid colours of nature and listening to the voices of the universe. They were telling her stories that she liked to hear. The best music for the living soul. She was looking at drops falling from wet leaves, sparkling like a mirror on her pale face. This is the best holiday for her spirit. She likes this place, the presence, the spot, her life, her soul. This is her home. Somewhere in between reality and fantasy, in a dimension the human brain cannot comprehend, there existed her people, people of light— the Immaru nation. A place without time, negativity, worries; only joy, and happiness.

Urruh was satisfied with herself. She loved her friends who chose to visit Earth again, but she has decided not to go there anymore unless she was sent by her teachers. She reached a level where she could choose, make her own decisions, and create her own plans for the future. Even though she was in a higher position, she respected the decisions of her teachers in every way. However, as she reached the point where she could make decisions about her future plans, she needed time to finalise her last decision.

She was a creature of light, an all-knowing being, existing in the physical realm with a physical body at the highest level of her existence in an unearthly frequency. Time no longer existed for her. She passed all her universe exams. She learned all the secrets of the universe and all its laws, resisted all temptations, and found peace within her soul. All she possessed were love, logic, answers, and forgiveness. She enjoyed peace of mind, tranquillity of her soul, and harmony with her body. She has travelled to every corner of the universe that her soul could reach while her Immaru body patiently waited for her at home. She had been away from home for a long, long time, and now, when she wanted to enjoy the reality she chose, her teachers were asking her to make a decision. She understood that her teachers had been in her position in the past, and they didn't regret their decision. They said it was the most beautiful decision they had made, bringing her into their lives. But Urruh enjoyed her current status, and knowing what is expected from her and where this decision will take her, she hesitated to move forward. She will not be pressured by anyone, and she knows that it is something she has to accept sooner or later–but not yet, not now. The music of the nature she was listening to was so healing, lifting her into a higher dimension. Not now… not now...

'Teacher, do I really need to be at this gathering?'

'Yes, we need you there.'

'You all have everything you need to make decisions that will be best for us.'

'No, we don't have it, and you know that. Why are you always so restless when you have to come with us to gatherings?'

'Because the place is making me tired. I lose a lot of energy and struggle to keep my spirit up when I go there. And those creatures... Ah, those creatures are making me so tired.'

'Don't you feel love for them?'

'I do love them, but I also love my pets at home.'

'But those creatures, whatever you call them, are on our planet too. What makes them different there?'

'They are our guests; we tolerate them here. We accept all of their faults and bad manners here, and I accept them as they are. I accept them on their planets as well when they are there, but I don't feel the same when I move into their territory. I feel like someone will steal something from me.'

'You know that they are not thieves. They have chosen to live in a different way. To utilise talents, belongings, and physical bodies, they live in various ways, but they are still spiritual beings. In the end, we all end our circles at the same spot. Perhaps at a different time and in a different way.'

'I believe that time is what makes me feel insecure when thinking about them. And their bodies?! They use them. I don't like that at all.'

'Don't you love your body?'

'I love my body very much, and this is why I have a deep respect for it.'

'However, you don't use it. You know that we can accomplish so much more if we utilise it.'

'I can accomplish tasks without relying on my physical abilities. I can lift materials, I can build, I can travel, I can learn, I can teach, and I can protect myself and others. What else should I need a body for?'

'How about multiplication?'

'Teacher, I haven't made a decision yet.'

'You will not lose your spiritual level, only your hierarchical position. You will simply swap priorities and duties. We need more of you here. For a brief period, you achieved this status. You were very quick, and this is exactly what we need.'

'You will have me in the spiritual realm. You know that if you need me, I will always be by your side. I don't want to be caught in both worlds, and I don't like the physical world. It is very painful.'

'I brought you into our world and sent you to educate yourself across the universe. I was worried that you would have to face all your challenges, but I knew you would pass all your exams. After all, is there any other way than to take exams and go home? I knew that sooner or later, you would come back to us, to our home and be a part of us. I always knew you would go far and reach your true potential. You did this now. You are free. Don't you think it would be nice to share the light of your soul with others as well?'

'Teacher, not all creatures of the universe have the same kind of soul. They do not have the same understanding or the same needs.'

'No, dear. Not all creatures of the universe have the same standing point on the meaning of the soul.'

'I don't feel safe among them.'

'They will not steal anything from you.'

'They will drag me back to a lower level, teacher. This is what scares me the most.'

'If this is the case, if you are uncertain of your status level, I encourage you to challenge yourself. You have to come with us to this gathering. No negotiation.'

"Urruh, What have you done to yourself?" She screamed at herself silently. "Your teacher is your creator, but your teacher is also your judge and examiner. You should not have said that you feel fear. You have just condemned yourself to more physical misery."

Standing behind her teachers, alongside other adepts, in the Planetary Council of Solace amidst various species, Urruh kept her head down, burdened by the guilt of not keeping her deepest secret. As she tried to blend into the background among the other beings, she recognised someone who had been a part of her past life. Past life! What irony! She has to love all the struggles she had in her past life. Her teachers never gave her a chance to hate it. It was just an exam that she successfully passed. "Accept it! These beings, these lower creatures, have also been your teachers in your past life. They said, "Accept it" too." All the misery they gave her, she has to endure now. Countless obstacles and challenges, ups and downs, all to teach her how to make the right decisions. But it wasn't only for the decision's sake; it was the shaping of her soul. She didn't like that back then, and she doesn't like that now either. Was she a fraudulent adept? This thought crossed her mind. She looked around; this was not her thought. This is a message from someone in the crowd. She looked around and met someone's eyes. All of these beings had the same humanoid shape with different body variations, but they shared the same spiritual ability to communicate with each other on a mental level. Some of them could communicate using their bodies or their voices, while others relied on their mental abilities to produce voices. However, when they needed to communicate with all members of the Council, they utilised a shared communication ability.

"Fraudulent adept!" This thought came from someone in the crowd. Urruh was genderless while in the physical realm, looking more feminine in appearance. The being sending the message appeared more like a human man. In the language Urruh used to communicate on her planet, gender didn't exist because there was no physical concept of gender in their world. As she lived among all these planetary nations, races, beings, and creatures, she was aware of genders, reproduction, and the emotions of love and hate. She refused to think about that in her own world. She felt nothing but love for others, but this love was of a spiritual nature. She viewed physical love as animalistic, primitive, dirty, and an act of soulless beings with base desires. It was a part of her past, a life she was a part of. Something she wishes to forget. Since her uprising, she was afraid to interact with beings who could cause her descending. The thought that came into her mind caused exactly this. Was she so uncertain of her position and her worth that she was afraid of thoughts entering her mind?

"Fraudulent adept!" The message from this humanoid being came to her mind once more. This time, she felt his feelings: hate. She replied to this message.

'Why are you hating me? Did I hurt you in any way?'

'You cannot hurt me. Look at you, neither a man nor a woman. Maybe an androgynous woman? You have no ability to hurt me. You call superior to me. Look at you. A woman. How can a woman be superior to a man like me?'

'Why would you wish to hurt me? Why these hurtful thoughts toward me?'

'You call yourself superior to us. You call us lower beings, your pets. You set up rules for us. Tell us what is good and what is bad for us. You think you know everything. You always patronise us. Animals are better treated than we are treated because of you.'

'Do we really do this to you? And what harm could be done if we teach you to distinguish right from wrong?'

'We die because of you! We disappear because of you. Other nations are fighting with us because you incite them to give us a lecture. We constantly have wars with others because of you. They call us savages, primitives. Our worlds are developed, if not equally, then beyond theirs. We cannot exist because of you.'

'Perhaps you need time to learn, just as we do. Perhaps you need to struggle and face death in order to transcend and live as higher beings.'

'Why should your path be the only path? Why should your thoughts be our thoughts? Why should our ambitions align with yours? Why should your world become our world?'

'Because we carry the secret of the universe. We are the only beings who know the truth of existence.'

'You act as lords of the universe and existence.'

'Perhaps we are that.'

'No, you are not!'

'We are lightworkers and light teachers. We are carriers of all good and positive, love, care, and compassion. This is why we are called whites.'

'Anyone who is not on your side is considered bad. No gratitude that your importance comes from our side.'

'Our value is always appreciated and accepted. We don't need you to act on our behalf.'

'We don't need you to teach us how to live. Keep your ambitions away from us, our people, and our planet.'

'I am sorry, I do not have the authority to do that.'

'Are you aware of why you are here?'

'I accompany my leaders. They need our opinions to make their decisions. Not that they are unable to make decisions without consulting us, but this is how we govern our worlds - old and young working together.'

'This Council has convened to make a decision regarding our existence in the universe. And you don't know anything about us.'

'I know enough to have an opinion about your world. I have been following you long enough to know.'

'I know you, Urruh, too! If my world suffers because of you, you will also face your deepest fears.'

Shivers ran down her body. This feeling was forgotten for a long, long time. Her name was a secret, known only to her teachers. Her name was a mathematical mark on her being and following, on her body as well. It is a binary code that was given to her at the moment of her existence. It was as if her identity number was connected to this code name. In her world, she was simply called a friend. Only her closest companions knew her name. It was a right and a privilege to know all about her. Who is that creature that he knows so much about? He knew her name, so he knew all about her: her past, present, and future. But the creature disappeared from her site. It wasn't enough time to warn her teachers, as she had to act quickly. She established a connection with other fellow adepts of her world, asking to find the creature in the crowd. She gave them a mental picture. They trusted her and left the presence of the teachers. In the moment of their absence, the teachers were confused and made a decision on the Council that had a deep impact on the universal order. While the adepts, along with Urruh, were searching for a stranger, the teachers were unable to fully comprehend all the complexities of the universe on their own. They needed assistance from the adepts, but being alone, their decisions became confusing, vague, and incomplete. Trusting in them, the majority of Council members made the decision to eliminate the stranger's planet. The decision stunned everyone as this had never happened before. They understood what this means. So, Urruh stopped, too. The time started again, and she heard her heartbeat. "What have you done, Urruh?! The Council made a decision to destroy the entire planet! That is not possible! That is not possible!" - She ran back to her teachers. They looked at her, confused and scared, with questions in their eyes. "Where are the others? Why aren't you beside us? We needed you. We will also be punished."

The decision was made. The planet of the stranger should disappear from the universe, along with everything that belongs to that planet. All the weapons available on other planets will synchronise their shooting at the planet until it disappears. Urruh and her teachers have listened to the decision, which was made after receiving input from her teachers. All caused by Urruh. For the first time, she understood how deeply her actions had impacted the existence of other living creatures. Her nation is supposed to be above these creatures. They were supposed to balance the universe. They were supposed to counsel other beings on what should be done and how peace should be established. They were teachers of universal order. But they failed. They caused the opposite. They caused the destruction of the universe and the disappearance of other living beings. They had rights, but the universe had even more rights than they had. By causing the misery of others, they brought about their own self-destruction. Sooner or later, trust in these lightworkers and peace-bringers will fail, and all the rage will turn against them.

The entire group of lightworkers gathered peacefully in a separate room of the Planetary Council of Solace.

'What have we done? What happened? Are we not supposed to know everything? Are we not supposed to give directions to others that are good for the peace in the universe? Urruh, why did you disobey our orders? Why did you disappear? Didn't you know what you have to do?'

'I deeply regret everything I have caused. I am aware of everything. I take full responsibility for the situation.'

'This will not be of much assistance. Before we punish ourselves by disappearing from the universe, we need to work together and find a solution.'

'I was distracted from my mission. I deeply apologise and ask for your understanding in for not following our rules. I ask for mercy and forgiveness for my fellow adepts who trusted me. I know I am not worthy of my presence, and I accept the punishment.'

'Our nation needs you. If you punish yourself by disappearing from the universe, our planet and the universe will be weakened. I am afraid that our galaxy will also disappear. No planet will survive in this neighbourhood galaxy. I humbly ask for your assistance in speaking to the Council. I hope for their understanding and for them to withdraw their decision,' one of the Adepts spoke.

'Your idea could be promising, but we need to understand the level of commitment you have towards implementing the punishment.'

'I will accept any decision that you and the Council make regarding the withdrawal of their decision.'

'In this case, we will ask for a second hearing where you will be allowed to speak.'

The decision that the Council made was final; however, for some reason, they decided to listen to Urruh's speech. They didn't know her, but since the decision was very important, they wanted to hear every opinion on it. While speaking in front of every member, she looked at them, paying full attention, and explained what had caused her teachers' distraction. She couldn't help but feel unworthy of being present in that place. She felt like a naughty child, causing worries for her parents and giving childish explanations to these respected members, representatives of planets and nations. She was a soldier of her people, her nation, and her planet. She was a lightworker who ultimately did not succeed. She deeply regretted her actions and asked for the decision to be reconsidered. The council granted her wish. They asked her, in her opinion as an unworthy lightworker, what kind of decision she would make if she were in their place.

'If I could be a part of the Council tasked with making such a difficult decision, I would act as you would. However, as none of us is equal to the creator, and none of us is a creator, we do not have the right to act as if we were. Only the creator should make decisions about existence; the rest of us should obey. None of us, as not being a creator, should work against life and existence. We are not worthy to make decisions that could harm other living creatures, regardless of who they are, where they live, or what shape they take. As we are not life-bringers, we are not allowed to be life-destructors either. We should strive to live together, finding ways to communicate effectively and avoid conflicts. This Council has proven that communication among living creatures is possible. I understand that the creator has created duality in order to comprehend the purpose of our existence. I understand that living creatures bear all the fault for not understanding the balance of duality, and therefore, all the conflict among us is happening for this reason. Ruling each other comes from an inability to understand the duality law of the universe. It is not possible to rule over each other, as it is not possible to break the law of duality. However, by balancing this law, we can bring peace to all of us, our galaxy, and our universe. I cannot exist as a lightworker without darkness. Darkness cannot exist without light. All creatures in the universe carry the struggle of deciding who to lean on. All of us are drawn to the light, but we cannot truly appreciate it without experiencing the challenges of being in the dark. Whoever lives in darkness has to understand that only their decision can stop all the challenges they face in the dark, and the light will come. We cannot hate one person and love another. We must not oppose each other. This is not a universal law. Balancing is.'

'This is not enough to change our decision. We gave a lot of warnings to this nation. They ignored our warnings. They made decisions that had an impact on other nations solely for their own selfish benefit. They are a part of us, and therefore, they have to work with us for the benefit of the entire universe. If they jeopardise the existence of other nations and planets, we need to eliminate them. If individuals engage in constant conflicts with others, they are not deserving of existence.'

'They are intelligent and productive creatures who have managed to construct a flawless physical form in order to overcome the laws of nature on their planet. They have the right to exist in this universe. They are not perfect. But they will be in the future. If we take away this right now, we will be facing our own failures. Consider them pioneers in material engineering, explorers of new possibilities, and builders of universal theory who can put words into practice. They fight with others because they do not understand the importance of cooperation. As my actions led to your decision, I request that you punish me instead and give them an opportunity to improve themselves.'

'Considering that our decision is not for the benefit of the universe, our galaxy, planets, and nations, your wish is granted. We will give them another chance under the condition of if they accept our supervision. We will also request to be involved in their decisions related to interplanetary projects. Due to the confusion caused by you and your peers caused, we kindly request that your teachers make a decision regarding your future. We ask to be informed of their decision, but we will not interfere in the decision.'

The decision was made: adepts should be handed over to the ruling council of strangers as slaves, stripped of all hierarchical benefits, as unworthy creatures. They will be abandoned by their nation and forbidden from contacting, communicating, or being mentioned as members of their nations. Urruh was thinking, is this what happened to the "falling angels" in the stories she had heard while she was on Earth?

No, this is not possible. She should be eliminated. This is worse than she could have imagined. She hoped to transcend her physical body and exist in a spiritual realm, perhaps even becoming a teacher. However, the idea of being caught between two "wicked" worlds, this was a fear she couldn't shake. Her body was not solid and could change shapes. It was intangible and flexible, constantly in light. Even though she had a humanoid shape, her soul was the driving force behind it. She was a Breatharianist who didn't have human needs. Knowing all of that, she wondered what would happen in the future. Where will she be? Who is she going to be?

***

'Welcome to our planet! Welcome to our nation! Welcome to our world!' One of the councillors greeted her with respect. Despite circumstances, he was genuinely welcoming guests.

'I don't know how I should respond to your welcome. "I cannot say it is good to be here,"' Urruh responded.

'Even though we found you responsible for the Planetary Council of Solace's decision, I still have to thank you for their withdrawal of that decision. It is not what we had hoped for when we joined the Council, but we will obey their decision.'

'You will be monitored, as far as I understood. Isn't this something you didn't want to do?'

'It is better to be monitored than to be destroyed. Would you agree with this?'

'Yes, absolutely. I don't understand how you could push your agenda and make other leaders so furious. Are we not all in the same space?'

'Ah, I can't believe you don't understand. You have the incredible ability to understand everything and everyone in the universe. Or maybe you are just engaging in an unofficial conversation with us.'

'Yes, I absolutely understand. I apologise for using that phrase.'

'Since you are our guest, I am wondering how we can accommodate you. Do you have any specific wish?'

'How lovely does this word sound, guest... I am an abandoned guest, given to you as a slave. You can do whatever you wish with me.'

'Still, we cannot do anything we want. But even if we want to, we cannot. You feel no physical pain, and it is impossible to harm you in any way. Isn't it?'

'I have already been punished. Not being a part of my people, my entity, my planet, my home, that is a punishment.'

'Well, I completely understand your struggle. However, we don't need you here either. The only thing we can do is offer you up for auction. I believe we already have a buyer.' The councillor acknowledged the presence of the stranger.

She immediately knew what had happened and why it had happened. She knew her past, present, and what would happen in the future. What she didn't know was how this stranger was managing to evade her abilities. She was handed over to him and confined in a dark metal box without windows or light. The vehicle soon brought her to another place and placed her in a dark, pitch-black underground box. She lay on the floor. After a while, she tried to escape from that place. It wouldn't be her first time. Her body had the ability to pass through walls, and her soul could escape through cracks and holes. But leaving her body in an unknown place was not something she would do this time. She always left it at home, but this is not her home. She was unsuccessful. The material the box was made from is not something she can escape easily either. This planet, this world, has time. She must be patient and wait for the opportune moment to take action. There's not much to do in that box anyway. She can think. She can sing. So, this is what she did. After a long period of time, she became tired. Leaving her world always made her tired. She needed her creek, her waterfall, her forest, her sky. They had never experienced darkness in her world, and the colours of nature were so vibrant. She was fuelling her energy with high vibrations of colours and sounds of nature. Darkness had a negative impact on her. It made her tired, lethargic, and a bit sad. No matter how much she fought against these feelings, she had limits she couldn't surpass.

A small door above her head allowed limited light to illuminate her body. A sense of hope rose within her. Time is working in her favour. No, not again. They closed the door. She lay down on the floor again, struggling with herself. She was unable to die because she had an ethereal body, and her physical body was influenced by her spiritual abilities. They both have been weak and tired.

The door was opened again, and someone picked her up and brought her into a dark room. She felt the presence of a stranger.

'You are not so special after all. Look at you. You look like hell. Put a light in the darkness, and the darkness will dissipate. So weak... So weak... Pity.'

'But you are so strong now!? And happy when you see that you have defeated me.'

'This is just the beginning. You haven't experienced the real thing yet.'

'What have I done to make you hate me so much? Who are you?'

'Oh, the one who knows everything doesn't know my name?'

'I know your name, Arahdahl. I know it very well. How long are you going to hate me?'

'So you remembered me after all. You remember everything.'

'I don't remember everything, of course. But I will eventually re-member.'

'Good! So you will remember everything, including my promise to you as well.'

'We all had different journeys. You wanted something I couldn't give you.'

'Is it because of your ambition?'

'No, because of my fear.'

'So, you escaped from me.'

"I had my own path, so you should have yours too."

'Have I not been good to you?' Arrahdahl was furious.

'We are different species.'

'We have both been humans on Earth. We both had the same purpose. We were aware of our differences, but you let me down. You were supposed to come back with me. You decided to leave the Earth forever. Why? I lost you and could not find you until your ascent.'

'It was such a long time ago. Why haven't you moved on? You shouldn't have harboured that hatred.'

'You promised me that you would be with me in every life, in whatever form, no matter what. Do you remember that? Isn't this enough to exist? You promised me that we would rise together, that we would support and defend each other, and fight side by side... But you let me down.'

'That was a fleeting emotion. It should have disappeared from you by now. It disappeared from me a long time ago. I have had no feelings for you since we parted ways. It wasn't love; it was just a short-term need.'

'Yes, I know. You had a chance to find me. You knew where to find me amidst our lives. For you, it was only a game, an exam to pass.'

'There were many species and entities that I both loved and hated. No one deserved my sacrifice. I lived for a higher cause. I didn't want to waste my time. I would say I am sorry, but I am not. You have to realise your purpose in existence as well.'

'My time stopped after you. In every life, I was searching for you. Each time I found you, you escaped from me. Not this time. You will pay your price now.'

'I am a slave now. You can do whatever you want. I don't exist any more. I cannot feel pain or love for anyone.'

'Love is your essence. This is what you are made of. You will love me again.'

'It is not what you want. I love you and others for being who you are, but I struggle to differentiate you from others. I cannot feel physical or emotional love for you or anyone else. I am done with the material world.'

'No, you haven't paid for everything that was done to me.'

'You live in your own world, which is different from mine. You wanted something I didn't. I lived for a higher cause, while you desired earthly pleasures and power. I wanted to have power only over myself, but you wanted power over others. We were different. We still are.'

'I have to admit, it is true. I desired earthly pleasures and power. But it was you who had power over me, not the opposite. We made a promise to each other that we would take care of one another and stay together through every situation to achieve our goals. You left, but I stayed. You took a chance to become who you are now, while I remained in the material world, never straying from my true essence.'

'We are different species.'

'Liar!! You are just a liar!!' - His arm swung at Urruh's head, but it passed through her body. - 'I could have been in your place now, together with you!! I could have been a lightworker, too. But I am not. I am stuck on this level!!'

'We are different species. You have to understand this. We cannot serve the same cause.'

'Liar!! You are just a selfish coward and a traitor! You found a way to escape all the pain that I have been through. And I am still going through it. I couldn't let you complete the circle. It is not done yet. You cannot move forward without me!'

Before she could say or do anything, she found herself in a dark pit. Who knows how long she has been there? Her body and soul were growing weaker and weaker. She couldn't fight, think, move, or beg for mercy. Someone occasionally poured water into the pit. She felt cold. This was not a good sign for her. It meant that her body was deteriorating, becoming ill, and her soul was departing. She would be stuck between worlds, unable to move forward or return. She was whispering to herself while her body shook: "It is not over yet; fight; don't let him win; don't lose yourself; don't go back..."

The light came back once. Who knows how long it could've been? Arahdahl gave a command to his men to carry her out into the light. He was looking at her as she lay on the floor. She wasn't alright. This is not what he had in mind. He thought she was strong enough, but she wasn't. Her white aura vanished from her body. She looked like the weakest earthly human. She looked very unattractive, he stated. She is a lightworker, able to thrive only in the light. She is disappearing into darkness, but she will not become a worker of darkness. She is stubborn; she will not change her nature. This is not what he wanted. He wanted her to shine. He wanted her to be true to her nature. He wanted to crush her, but he also wanted her to live and be by his side. No one in his life made him feel as weak as she did, and no one could make him feel as powerful and strong as she did. No one ever made him as confused as she did. No one lifted him up as she did. No one cared for him as much as she did, but no one betrayed him like she did either. If he wasn't connected to her, if his soul, or at least what was left of it, didn't desire to be near her, he could have found peace and moved on. But he was stuck. He made many life circles over and over, repeating the same mistakes and failing to learn from them. He couldn't grasp what he was doing wrong, which resulted in him being punished repeatedly. While she was with him, she served as his guide and interpreter in life. He leaned on her, trusting that everything would be alright in the end and that they would be laughing when they finished the game. However, he was left alone. She escaped.

He lifted her in his arms and carried her to the crystal-clear water. He put her body in it and waited. The sun came out, and its rays illuminated her small body. But her white aura hadn't come yet. He was hoping for any colour, but no, nothing happened. He laid her down on the green grass, surrounded by flowers and beautiful bushes. In one hand, he held a pot, pouring fresh creek water on her face and body. He was touching her face with his hand. Her face had a dark complexion. He doesn't remember if she ever had such dark skin, even when they were living on Earth together. They were earthly companions in multiple lives, struggling to survive, to learn, to exist, and live. But then, she decided not to enter his life, leaving him all alone. They were soldiers: simple peasants, sometimes of the same gender, sometimes of different genders; sometimes siblings, sometimes partners. They were ordinary humans facing earthly challenges. Sometimes fortunate, sometimes unfortunate. Suddenly, she left him. His soul felt lonely. He was searching for her, making a lot of mistakes and making horrific decisions that, instead of moving him forward, pushed him back. While she was enjoying the end of her journey, he was still struggling to move. It took him twice as long as her to reach his current location, but then his people ordered him to stop imitating other species and return home. He could have been more. He could have given more to his people. Instead, he is nothing more than a materialised being. His soul hadn't evolved much since he left his planet. He was aware that he could not be equal to her, but he enjoyed her company. It was enjoyable to experience life on Earth. It was just a game. But when she left, the game was over, and everything became so serious. Selfish being!

The night was approaching, and the sun had set. He carried her in his arms and brought her inside his house. He was a highly-ranked military commander and didn't answer to many individuals above him. He possessed great power and the ability to make decisions that had a significant impact on his people. He had a wife and children. His wife was a virtuous individual, well-suited for his social status and position. She provided him with whatever he needed, but she was also aware of his hatred and obsession with Urruh. She was jealous of Urruh, but she knew that she shouldn't disobey her husband. She showed him respect and honoured him. He was not a soft-hearted person who would allow anyone to challenge him. Everyone respected him, including his family and children. They knew where they belonged and what limits were in front of them. He wouldn't hesitate to eliminate them from his life and from life in general. No, they didn't like that Urruh was on their planet and in their lives. As long as she was not in their home or sight, they tolerated the situation. They had to. Arahdahl also knew that it wasn't right to make his wife jealous or to make his children take sides. Even though they didn't need their parents any more, he knew that children would have their own opinions on his decision. He needed time and space to solve the issue, and despite his family knowing what was going on, they didn't make him regret his decision. They had to wait for him to finish what he started.

It took Urruh several days to open her eyes. Arahdahl carried her body to the water, which was the cleanest, shiniest, and bluest. He did this by himself. None of his men accompanied him. Even the high priests didn't participate in her revival. He stood by her side, gazing at her and reminiscing. For some reason, he was able to remember everything, but she had difficulties doing so.

'I can handle your hatred because I comprehend it, but I am perplexed by your current expression.' – said Urruh.

'I want to hate you, but I don't know how to keep hating you.'

'How about loving me?'

'I don't know how to love you. I love my wife, my children, my people, my life. I don't know what to do with you. You betrayed me.'

'You could have left me in the pit. My body would dissolve.'

'I don't want your body; I want your soul. If your soul were to leave your body, I would never be able to find you again. And we have an unsolved issue.'

'You can't take my soul, and you know that. Many have tried. No one understands that this is not something one can possess. You can take someone's mind, body, feelings, and thoughts, but their soul... that is not possible.'

'This is the only thing I want from you. I wanted to be like you. I wanted to be your soul.'

'Ah, Arahdahl... You have to conquer all universal laws to understand the meaning of the soul. You have a lot to learn.'

'Why don't you and your people share this knowledge with anyone in the universe? It would be helpful to prevent conflicts. You possess all the knowledge, yet you are selfish and refuse to teach us.'

'It is not possible to teach this knowledge to anyone. There is no language to describe all universal laws. There are no letters to write books about it. We are the knowledgeable. It is a secret within us that we must uncover.'

'You discovered it. Why couldn't the rest of us?'

'Because we are the chosen ones. We are chosen because we do not want to live in a materialistic world. We don't want to lead or have power over anyone, possess properties or other humans. We don't want to be superior to anyone, and we certainly do not want anyone to be above us. We cannot be leaders, nor do we want to be led.'

'We can't be equal because we are all unique. We all have different minds, needs, and thoughts. Some people are leaders, while others are led.'

'Do you remember that in one of our past lives, we discovered a case of gold? We wanted to take it with us, but we decided to leave it behind because it would slow us down on our way, and we needed to run very fast. Have you changed your mind now, after so many experiences?'

'I still think it was a mistake not to take it with us. It would have changed the course of our lives.'

'And I think our decision not to take it was a good one. And this is why I am here at this level while you are at that level. We argued for many years about this decision and how it could have changed our lives. I have had regrets many times for not listening to you, but now I think the decision was correct.'

'Was I always wrong in making decisions? Was I always so wrong, and you always right? Is this why you escaped? Would I slow you down if you stayed?'

'You have changed the course of your life. I didn't want to be anyone's teacher. You started being a teacher, remember. You have chosen a life that puts you in a position where you can either take someone's life or give them a life. People died because of you. Have you forgotten? I wanted to experience the power. I didn't like it. The difference between you and me is that you enjoyed having power over other souls, just like now, and you never had any regrets about the decisions that deeply impacted their evolution. I had no choice! It was a difficult decision to choose between my own life and the lives of others, but ultimately, I chose to prioritise my own. I didn't like it. It was painful to see how these humans abandoned the Earth. You stayed and enjoyed it. You wanted more power. From being a small dictator, you became a big one. You didn't choose the place, the time, or the aim... The most important thing for you was to learn how to become a leader. You cannot deny it!!'

...'We promised not to be teachers to each other, but we were. You started at first.'

'Yes, I have. It was the wrong decision. You expected me to produce an heir, but I was unable to fulfil that expectation. Someone else gave it to you. I felt abandoned and betrayed, so I decided to take my own life. You never noticed that I left your life.'

'I didn't know about it... That's true. I was fixated on my success.'

'But this was not the first time you betrayed me. I came back to you. It was you who ended my life by pushing me down the stairs. You hated me; you couldn't stand my soul. In my next life, I was near you and saw what you had become. A murderer, a criminal, a deceiver, a thief, a liar... I was ashamed of you. I didn't want to be near you. You have forgotten your purpose on Earth. You were the one who left me.'

'Where have you been? Why was our connection cut off?'

'Did I cut it off? I asked my teacher to cut our karmic connection. I moved to another species, on other planets. Earth was not the only school and playground in the universe.'

"I tried to find you amidst circles. I couldn't believe you left me. I kept telling myself she wouldn't do this to me. She will find me if I don't recognise her first. Every soul who came by, I trusted. I thought, 'This is her. She is my soulmate.' But no! I survived the hell on earth."

'Didn't you say that we promised not to be teachers to each other? That meant we wouldn't hurt each other. I wounded your pride; you harmed my body and soul. From being soulmates, we became enemies. Look at us now! You are still trying to hurt me because you are also hurt.'

'So now, am I being blamed for everything? No, you will not escape this time so easily. Everything we did wrong on Earth, we will make up now. If I have been a bad marriage partner, you will teach me how to be a good one? If I were a bad parent, you will teach me how to be a good one? If I were a bad leader, you will teach me how to be a good one? If I were a bad person, you will teach me how to be a good one?'

'No! This is something you have to learn on your own. I am done. I am at the end of my cycles.'

'No!? I know I cannot possess your soul, and I know you don't care about your body, but your future is mine. You can't negotiate. Whether you want to or not, you will become a Teacher!'

Urruh was a bit surprised to see Arahdahl by her side every day. His feelings have been confused, and his mood has been fluctuating from low to high. He was very clear with her. He told her everything he felt directly to her face. Sometimes, in his passionate attempt to hurt her and suppress his emotions, he would become physically abusive. However, as he swung his arm towards her, her body seemed to disperse and then reassemble. He knew about this, and he also knew that he could not physically harm her. But still, old habits remained.

He was resting his body on a marble bench with his eyes shut. Urruh didn't know if he was asleep or lost in his thoughts. He looked so peaceful in their home, which was made of flowers, various trees, bushes, and plants. There were many birds singing and artificial lamps to mimic Urruh's natural environment. Fountains made the sounds of running water, while the glass roof showcased the beauty of the sky.

'Arahdahl! Do you know why we exist?'

'No. Why?'

'Out of Universe selfishness.'

'Really? I thought we have to learn.'

'Every time I came back home to my Teacher, I asked the same question. And he always told me a story.'

'Do you miss him?'

'Yes, I do.'

'Can you be sad?'

'When I do not feel love, I experience emptiness. I suppose you could label it as sadness.'

'So, what did he tell you?'

'He was telling me the story of the universe. I don't know who made the Universe, but out of his boredom, he made galaxies. Then, he created planets. Planets, due to their nature and position, create days and nights. The time was measured. The universe was still bored and lonely. So one day, he made us, Light workers. He was still not amused. One day, he said, 'They are naked. I will give them bodies so I can see them.' So we got these bodies of light. He brought us to a planet where only light existed to see us. But he couldn't see us despite having bodies. So, the Universe decided to send us to the planet of night. We were shining there, and we were amusing the Universe for a while, but we couldn't survive for a long time. We were dying there. He got bored again, so he decided to create light and darkness, white and black, and scatter us across different planets. At first, Lightworkers lived on the planet of light, while Darkworkers lived on the planet of night. But the Universe was not amused; he couldn't see us, so it

swapped us. Lightworkers went to the planet of night, and dark workers went to the planet of light. None of us liked that. So both groups,
the light and dark workers, started escaping from one planet to another. We looked like fireflies, always jumping and escaping, trying
to make things right. Sometimes, we lost time and direction, so we got
lost. We were dying. The universe didn't like it when we were lost or
dead, so after a while, it got angry at us. We were no longer entertain-
ers. We were his troublemakers. He punished us by sending us from
one planet to another, asking us to create more colours. Both groups
had to work together on this project. So we went looking for the most
suitable planets. Light workers could thrive during the day, while dark
workers at night. So, the Universe made a compromise and brought
us to a planet where both night and day existed. Once we arrived on
that planet, we pondered how to create more colours. The Universe
has bestowed upon us intelligence, and we have had to cultivate our
creativity. We have discovered how to harness the resources of the
planet, including water and minerals, and have successfully cultivated
various plants. Light workers worked on the project during the day,
while night workers worked during the night. Our project was successful, and the result brought joy to the Universe, filling it with vibrant colours. We have managed to create a pleasant environment
where we could live in peace and harmony. We didn't escape any
more, we all were happy and the Universe was happy. Just as we settled down and started enjoying ourselves, both groups, the Universe
became unhappy once again. Maybe jealous of us, maybe bored again,
and maybe frightened because we didn't fear him. And maybe the Universe found that it can be amused by our fear. Who knows, but the
Universe has driven us away from that planet, urging us to put in more
effort, discover a suitable planet on our own, and create other entities

like ourselves. We had the knowledge now. We knew what we were looking for, and we did it again. As we created flora, we also needed to create fauna. We were struggling to make both of them sustainable. In order to make them larger, we established multiplication. We didn't know what that was, as we were made of light and darkness. The Universe made us, and together we created life. Unfortunately, we haven't been so successful in keeping life sustainable, so we have created life cycles, multiplication, and duality. We thought, "Now the Universe will be amused and happy." Colours are here, and new entities have arrived, but no, we still haven't managed to satisfy it. The Universe was mad at us. How can fauna survive solely through reproduction? It needed desire, and hunger, and fear. We experimented with various shapes. The Universe ordered us to put on the suits we had made, but we refused. In return, we breathed life into them and infused them with a bit of our soul. We refused to be confined in a disposable form. The Universe was angry with us. We were united and determined to tell our creator that we had enough of this game. No matter what we did, we couldn't satisfy the Universe. So, we refused to obey his orders. The Universe started to fear us as we gained power after disobeying his orders. We possessed intelligence, creativity, the ability to learn independently, and the desire to be united. So, the Universe had enough of us and ordered us to stay where we were. For a while, we enjoyed the freedom and our creativity, but our bodies couldn't sustain it for long. We couldn't go back home because we didn't have one, and we couldn't stay. We had to work with time and make it work for us. We experimented with different bodies and finally created a human body worthy of us. Again, to make the body and life sustainable, we created life cycles, reproduction, and duality. As both light and dark workers, have cooperated since the beginning of existence, we both have made a decision to share our lives together. And here, the fight between light and darkness begins. The ultimate goal of lightworkers was to await forgiveness from the Universe and the remission of punishment. While waiting, they were in humanoid bodies. However, the dark workers understood that bodies could bring them satisfaction and amusement, so they opposed the initial agreement. Not being able to maintain balance, the light workers started to destroy everything they had created. Dark workers went behind, mending what was destroyed, asking the Universe for attention. The Universe felt bad about the situation, so it made a decision: "Anyone who successfully passes all exams on Earth and is willing to return home can do so, but only after completing all the challenges of the Universe!"

'And so, the Universe got its own amusement! I always thought that the Universe has a wicked sense of humour.' Arahdahl was reflecting on his past lives.

Now that she lived in the present, Urruh asked herself, "Is this how my life is going to be?" She has been treated fairly by Arahdahl, but she felt trapped in his presence. She was unable to hate as she transformed her nature and suppressed it. No action on his part could make her suffer. Understanding this and questioning his actions towards her, he became less angry and violent. He still had this strong, leader's, almost dictatorial character. Being constantly in her presence and influenced by her silence, he started listening to other people. He always made the final decision, and no one could oppose it. His family hasn't been honoured by his presence, but they didn't dare to question him. They also didn't dare to visit Urruh. Understanding Urruh's ability, his wife, Tarah, sent a mental message to her, asking to be seen. At first, Urruh ignored these brief calls. Messages with intense emotions persisted as time went on. Tarah was desperate, sad, angry, confused, and almost tired of life.

'Arahdahl, I would like to visit your temple.'

'Is it time for you to do that?'

'Yes, it is. It is for you as well.'

'I am doing well now. I don't need words any more.'

'But you are tired. You need comfort now.'

'No, it is not me who needs comfort. Just go.'

Despite being the companion of a dark worker through her life cycles, she has never visited his home planet. In lonely moments, she visualised it based on Arahdahl's character, but she was actually surprised by what she was seeing. Asbu nation, equal to hers, was technologically developed. While her nation used laws of nature to synchronise their presence on their planet with nature, the Asbu nation used nature to conquer weaknesses of the atmosphere for their benefit. While the Immaru nation made their homes look imaginary, Asbu architecture looked intimidating and powerful. Immaru used mild and colourful shapes of buildings, but Asbu used sharp and dark colours to glorify their existence and presence. Looking at the faces of the Asbu people, she noticed similarities in their expressions; both of them had respect for each other and took care of the weak and powerless. She was surprised to notice that both nations cared for their people and respected each other. She would never have thought they hadn't been so different after all.

In the darkness of the temple, solitude was pleasant to the wounded soul. But this place was not a place of worship; it was a place of knowledge. Crystals kept as ornaments in their original shapes, spread across the building, were used for power supply but also for healing and meditation, in which a soul was brought to a state of acceptance, revealing the deepest secrets of the universe. Teachers of the nation, priests and priestesses sometimes gathered there to discuss the most important issues. Despite their differing opinions, the place absorbed their negative emotions and energy and transformed them into the purest, most positive, and cleanest thoughts. The sanctity of the temple emanated from an energy that radiated only goodness and positivity. There was no fear, love, or hate in the temple. It was all taken away the moment someone stepped inside. A soul took its original shape and stood naked in front of the universe. The shape of the temple was ancient, even though the technology surrounding it was unimaginative and inconceivable. It was surrounded by an invisible, energetic curtain that created a mirror effect, allowing only high priests and selected officers to enter. No ordinary people were allowed there. This place was not a place of religion, even though only the most spiritually inclined individuals were allowed to enter. It was not the place of education where the most educated could gain more knowledge. It was not the place for politics either, although sometimes politicians could enter. It was a place of wisdom and purity for those who were capable of imparting this wisdom to others. People who were allowed to enter were not chosen by anyone living but by the universe. People used to say that a temple is a place for the chosen one. And that was why it was worshipped.

Urruh's radiant aura made her look ethereal as she stepped inside the temple. Even though her physical body had the shape of a humanoid being, her figure was gloriously unrealistic. She could walk, fly, disappear, transpose, or change shape. But she loved to be "natural," to be seen as an equal, to have others look into her blue eyes, hear her melodic voice, and feel her gentle touch. She looked like a celestial bride, gliding in her ethereal white gown while her long, flowing hair trailed behind her. She forgot whether this is how she should be or if she has chosen to be. Her friends constantly changed their shape, but she learned not to mind their appearance. She recognised them only when their souls spoke to her.

Tarah was lost in Urruh´s thoughts and imagination, but Urruh had never encountered her soul. She was wondering if she could recognise her. She used to have the ability to recognise a person based on their appearance and then connect with their soul through their gaze. She lost this ability at this stage.

The interior of the temple was also pleasing to Urruh. She wondered if the people inside would mind her presence. They looked in her direction; they bowed down out of respect, but no words were spoken. They continued contemplating as before as if she wasn't present. They believed that this place was worthy of a sacred soul's presence, and everyone was welcome to be there. In the darkest corner of the hall, there was a mysterious silhouette watching her intently. Every living person would describe this individual as a tall, pleasant-looking, brown-skinned humanoid woman. She wore a light, long dress, showing her status as a priestess. These two have been looking at each other from a distance. No words have been spoken.

'I was wondering how you look. Thank you for coming to me.' Tarah approached Urruh first.

'Tarah!'

'I was always curious about you and your personality. I am confused now. I don't know what to think. I don't know how to feel.'

'I understand how you feel. I know what you will say to me. I also know what I will say to you. I came to pay tribute to you and to show my respect for you.'

'You killed my son... my pride... my family... my life... my future... I want to hate you... How can I hate you?'

'I will listen to you, and you will decide if it is worth hating.'

'How can a mother hate someone? I have brought a life into this world. Why is my heart not as full of love as yours? You never brought a life.'

'I am on a different path than you. We are different.'

'Yes, we are different. You take away life.'

'Tarah, you can blame me, but have you ever thought about how much responsibility you have for your own destiny?'

'I have only one fault: too much love. I loved my husband so much. I loved my son so much. And you took them away. He was always chasing after you. He was never with me. While I was waiting for him to come back home, he was with you. I was waiting and waiting for his love, his affection, his time, his attention.'

'Are you sure he was after me? Did you ever understand your husband and son?'

'I loved both of them. I was the happiest person on the planet when I had my son by my side. My husband spent some time with his son, and one day, he informed me that he had to leave. I was thinking that a man can leave his wife with a small child solely because of another woman. I realised that this was solely due to my shortcomings as a wife. I remained silent. I was hopping. Every time he came back, he had changed, for the worse. He didn't have time for me and his son. As soon as he came back home, he wanted to go back. I was alone, raising my son. One day, my son said, "I will go after him and find him." My husband came home and realised that our son had left. He was furious. He accused me of being incapable of raising a child. He went back to search for him, and when he found him, he brought him back to me. My son has undergone a complete transformation, and my husband was furious with me. He said I had disappointed him again. Our son also disappointed him. He left us again and told us not to search for him anymore. So, my son decided to leave us for good blaming himself for not being strong as his father was. He escaped from us forever.'

'Tarah, I heard you, and you left many words unsaid.'

'Yes... I have... it is too painful to think about it now...'

'It is much easier to blame someone else...'

'...I was also guilty... I told my son that if he were a daughter, he would be much more loved, and his father would stay with us...'

'So, he went to Earth, where unevolved humans lived, who messed with his mind, confused him, and changed his personality and his perception of good and bad. It was like sending a lamb into a pack of hyenas. He was not ready to leave home, and you know that. He had your blessing when he left. He lived the worst life he hadn't chosen. He wasn't prepared for the challenges. He was not strong. He didn't have a goal. He thought that when he went to Earth, he would remember his purpose, but he became lost. He lost his mental and spiritual compass.

'Yes, I blessed him...I thought he was the son of a great leader. He will be good, just like his father.'

'Usually, great leaders have dysfunctional families, only because they are too tired to spend time with them. They have no time to pass on their knowledge to their children and encourage them to be as good as they are. Great leaders need to have great assistance as well. Have you been there when you sent your son after him?'

'No, I haven't. I was blinded by jealousy. I asked him if you were a woman. He answered, neither a man nor a woman. And again, you have been both a woman and a man. I didn't understand what he said. I was trying to raise my child to embrace both masculine and feminine qualities.'

'I thought you knew that. But in case you have forgotten, souls do not have a gender. When we choose to be born into the physical world, we are tasked with selecting our gender, our family, the challenges we will face, and our ultimate goal. Sometimes, I was born as a man, sometimes as a woman. Arahdahl was saying this to you. But you gave your son permission to change his gender after he was already born. You disrupted his energy. He was born with negative energy, and you suggested that he change it into positive energy. He thought this is how it should be. "The universe has failed me, and I am a mistake of nature." You don't change energy once you are materialised; you endure and wait to be born again. If you are dissatisfied with your energy, simply wait for another life. In the meantime, live as the universe has instructed you. You cannot live as a woman carrying negative energy or as a man carrying positive energy. You are tampering with universal law, and the universe will eventually retaliate against you. This is what happened to your son.'

'I needed to lose him to this, obviously, even though I always knew the laws of the Universe. He took his own life. He broke the law again. He knew that. He has disgraced us. He was expelled from our society and asked never to return.'

'Again, as a High Priestess, you understand that death is not important to us. We're coming back until we finish our cycles.'

'Our son chose not to come back, at least not to our family. He blamed us. All he wanted was the love of his father.'

'No, Tarah. He wanted to make you happy. He was seeking your energy and authority. He wanted to be you! He didn't want his father. He wanted you, and you sent him after his father. You thought that if he found his father, his father would come back to you. You used your son to cope with your insecurities. You never understood that your husband's priority was his nation. This is why he was born. This is why he went on an experiential journey. This is why he came after me. Not because of me, but because he thought I would be a good companion in his studies. When I left him to evolve without me, after he had chosen his goal and gained experience, he was fighting with all of you. He was lonely, and you didn't support him at all; if you were, he would've forgiven me for leaving him. Would you be happy if you were him?'

'No, I wouldn't ...'

'You managed to be good partners after all. You had more children after your son left.'

'I became a priestess. I studied universal laws and laws of nature. I was not focused on pleasing him. I was happy when he came back, but I had my priorities straight.'

'Well, you see. This is obviously what he wanted. He wanted someone to be proud of, not someone who disappointed him.'

'How about you? Didn't you love him? Didn't you want to be with him?'

'Ah, Tarah... I never had a chance to be something different. He had more freedom of choice than I had. We are different species. I was given an order and expected to obey it. Whatever I wanted, I was denied. If I wanted to dance, I would have had both legs broken. If I wanted to sing, I would have lost my voice. If I had gone left, I would have been pushed to the right. Eventually, I stopped wishing. I was just a person who lived a life pretending to be free. They have sent me to travel from point A to point B and successfully overcome all the challenges along the way. All I know is what hell looks like... I have never loved anyone like you had. And I never felt loved. However, I have great love for all of you. Arahdahl is calling this "Loving My Pets". Honestly, I never had the feeling that he loved me as much as he loved you. He loves me as a companion, as a partner in battle, as someone who can guide him to his destination, as "pets love their owners"...'

'If you had the opportunity, would you love him? Or anyone else, like I love him unconditionally...'

'I don't think so. I am not made to experience these feelings. I have no freedom in this experience. I love spiritually and unconditionally, but not as different genders love each other.'

'And are you in harmony with this?'

'You see, both Arahdahl and I are soldiers. We obey orders. I would never challenge the wrath of the Universe, not because I am incapable or because I am exceptionally skilled, but because I have learned from past experiences that I will inevitably lose.'

'Urruh, I don't hate you and I don't blame you anymore. I understand that I am not on your level. I blamed you for a long time, but now I understand that I failed my exam. I hope my son will eventually forgive me and find his way back home to me. But if he decides not to come, I will forgive him, too.'

'Love is a weapon, my dear. The worst weapon the Universe has made. It works against us, but at the same time, it is the most sacred feeling we can experience. If we understand love, we will never hate. We will never bear the burden of hate. Duality is the universal law that we have to master. Both feelings bring us to the level we want to achieve. However, only love can bring us to the pedestal of soul evolution. Only love can bring us to the end of our circle. Arahdahl thought I was unable to love, only to hate. He challenged me while we lived on Earth. He wanted to see how much I would give of myself, and how much I would sacrifice in order to succeed in life. He still does not believe me when I say that I am incapable of feeling hate. It's not that I am unable to hate, but rather that I choose not to. It is a burden I no longer want to bear. It doesn't mean I will forgive and forget. No, I will remember this, but I will not be pulled down again. I will leave it to the Universe to avenge me if it comes to that.'

'Would you like me to speak to Arahdahl? I don't understand his obsession with you. He has to make a decision about you. He keeps you trapped like a bird in a cage.'

'He is unable to let go of the hate. Not only was he unfair to you, not only did he have to grow up without me, but I also believe he is aware that we need to go our separate ways. This is my final cycle, and I long to transcend. I am so tired that I cannot put it into words. He cannot say goodbye to me. This is what has shaped him into who he is.'

'Now, I understand this as well.'

Days turned into nights, and nights into days as time continued to pass for the inhabitants of the planet. Not for Urruh and Arahdahl. The time didn't go anywhere for them. Nothing changed for them. He had mood swings, not knowing the source. He was blaming one person for the actions of another and punishing someone else entirely. He was confused and could no longer understand himself. He understood that he was losing control over himself and that he had to change this quickly. He didn't want to be the cause of serious actions, and he needed a clear mind. He had to let Urruh go, but he couldn't. He wanted her for himself, even though he knew he could not keep her by his side forever. She didn't belong to anyone but the Universe. She was just a guest who had to leave. How can he say goodbye to her? She was his Teacher and Guide. He needed her. He was lost without her. He can't lose her again. He lived without her, and he survived. He lives with her now, and he is even more confused. He didn't need her like he needed his wife and children, his friends, his people. He needed her like he needed to breathe. He was completely broken. He knew what decision would bring in the course of time, but he prolonged that final moment.

'Arahdahl, is this how it's going to be for you?' - Urruh helped.

'How can I let you go? How can I say goodbye to you? Teach me how?'

'Easy. Just say, "go." Say goodbye!'

'And will you go?'

'Yes, I will go.'

'No regrets? No wishes to stay? No sorrow?'

'No, sorry. Not for me. I am looking forward to ascending.'

'You will not recognise me from that place.'

'I don't know. I hope I will.'

'No. What kept me all this time is the possibility that I will see you one day. And it happened. In the place where you wish to go, there are no longer any cycles. When I left one life, I knew I would see you again. I know it won't be the same this time.'

'You may not see me, but you might feel my presence. I will still be of energy. Not of light anymore, but you could still feel me.'

'Not good enough for me. I am not on your level. You cold-hearted creature!'

'So, what is your solution? You are falling apart.'

'I want to be at the same level once again.'

'Hah, you want me in the matter again. Why?'

'I need to stop hating you. I need to stop blaming you for my karma.'

'It's all about you, again.'

'No, not this time... I was chosen to become who I am today. It has been a great burden for me to lead people, and I believe I am failing. I am not happy with the results I see.'

'You have your consultants. Why do you have no faith in them?'

'None of them are on your level. I need to learn how to better myself. I need to be an enlightened leader.'

'I never had this ambition. This is something you've always wanted. I have no experience in this. I don't know how to teach you.'

'Maybe you don't have experience in teaching a leader, but your personality and character will help me steer myself in the right direction. I will go from there by myself.'

'Do I really owe you so much that I should compromise my future just for blame? You can find millions of people around you.'

'You are fearless. They are not. Your words always hit me in the head. I always come back to my senses. I know you think you have fear, and that it has prevented you from ascending, but you are wrong.'

'I had a fear. It disappeared since I am here with you.'

'What? How?'

'Obviously, you have been the cause of my fear or the source of my fear. But now I understand this, and it is all gone. An Adept should have all understandings and emotions under control. I am done now. I am ready to go now, if you excuse me.'

'So there is nothing that could keep you in matter or light?'

'No.'

'Do you just need an excuse from me so that you can go?'

'Yes.'

'No! No! No! I am not ready to let you go. I don't trust you.'

'How about this: a condition? I will go down for your sake. For the sake of your peace, not for the sake of my ascending. If you recognise me when I am down, you will have me. But I will not help you recognise me in any way. I won't make it easy for you to find me and to recognise me. You choose your life, your life bringers, your geographical area, and your goals. I will choose mine.'

'Should I believe you? What if you leave me in hell again?'

'It's your choice. I have enough time. I can wait.'

'How will you recognise me?'

'Come on, Arahdahl. Now you insult me. I am able to recognise every soul that has ever interacted with me in any of my lives. How can I not recognise you? You are the trouble of my existence.'

'So it is up to me to recognise you?'

'This is my condition. You have to figure out how to recognise me, and then you will have my help or you will forgive me and let me go.'

'If I do recognise you, how can I have you? In what shape? What am I allowed to do?'

'I will not come as a cat or a parrot. Don't worry. I will be a human as well. I promise I will be the opposite gender as well.'

'Oh, what a relief.'

'If you ever lay your hands on me again, I will make you pay for this. This is something to worry about! If you do something to me that I don't approve of, hell will seem like paradise to you. If you fail, remember that, your entire nation will fail. Remember that!"

Chapter 2

Maria was the first child of young parents. Born in a small village on the Bosnian Mountain Dinaric Alps in the early 1970s. Her parents were devout Roman Catholics, committed to the Catholic Church. Attending Sunday Mass was obligatory. Her mother met her father at school, and they continued to see each other while she attended church. They got married while still young and in love without fully understanding the complexities of life. Her mother was 18, and her father was 19. Her father had to fulfil his military service, which was a significant obligation for every man born in Yugoslavia. According to stories, many great loves ended during this period because women would find other men and marry them. They didn't want to be a couple who split up because of distance, so they decided to get married. Maria's mother lived with her parents in a small mountain village consisting of about ten old houses, while her father lived in a larger, more urban community. Maria's maternal grandparents made a living through livestock breeding and dairy production, while her paternal grandparents had the privilege of working in the industrial sector. The young couple faced opposition from the paternal grandmother, who wanted them to marry into a more well-off family. The young couple, being Catholic, had to have a church wedding. However, these marriages were not recognised by the law; only civil marriages were. Prior to the wedding, the couple sought permission from a local priest to grant the ceremony. However, the priest denied their request due to a request from Maria's paternal grandmother. Finally they decided to get married at the registry office as Maria was on her way. Her father soon went off to military service, leaving her mother to live with his parents. It was customary for a wife to live with her husband's family and serve them as if they were her own parents. Every decision in her life was made by the lady of the house, from leaving the house to dressing appropriately, interacting with neighbours, and even visiting her parents. Grandmother took control of mother´s fate, causing her to regret choosing her son as a husband. However, being a Bosnian woman meant enduring a great deal of injustice from all sides. After completing his service, Maria's father returned to his small family and did his best to live happily despite his mother's objections.

His father, Maria's grandfather, held the official title of the head of the family, but in reality, he was merely a puppet controlled by his wife and carried out her decisions. He believed that they couldn't survive without money, so he pressured his son to go abroad, using manipulation and threats at times. He had many acquaintances and friends who left their homes to work in Germany. They were referred to as "gastarbeiter" in the German language, primarily referring to the Yugoslavian labour force. Her father had no other option but to take a chance and try his luck. Before leaving, Maria's mother requested that he speak to the priest and have baby Maria baptised. Her grandmother was unable to refuse this time, not only because of her daughter-in-law but also due to the presence of the priest, church members, and villagers. The task was completed hastily, without any celebration, to allow her father to continue his journey.

The only means of communication during that time was through mail. Phoning used to be very expensive and was only used for urgent matters. The village lacked a post office, so anyone who needed to use a phone had to take a one-hour bus ride to the nearest town. People who lived in towns had the privilege of having phones at home. However, if they wanted to make international calls, they had to contact the international central office and provide them with the number. The central office would then call back once the line was established. People used to spend the whole day waiting for the call. The bill for international calls was always so large that they were only made in the event of a tragedy and the need for someone to attend the funeral within a couple of days. Maria's mother's ability to hear her husband's voice depended on her mother-in-law and her mood, making it uncertain until he returned home. He sent money to his family, but she never had the opportunity to see them. He continued to send letters, but once again, they were withheld from her. When her parents visited, she asked them for a favour - to give her some money so she could send a letter asking him to come and take her with him. The letter was sent to him, but instead of sending a letter to her, he chose to send another letter to his mother. Being angry at her for such disrespect, she beat her. Maria's mother became very angry with her and left home, taking the baby with her. Her parents disapproved of her actions and were afraid that the villagers would gossip and tarnish her reputation. They made the decision to secretly send her to her husband in Germany. Maria stayed with her grandparents in a mountain village.

When her mother finally located her husband, he was furious upon seeing her. She left his mother, who needed her care, and she spent unnecessary money that he thought was meant for his mother. However, since they were married, he was unable to send her away. He was staying at the company's hostel with other foreigners, actually wooden barracks, without having any privacy, but after his wife arrived, he had to spend a significant amount of money on rent. He worked in a factory but dreamed of a world full of possibilities, fuelling his ambition. He wanted to purchase the most expensive car available to create the impression of success when he returned to his village. Maria's mother loved the idea and wanted to dress up, too. She found a job as a janitor. She was unable to find any other work because she did not speak German at all and was illiterate. They were accustomed to a life of hardship and hard work, having grown up in a village. His mother was accustomed to his wealth and became concerned when she learned that her daughter-in-law was now involved with her son. She worried that she would no longer have access to his money. She sent letters requesting financial assistance for his father's medical expenses and their daughter's needs. Maria never received the money. When her mother discovered that the money they had been sending never reached her parents, where the baby was, she began arguing with her husband. Both were angry with each other, and their relationship ended very quickly.

After their divorce, Maria's father remarried a German woman within a year, whom she secretly met while still married. He quickly started a new family and had no interest in hearing about his daughter. Daughters in his primitive village have not been considered important and worthy of father's love. Her mother made every effort to pay her rent and send money to her parents for the baby. She soon met and married an older German man. He was aware that she had a baby, but he gave her a choice: she could either be with him and care for him or go and take care of her baby. He didn't want the baby to be near him or her, and she was not allowed to visit her parents or the baby. If she wanted to be with him, she had to give up on the idea of having an-other child. It is unclear what she was thinking, but she made the de-cision to abandon her child.

Maria's maternal grandparents learned about their child's decision through word of mouth from villagers, as her paternal grandparents shared the joyful news. They were illiterate, making it impossible to write a letter and explain what happened. They took the toddler and brought her to the doorstep of her paternal grandparents. She was their granddaughter, their own flesh and blood. However, they returned Maria to her maternal grandparents' doorstep in the dark.

'If you bring this worthless being at our home again, I swear to God, I will throw her to the wolves. She is a girl! Your worthless daughter couldn't give me a grandson like the new daughter-in-law, but she gave me this creature. What should I do with her?'

'She is also your blood! If you refuse to take her, I will report you to the priest.'

'I already told him that I am not taking her, and he responded with "fine".'

'I am unable to care for her. She needs a doctor, clothes, food, and medication. I live on the mountain, while you live in the village. She will die here.'

'So let her die then. You have been taking good care of your daughter, so make sure to take care of this as well. If you do not want to, then kill her.'

How could she harm an innocent child? She was the daughter of her daughter. How can she be so heartless? She can't do that. No one wants her. She can only keep her. She knew how cruel this woman in front of her could be. She had the option to surrender her to the state, where they would provide care for her. However, this would mean she would never have the chance to see her again. They may send her away or put her up for adoption. Her blond hair and rosy cheeks were adorable. She was a well-behaved infant. She didn't cry; she ate everything she was given; she stayed where she was left. She had a playful nature and enjoyed laughter. She enjoyed playing with lambs and their large guardian dog. Her grandmother ultimately chose to keep her.

The only baby in the village of ten old people was treated as a rare and special being. The village was huge some hundreds ago. It was almost a huge mountain town with wooden huts, but modern times didn't bring a road to the top of the mountain, making it hard for people to establish new lives and live from cattle breeding, so young people left. After the Second World War, the village slowly died with old people. For this reason, the little baby Maria was special to everyone and treated as if she belonged to each one of them. She was a new life, a new light and hope. If she was hungry, she could go to anyone and sit at their table. If she was tired, she could go to any bed. Her grandmother would go from house to house, asking neighbours where she was. She was safe wherever she went. Her grandfathers treated her no differently than if she were a boy. She was taught from the beginning to cut wood in the forest, mend their house, feed animals, and work diligently. Grandmothers used to teach her how to prepare food, make clothes, and knit woollen garments. She used to refer to them as her grandfathers and grandmothers, treating them as if they were her own family.

Her grandmother, being the youngest in the village, would go to the town every two weeks to sell dairy products on the open market. Maria was at her company. Lacking a road, both of them had to walk across dense forests, facing wild animals and dangerous mountain roads, while they had wrapped dairy in a woollen scarf. It was a woman's job to carry a heavy load on their back and sell it, as men had to stay at home carrying livestock. Her grandmother hoped that if she could be seen by another grandmother, maybe she would receive some assistance. But she couldn't thaw her icy heart. Eventually, she thought, at least, she would be used on people other than her old villagers. She would adapt to modern life despite living in a place that resembled medieval times. Their house was made of wood and had a stone plate roof. They had two rooms: one for living and one for storing their clothes and linens. In the middle, there was a kitchen cupboard. The floor was made of mud to provide insulation and was covered with a thick carpet. They always wore gumboots, as they were the most useful footwear most of the time. During the summer, they wore rubber peasant shoes with thick woollen socks. They had a garden for growing food and a large orchard. The stables were located separately from the house but in close proximity for easy maintenance. The only problem was water. The village fountain was located a distance away from the houses, requiring residents to regularly fill their tanks. Maria had the responsibility of taking care of this duty. As she couldn't carry enough water for everyone, she resorted to pushing a construction cart. They also had donkeys, but because she was very small, the villagers didn't want her to be near the larger animals. They were used to transport water to other animals.

She grew up rapidly, like a mushroom after the rain, and soon, it was time for her to start school. It was not uncommon for children from neighbouring mountain villages to walk one hour to school. Maria was the only one in her village, while the rest of them went together. Her grandmother once again asked her paternal grandmother to take her home so she wouldn't have to walk through the woods and encounter wild animals on her way. But the cold woman said again "no". They stopped asking and had to accompany her to school. Early in the morning, she held a warm loaf of freshly baked bread with white cheese in one hand and her grandfather's hand in the other, with a heavy school bag on her shoulders. Children of other neighbouring villages were waiting for her halfway down, accompanied her to school. Someone from the village waited to escort her home on her way back. She enjoyed attending school, not primarily for the purpose of learning but rather for the opportunity to interact with other children. Her school was a small, single-story building with four rooms made of stone plates. The structure was slightly raised above ground level to prevent moisture from the bare ground. The coal furnace had emitted a strong odour similar to a locomotive, but it failed to effectively heat the room. Windows had broken glasses, making the room even colder. Children were shivering in the frigid room but didn't care so much as long they were respected by their friends and teachers. Despite the teachers' efforts to make the room cosier, the school couldn't afford to improve the quality of the building. This building served as her window to the world for eight years, simultaneously imprisoning her desires and serving as a playground for her friends. She walked past her grandparents´ home without ever looking back in their direction. They were strangers to her. As she was growing up, she frequently saw a beautiful foreign car parked in front of their house. Their house became increasingly beautiful and eventually became the most beautiful house in the village. Eventually, she witnessed two children conversing in a foreign language and engaging in play to-gether. They were dressed nicely and appeared to be looking down on others. Parents and grandparents were constantly yelling at them, urging them to be cautious and mindful of their clothing and footwear.

'Oh, hello! Have you come home to visit your parents? Nice. Nice. You are a good son. How are you?' Her grandmother nudged Maria towards a stranger in the churchyard. Maria was looking at this man who was smiling and proudly introducing his family to the villagers. He didn't expect to be approached by an old woman. He was some-what surprised and acted a little awkwardly. You could see that he wished to escape from this situation but noticed that other villagers were looking in his direction.

'Oh, hello, mother. How are you?'

'I am very well, son. I wish you had asked how your daughter Maria is.'

'I am sure she is fine. How can she not be fine when she has such a grandmother? How are you, little one?'

'You could have visited her sometimes. Or send her something occasionally.'

'Yes, yes. I am sending it to her by mail. Didn't you receive what I sent to you? Just a month ago, I have sent a big parcel to her.'

'No, son, I never received anything from you. Since her birth, I have been taking care of her.'

'Oh, I am so sorry. It must be the post office's fault. Probably someone was taking all the parcels I was sending to her. I was also sending her money. I don't believe you have never received anything that I have sent. Money? Never?'

'No, I haven't received anything you sent to Maria.'

'Oh, I have to speak to the mailman then. I will go to the post office in town tomorrow morning to inquire about the undelivered item I sent to her. Well, little one, here, I am giving you five German marks for chocolate.' - He put the money in her pocket. Maria took it from her pocket and threw it in his face. He picked it up from the ground and placed it in another pocket. 'Take it. It's for you.' But then she kicked him in the leg and threw the money at him again.

The priest realised that this was going to be a theatrical show, something that the villagers would talk about for the entire year. He approached them and signalled for them to return home. This was the only time Maria had looked her father in the face. Two children stood beside their mother, looking at her with disgust and disdain, not un-derstanding why she was being so disrespectful towards their father. They looked at her church dress. Her grandmother, despite being poor and struggling to provide her with a better life, gave her the best she could afford. Maria didn't ask for much and didn't care about her ap-pearance, just like the other children from the mountain and the vil-lagers who didn't look any better. Children in the town were different, so she knew where she belonged. These two children, despite being so small, already knew their place. Town children are coming to see muddy roads and villagers dressed in clothes they haven't seen on tel-evision or in magazines. They have already placed themselves in a higher social class only by their appearance. Maria looked at them and thought, "Well, if I have to have this man as a father, I would probably be an idiot like them. I don't miss anything."

Time was passing by quickly. Things were happening. The life cycle ended for some of the villagers. Their children and grandchildren used to come sometimes to visit them in their town clothes, arriving in nice cars on muddy mountain roads. Most of the time, these cars that haven't been made for mountains stayed down in the village. They looked funny carrying suitcases and bags up the mountain. They thought their parents and grandparents were lacking clothes and food, but what they truly missed were the familiar faces of their family members. When they were leaving, they carried their bags and suitcases filled with meat and food they had received from their parents. Maria used to play with these children, but she couldn't establish a connection with them. She didn't have any mutual interests with them. Obviously, they liked her as they always left her teenage stuff, magazines, school accessories, their clothes, and a promise that they would write to her. Letters came immediately after they left but stopped after the second one. These letters used to come to the school and intrigue other children. Each time she received it, they would ask, "Is this from your dad?" "Or Mum?" No, it was not for her; it was for her other grandparents. Eventually, as they died and were buried, these letters stopped coming to her. She was forgotten.

Life ended for her grandfather one day, too. She was eleven. He felt sick, went to his bed, and after a few hours, he fell asleep. He never opened his eyes again. It was snowing, and she was running through the snow-covered woods. Wild animals were observing her from a distance, noticing her silhouette with a lantern. She practically kidnapped the priest, thinking he could bring him back to life. However, by the time they returned after three hours of walking, he was already cold. There was nothing to do but pray for his soul. Villagers from the valley came in the morning to bring a coffin and exhume the grave. No one knew the reason why he died. No one cared to know, as it was all finished. The truth will not bring him back, they said. He died because of old age. Simple life, simple mind, simple solutions to every issue. Simple minds always accept life as it is.

As villagers were dying, Maria was the only person who could help the others survive. Still being a child at the beginning of her teenage years, she was considered a young woman. She had to confront her fears when she used to come back home from school alone or when she had to pass through the woods, especially in the pitch-dark morning. No one could accompany her to the meeting point, so she had to learn how to confront her fear when she looked into the eyes of wolves, bears, or wild boars. She used to carry a long stick as a weapon against them. She heard from others that animals will only attack her if they feel threatened or if they are protecting their young. It was her reality, so she had to face it.

As her grandfather was no longer alive and her grandmother was weaker, all the responsibilities fell on the young girl. She tried to learn and do school chores, but she was depending on daylight. While children of her age, somewhere in modern life, were going crazy for unimportant things, she had to study by candlelight during the night or wake up very early to catch up sunlight before her choirs. Most of the time, she was walking to school with her book in front of her eyes to prepare herself for classes. She had been running all day, trying to accomplish everything she needed to do. Not a single moment for herself except to go to church. Her grandmother was getting sicker every day. Maria asked the priest to speak to her grandmother and have her sent to the hospital in town. She obeyed, but when the doctor informed her that she was not eligible for free medical treatment and would have to pay for everything, she changed her mind and decided to stay at home. Medications were costly as well. The pressure she faced made her ask her teacher for an exemption from going to school. Her teacher, determined to bring her back to school, visited her in the mountains. She knew that all these children were involved in adult responsibilities and didn't have time to enjoy their childhood or teenage years, so she wasn't surprised to see Maria washing the clothes by hand outside in the cold.

'Maria, I would like to speak to your grandmother.'

'Teacher, she is not feeling well. I told you she is sick.'

'It doesn't matter. I want to speak to her and convince her to let you go back to school.'

'I don't keep her here, teacher. She could go. I will work as much as I can.'

'If she doesn't finish school, I will have to report you to Social Services. They may take legal action and compel Maria to attend school.'

'I know that teacher. But what can I do? I cannot force her to go.'

'Convince her to go for one more year. At least finish elementary school. This is a must in our country; you know that. At least she will be able to read and write.'

'Maria, your teacher is right. You have to go to school until you finish your education. You will not be able to continue your education, anyway.'

'How am I going to go when you are so sick? Who is going to take care of the animals, do the laundry, tend to the garden... and who will sell dairy in town?'

'I will speak to Social Services. They will provide you with financial assistance, which should be sufficient for you to stop working so much. You will be able to help your grandmother take care of her, of animals and still attend school,' the Teacher proposed.

'If this is the case and they are willing to help, I will go back to school.'

So, this is how Maria finally finished her elementary school. Immediately after leaving school, she was considered old enough to take care of herself at sixteen, both officially and unofficially. She increased her livestock, produced more dairy, worked in her garden, went into the forest for wood, took care of her grandmother, and buried the rest of her villagers. She was so busy that she didn't know what mourning, depression, or what life might look like for others. This was the only life she had, and she never had time to dream for a better life.

Healthy as dogwood and strong as a bull, villagers from the valley would say behind her back as they watched her during Sunday mass. Boys started looking at her, as did some of the older women, too. She would have been a good match for their foolish and lazy boys. Some of these women went to visit their grandmother and threw in a few words in conversation. Her grandmother understood that it was time for this talk.

'Maria, is there anyone in particular that you like in the village.'

'No, Grandma, I am never going to get married. Forget about this.'

'You will be old one day.'

'Whether married or unmarried, I will grow old regardless.'

'But you will have to start a family someday. Children... Grand-children...'

'Why?'

'This is how life is, my sweetheart. I had a child, my child had a child, and now my grandchild has to have her own child. This is how life is.'

'Is it written somewhere in the Bible that I have to get married? Or to have children?'

'No.'

'I will become a nun. That's it.'

'Don't be so cruel to me. Don't punish me like this. A nun?'

'I am telling you. Whether you like it or not, I will become a nun.'

***

If the water were not agitated... If people wouldn't swim in it... If they were smart enough to recognise the enemy in their ranks... If they minded their own business... If they understood who their true enemy was... If they knew how to escape drowning in this agitated water... Bosnia is rich in fast waters and abundant nature. God didn't spare any effort when He made this place on Earth. If this were true for people. They were dry powder, ready to explode at any moment. History re-peated itself again, and again, and again...

'Maria, quick! Leave the animals and come with me!' – shouted a neighbour from the village down in the valley while walking towards her in panic.

'What happened, Uncle Mustafa? Why should I go with you?'

'Stop talking! Quick, we don't have time!' - He forcefully grabbed her hand and began dragging her towards the valley. 'They will come after you. Walk!'

'No, uncle. If I have to come with you, at least let me take some money and pictures.' - She was going back.

'Oh, crazy girl! We will lose our heads because of her pictures.'

But she knew that this is the only priceless possession she has and she needed this more than her life. Pictures of her grandparents holding her in their arms. It was worth the risk. While her friend's father was chasing after her, they heard the first gunshot and the first bomb. It was in the opposite direction. She quickly took her treasure and opened the door to the stable so the animals could roam freely in the mountains. From far away, they could see smoke. A house was burning. They lost more than half an hour due to her decision. They knew that by the time they came back to the village, a disaster would happen. They stopped at a visible distance, far enough to be safe but near enough to hear gunshots, human voices, and the silhouettes of soldiers. Military trucks, tanks, cannons, and hordes of wild soldiers covered the roads and streets of the village. They could see that people were being shot on the streets. Voices could be heard coming from the houses. Pleading, negotiating, crying, and begging didn't help much. Maria looked in Mustafa's direction and subtly nodded, silently asking about the whereabouts of his family. He replied by lifting his shoulders and shaking his head. You could see his tears and his face. His son! His son was taken on the main street. Soldiers asked all young men to lie down on the road. It was over for him. Maria was screaming in her head, thinking that this was only a bad dream. It is not possible! Not Sinan! Not him! He was a good boy who always helped her. Not him. In that moment, they heard branches breaking behind them. They froze. They have been discovered... An older man, two young girls and an older woman in Muslim clothing signalled with their hands to come down as they lay on the ground as well. They watched everything from the safety of the cliff until it got dark. Soldiers took young men with them on the military bus and left. Young girls, all of whom Maria knew, were raped on the street and then slaughtered. She noticed smoke coming from the direction of her paternal grandparents' house and glanced at her friends. They understood what she was asking and signalled their agreement by shaking their heads.

The houses were still smouldering, but there was no sign of any living beings nearby. It was pitch dark. Military action took the entire day, and now the tired soldiers went to sleep in the safety of their barracks. Some drunk and drugged ones were left behind to watch out for dead bodies. Not knowing what they were doing, they started playing with them. Eventually, they were tired as well. The old man among the women gave them a signal to crawl back as silently as possible and return to the mountain. Maria was thinking, if she didn't go back to take her photos, would she become one of the victims down there?

Under cover of pitch darkness, with heightened senses and familiar with the woods, they walked cautiously towards the location where Mustafa believed they would find safety. The old man Milan, being of a nation the soldiers in the village were shooting, whispered that he would go back home to help bury victims and find someone to help them get into safety. He agreed that the best idea was to go to the village Uncle Mustafa mentioned. He heard that people are going there, so maybe they will be safe there too. However, as it was dark, they were scared to leave Milan and go back to their village, but as he promised that he would wait for the morning, hiding in bushes, the group had to make a decision to move on. They didn't feel hunger or coldness; adrenaline was helping them move quickly and silently. They approached a village in the early dawn while a beautiful sun was rising, but they heard the same. Military trucks, gunshots, human voices, smoke, pleading, begging, screaming... The voices were getting closer to the women hiding among the trees and bushes. It was early autumn, and the leaves were falling. The colour of nature helped them blend in with the leaves as soldiers approached with captives. They practically stopped in front of them. Young men, all in their prime up to their early thirties, stood with their hands behind their backs, on the ground, waiting for their final destination. Maria was looking at them. Her mind was screaming, "Get up! Fight! Do something! Don't wait! Get up! Get up! Fight with your legs! If you have to die, at least die fighting." But no, they waited for the long knife under their neck. Only one of them didn't make it easy for them. He was apparently a martial arts fighter, and he gave a hard time to six soldiers who tried to kill him in cold blood. He had free legs and managed to break the legs of two soldiers, but the other four shot him dead. While he was fighting for his life, ten other men were watching and waiting for their turn. They didn't try to fight or run away; they just waited. Maria was thinking, "What is wrong with you, idiots?" Angry that two of their comrades were injured, nine of the captives were shot.

But the last one, he paid the price of the other twenty. In front of the women's eyes, he was butchered into pieces. His voice, ah, his voice…Maria was thinking:" Every time I had to slaughter an animal, I never let them suffer. I did this quickly so that the animal wouldn't suffer. But these people, they are not humans. They were devils.

Hiding in the woods, feeling hungry, cold, and demoralised, they finally reached their destination. At least, this is what they thought it was. Then they moved to another place, and another, and another. They haven't been alone. Their group grew larger, gathering refugees from the mountains and forests. How many bodies did they see on their way? How many screams, executions, rapes, and destruction did they witness? They thought it was all over when they finally reached their destination, a big town comparing to their villages. Many people gathered in the town, all tired, demoralized and secretly wishing for their destiny no matter how would look like. They were looking at uniforms and commanders that made them afraid with hope that they will show some mercy on them. Among them, Blue Helmets were ne-gotiating the destiny of unfortunate people. Buses came, and people got on. No one asked where the buses were going. Civilians formed a line and boarded the buses. Maria was stopped.

'Where are you going with them?'

'What do you mean?'

'They are dirty traitors. You are a Christian,' – a soldier was look-ing at her cross around her neck.

'We are from the same village.'

'You shouldn't be with them. If you go with them, you will not survive.'

'It will be God's will.'

'Put them on that bus. But the man cannot go with them. You! Escort him to the other bus.' - the soldier grabbed her chain breaking it harshly and re-directed her to other bus where all the men were waiting in line.

Maria turned her head and saw familiar eyes. On her side stood a foreign soldier carrying insignia of Switzerland and the Vatican on his uniform. He was a tall, strong, and respectable man, with his arms crossed behind his back, monitoring the situation. There was no sentimental connection, just a recognition. But in that moment, Maria felt a spark - not love, but a jolt in her body. She was a bit confused. She looked at him again and noticed that he was also looking at her. She was pushed onto the bus by other men eager to get in as they were heading towards freedom. The only thing on her mind was, "where did I see him, where do I know him from".

But freedom came nearly half a year later...until one day, she crossed the border with Croatian flags and reached the free zone. She was feeling physically tired and hungry, but she was relieved because she didn't have anyone to worry about. A few months before she left home, her grandmother died. She knew what would happen, so she left. She was battling her illness, which went untreated due to a lack of money, so she passed away naturally, in agony. She had been taking care of her for many days. The priest would come, and her friends would bring her medication. One of her fellow villagers from the valley, Milan, who was an orthodox Christian, paid for a doctor and a nurse to come and assist her. However, their arrival was too late. She was thinking. The only thing she could do while she was captured was to think. How beautiful neighbours she had. Three religions living in harmony, all taking care of each other. In the small village, there have been an Orthodox Church, a Roman Catholic Church, and a Mosque. All of them are brothers and sisters by blood. Strangers came and broke us apart. We let them do that. What could Milan do, anyway? Could he stand in front of the gun for us? Could he have saved us alone? He saved Mustafa and his family, but he couldn't save his son though. He ordered his family to flee with Maria. He wouldn't do as much as she would if she were in his place. Her neighbours were fighting despite being of the same blood. Her neighbours were the one who harmed others. Her neighbours were the one who helped each other at the same time. They were hating and loving, killing and re-viving, destroying and re-building. Who should she hate now? Who is the guilty one? Who should she trust? Was the nation and religion so important to abandon humanity? Were we all blind to realize how we were manipulated to harm each other so that all moral laws and human ethic was broken and ignored?

"I forgive all of you! I forgive you, but I will not forget. I will not stoop to your level! Not me. I will not allow anger to take my soul! Not me! Not me! I forgive all of you!" - This was the mantra Maria was silently shouting to her brain and soul.

Buses were coming and going to the place, sometimes worldwide known as the biggest fair in the world. The pride of international in-novation, worldwide business connection points, start-up technology showrooms, and the best and biggest world events have happened in the widely known fair, but during the war, this was the largest refugee centre. Women were brought by bus and were asked to stay in line and provide their identification to Red Cross volunteers. It was Maria's turn to provide her name and address, as well as her place of origin.

'Maria Novak.'

'Where are you from?'

'Does it matter?'

'We need to know who to contact to inform them that you are here and alive.'

'I have no one to contact. No parents, no grandparents, no villagers. The village was burned to the ground. I have no home. I have none.'

'Anyway, I need to know where you are from. We need it as evidence.'

'Oh, let her be Violeta. She is from my town. Just write down my address.' - A man who entered instructed his colleague.

'Come on, Boris, are all of them from your town? Where are you from, New York?'

'My town is even bigger than New York, trust me. You may have never seen it, but if you had, you would have believed me. Just give her the identification card and find a place for her.'

Maria sat on the mattress on the floor and covered herself with a blanket. She didn't shower for a couple of months. She didn't eat for a couple of days, and after she was given her food, she couldn't eat and she couldn't rest. She was all broken. She was given a box, and inside the box was everything she needed for that night. The hall was filling with women and children, all confused, all worried, all having lost their mental compass. You could hear the joy of reunion and the screams of disbelief. She left the mattress and the box on top of it and went outside. All she could hear was noise. The noise of people. The noise of buses coming in and out. The noise of cars passing nearby. She turned around and noticed that she was in a bustling metropolis. Wow. In a huge city! A couple of months ago, she lived on the mountain. She used to visit her village in the valley and the nearby town, but she never imagined that she would be going so far away. She was thinking about what the world looks like, but she knew it would always end in aimless wandering.

In a couple of days, she was moved to another place, which was more like a hostel. Huge fair halls have not been suitable for humans to live for a long time. She was given new clothes and some money. She was free to move around, but if she didn't want to miss meals, she had to come back at feeding time. She met other girls of her age. They had different things on their mind, so she couldn't be so attached to them. Humanitarian agencies were all the time around them. Doctors, politicians, soldiers, journalists with cameras, both domestic and foreign, all wanted to speak to the refugees. They were bombarded with information and questions. Most of them wanted to escape the hell they had endured. Questions they were bombarded with have been too much for them. They were hoping to immigrate to western countries like the United States, or Canada, or Australia, so some of them took the opportunity to collaborate with foreigners, hoping to achieve their goal. The one who had money bought bus tickets and went to other European countries asking for asylum without loosing their time begging for help. They didn't wait for regular processes. You could see people from the town blending with refugees, presenting themselves as refugees from Bosnia to get a status which could bring those sponsors from the United States or Canada. Some Bosnians, who had a lot of money went immediately to rent apartments, asked asylum from foreign embassies and bought a plane ticket to freedom. People with money had choices, people without, had time. Streets have been full of people running in all directions. Foreign military uniforms blended with domestic ones. You could see fully equipped domestic soldiers, with trombones fixed on their guns, travelling in trams alongside civilians. You could see young boys pretending to be heroes in night clubs, killing each other before heading to the frontline, activating grenades while drunk or shooting at their friends because they said the wrong word. You could see mercenaries from various European countries who came to hunt people without any regard for who they were, all for the sake of money. They paid fifty German marks to have someone killed. Recruiters waited on the bus and train station to bring them to the Military office so they could kill for fun. For fun!? A human life was worth fifty German marks to human hunters and human hunters' recruiters. This was not a moral issue and a secret to anyone. Foreign journalists were filming news about a new military action from the safety of the UN Headquarters. They didn't have to witness the action first-hand. There was no moral or ethic issue if their words harmed innocent people. The truth was revealed by refugees who had just arrived safely to freedom so their point of view was valuable for people who earned blood money. Everyone used everyone for money, but true victims were silent.

'Hi, Maria. Look at you! You are alive! I am so happy to see you again!' - Sofia, Mehmet's daughter, who had escaped with her, saw her across the road.

'Watch out! Watch out! This is not our village! Do not run!' - They were shouting at each other on opposite sides of the busy street.

'Ah, Sofia. I am so glad to see you. How are you? How is your family? Is your father and mother alright? Have you found your brother?'

'Ah, dear. I have so much to tell you. All of us are alive, thanks to God. My father was in a concentration camp. It was horrifying what he experienced. My brother was beaten every day and humiliated in every possible way. We were taken to a concentration camp. All of us were raped. They said they wanted to clean us. I got pregnant. I had an abortion yesterday. They were preventing us from getting an abortion, but I managed to find a doctor who empathised with our situation and performed the procedure. My brother was in the hospital for a couple of weeks, how hard he was tortured. My father thought he had been taken away by Croats and killed, but in reality, he was in the hospital on the Serbian side. The Red Cross found us and told us where he was. So, we are all together now. The Bosnian Embassy has rented a house, so now six to seven families are living in it. They are helping us go to Scandinavia. We will all go together. Will you come with us?'

'No, Sofia. I don't know what I would do there. I hope to return to my house.'

'You know, I didn't want to tell you back then, but I can do it now. Please forgive me. When soldiers came to our village, they first went to your grandparents' house. They were searching for gold and anything valuable. Your grandmother tried to stop them. She was shouting that this was not hers; that it all belonged to her son; that she couldn't give it away. One of them smashed her head with the gun. Your grandfather took a hidden gun from the house and pointed it at them, so they shot him dead. Then they went after your grandmother and slit her throat. When they took everything, including all the furniture and belongings from the rooms and kitchen, the house was burned down. I'm sorry, but I had to tell you this.'

'…I don't know what to say. It is horrible what happened to them…She was so selfish…But I didn't want her to end this way. At least my maternal grandparents passed away naturally. I am really sorry for what I heard...'

'Also, I have to tell you some more bad news... Your house has been bombarded and completely destroyed. Animals were also killed.'

'Why?'

'Well, the Croatian and Bosnian armies entered your village and started shooting from the higher ground overlooking the valley village. It was the right position for them, so the Serbian army returned back.'

'So, I don't have a house any more?'

'No, I am sorry. We are all now homeless. This is why I asked you to come along.'

'You go first. Settle down and I will visit you one day. I owe you my life, my dear. I can't thank you enough.'

'No, dear, we all owe our lives to Uncle Milan. I have sent the message to him via the Red Cross. I hope they will find him. I hope he is alive.'

'He has also lost his house. He and his family are also refugees.'

Maria was transferred to another place, a new building outside of the city. She had to share it with another girl who was waiting to go abroad. She loved the new place and the new village, but she was just discovering the city. She loved walking in the town and discovering new things. Those things that she didn't have in her world, like riding in a tram, watching television, using the toilet in her apartment, and having shops in every corner. Despite currently having a modern life, she understood she didn't miss much. Parks couldn't replace her beautiful green mountain; bottled water couldn't replace natural mountain fountain water; zoos couldn't replace her animals; house dogs couldn't be equal to her guardian dog, who could eat these little dogs in one bite. Her house was ancient, missing all the comforts of a modern house, but it was made by the hands of her ancestors. She belonged there. It was taken away from her. A hope. This is all she had, a hope that one day she will return and build everything from scratch.

Her grandmother used to say, "There is no interest in mourning. Continue living!" Maria was bored with sitting and doing nothing after a couple of weeks. She was thinking of finding a job. The only job she could do was cleaning. She found a job as a cleaner in a shop, then in a building, then in a factory, and so on. Most of the time, she wasn't paid, despite she was promised. Sometimes, she was paid, but not as she was told. Sometimes, she was thrown out of the company when she asked for her money. She had to pay for the bus ticket from her own pocket, but when she wasn't paid, she had to walk. From one job to another, from one company to another, she finally managed to find a job in a textile factory. This got it only because the owner was a Bosnian guy who became a director of the company practically over the night, from a receptionist position to the owner of a huge plant. He belonged to a certain group of people who "helped" him to establish his empire in a short time. She didn't care that he had hidden abilities, but she cared if she would be paid. Despite his background he decided to be honest employer. Each month, on a regular basis, she was paid enough to pay her rent and buy some food. Good enough for her. She didn't ask for more; she was a modest person happy with small things. However, her job was dyeing fabric. Toxic fumes made her sick very quickly, so she decided to leave the company. She found another job in a private tailoring salon. She was working for twelve hours, six days per week. Work wasn't something she was afraid of but derogation and threat she will lose her job was very hard to endure.

'Oh, who do my eyes see? My country woman. Haven't you gone abroad?'

'Hello. Boris? Right?'

'I left a good impression as you remembered my name.'

'No, I didn't go. What makes you think I could've left?'

'Well, most people left. I left and came back. I can't live anywhere but here. I am from here, and I will not go anywhere.'

'I tried, but I was refused. I haven't been so persistent. I have family abroad and my friends left, but I will not go.'

'Why have you been refused? Where did you want to go?'

'I applied to Australia, the United States, and Canada. I tried for Switzerland as well. I was not accepted.'

'Why? Strange.'

'I am not educated. I don't speak their language. I didn't have money. I didn't have family there. So this is how it was.'

'What about Scandinavia? They would've accepted you?'

'They accept only Muslims, and I am Catholic.'

'Germany? Italy?'

'No, I don't want to go there. The whole Balkan is in Germany and Italy has its own issues.'

'Well, I am glad you decided to stay. I would be the only one from Bosnia here.'

'Come on. The whole of Bosnia immigrated to Croatia. Practically, there are no Croats in Croatia and Bosnians left in Bosnia.'

'They immigrated as well. You know, immigration is a very profitable business.'

'You could've gone abroad. Why did you stay?'

'I like being here. I was abroad, and sometimes I go "out," but I like to come back. Besides, the most beautiful girls are here. You see, if I wasn't here, I wouldn't have met you. I am a lucky, lucky person.'

'Really? I thought you had won the lottery.'

'Well, I have.'

Maria was thinking in front of the mirror about a conversation with the young man. He was tall, blond, with blue eyes. His face was always smiling, and this feature attracted women. While she was in the immigration centre, from time to time, she could've seen him. Girls were always around him, talking, smiling, and laughing. Why did he approach her? Young men from the valley village didn't dare approach her so openly. It took weeks, if not months, to look at her, nevertheless, to talk to her. She was thinking because she was not attractive. She had short, light brown hair. She looked almost like a boy. She was slim and rarely wore female clothes. She liked to look feminine, but the work didn't allow her to dress as a woman. She loved to have long hair as well, but it took her a lot of time to take care of it. She always looked practical in her appearance and that was her image that almost took her life away.

'Lilian, am I pretty?' - She asked her flatmate.

'Yes, my love, you are very beautiful. Look at these cheeks! They are so adorable. Look at this hair... so shiny, so healthy. Look at these breasts... Oh wow, where are they?'

'Come on… Am I attractive or not?'

'As a boy, watch out, girls. As a woman? You need some meat on these bones. Oh, you caught someone's eye. Tell me, tell me...'

'No, I was just thinking.'

'Oh, You like someone. Who is he? Where is he from? Who is his family? Is he beautiful? Tell me…'

'Well, someone approached me. Someone I met some months ago when I came here. You don't know him. I don't know him either. He just approached me. We talked. He drove me to the flat. Nothing serious.'

'Is that it? He drove you here, and nothing happened.'

'What do you expect?'

'A juicy story.'

'I am not a plum to give you a juicy story.' I just wondered: "am I attractive to anyone? Can I have a man's attention?"

'Well, with a little magic, you can draw anyone's attention. Let's start with your hands. My dear, your hands need a lot of work. They are all burned and scarred.'

'I work in a factory on a fume iron. These are working hands. The scars are from fighting with my Billy Goat. What should I do with them? I am using hand cream, but I can't change it.'

'Billy Goat? How did you fight with the animal?'

'Well, he never loved me, and I didn't love him either. He always chased me, so I had to have wood to beat him.'

'So, who won?'

'Oh, he always won. I was always in a ditch, in a fence, or in the hay. Once, he hit me so hard that my body rolled down the hilltop. He was a monster.'

'So these scars are from him?'

'Oh, not only from him, from a rooster, and from a donkey, too.'

'You fought with them, too?'

'No. They fought with me. I didn't fight with them.'

'How?'

'They were attacking me every time they saw me. Donkey always bit me when I fed him. I don't know why.'

'You are a peasant girl; how come you didn't know about animals?'

'Oh, I knew with them very well. All of them ended in a soup.'

'Donkey as well?'

'No, donkey, not in a soup. He is somewhere now, wandering in a mountain.'

'Ah, Maria. You are such a simple girl...'

If she could have stopped her heart from beating, made her brain think clearly, or visualised her future, she would have made the correct decision. But a woman's heart is so vulnerable to abuse, and her spirit is always naive, always wishing to find a saviour in a bad man. Simple minds, simple hearts, and simple desires are always attractive to complex, poisonous personalities. Maria stood as a blank canvas before a graffiti artist. She was far from being an unintelligent and mentally limited person. However, she was a woman. She was a woman eager for a man's attention. If she didn't have this need, she would've been able to live without an emotional scar. But how can she tell her heart not to feel, not to desire, not to wish... She knew all along that Boris was not meant for her, not for someone like her. But she dared to dream. Maybe... Maybe she was wrong. Maybe he found something in her that he needed, something other women couldn't give him. Maybe she was a unique person. Maybe he needed a pure, uncorrupted, simple person who was hard-working and honest. She could have looked beautiful with the help of the right outfit and makeup. She wouldn't have looked any different from any other model in a magazine. She had a nice, gentle face and an attractive body. Her personality was calm and steady, and she exhibited beautiful behaviour. Maybe he saw a potential in her, something she was not aware, but secretly she thought her quality is something he was after.

"Mother Maria," her flatmate used to call her. But this was not enough. Not for a man. Maybe only for Boris. But no other man showed any interest in her, and she was never approached by anyone showing interest in her. When she saw him standing in front of her door, her heart started pounding heavily. His smile melted her heart, and she was already prepared to go all the way, no matter what he asked of her. In the beginning, it was so simple - just hanging around and spending money in coffee shops. Then he introduced her to nightclubs and drinks. Then he spent money on her clothes. He gave her time, but with each passing moment, he desired more and more. She wasn't prepared for that. This is how she was made. Her father didn't have patience with her mother. She didn't want to make the same mistake. A ring on her finger, and then she will go all the way. She was giving him signals that this was the limit, but being a man, he obviously didn't understand. She pretended that she wasn't interested in him anymore, so he made excuses to be less with her. He called less frequently, rarely came to her door, and always seemed busy and tired. She knew, but she didn't want to acknowledge it; she didn't want to hear her own thoughts. She understood what her girlfriends were saying; the fight within herself, love and hate, but she made the choice not to be weak. She had been hearing from acquaintances that Boris was seeing other girls, and she trusted them. She said to herself, "It is all right. He can go with whoever he wants." She didn't understand the yo-yo effect within herself. He always came back to her. It took him a week or two to be with her, and then he was leaving. After a week or two, he returned to her. And she always took him back. She said to herself, "Maybe he will understand what the right thing to do is." This game of his lasted for about a year. Then, he proposed to her and married her in a small, intimate ceremony. No parents, no cousins, no family. Just a few friends standing in front of a priest in a small chapel. No celebration, no music, no gifts. It was a simple church ceremony, followed by a few drinks in a nearby pub. She had a ring on her finger. She had a Christian marriage, something her parents didn't have. She was somewhat happy because she got what she wanted. She was now an honourable woman with a man who desired her.

Soon after nothing much changed in Maria's life except that she was pregnant. She worked in the factory on a fume iron, ironing clothes and inhaling hazardous chemicals. She was paying her rent, taking care of her husband's needs, and giving her best. The war was still ongoing. She couldn't return to her home. She regularly met her new friends, but she was eager to see her friends from Valley Village. She heard that their priest was conducting a mass at a location two hours away on the border for his parishioners. She felt nostalgic as she saw familiar faces and hoped to hear about someone. She went without her husband's permission because he was never at home, and she couldn't reach him at work. He was apparently on the terrain the whole time. Being a humble person, she never doubted or questioned him. She knew where her place as a woman should be, and hoped he knew where his place as a husband was, too. She was not happy that he didn't bring his pay to her, but she knew that employers took advantage of people. They used to work for them as regular employees, but when it came to getting paid, it was a different story. They never had enough money to pay them. She thought, "What can we do? At least my employer is paying whatever he can." She paid their rent and bought food, and that was all they could afford. So, paying for a bus ticket and entering a zone where war was still ongoing, where a human life depended on the mood of a soldier from the opposing side, made Boris so furious that he raised his voice at her for the first time. She thought he was afraid that she might be in danger and, being pregnant, she might lose her baby. She stoically accepted the rebuke, remaining silent and feeling remorseful for making him angry. Apologising didn't help. He left the house as soon as he got in. So, she was alone again taking the blame that she didn't speak to him prior to her decision. She was feeling a remorse that she made him angry and he was angry because he cared for her and the child. No, this was not it.

Weeks turned into months, and soon, she became a mother to a little girl. She called her Lucy (Lucia). Lucia Tomić. She was the light of her life. She was her everything and made her the happiest person on the planet. However, due to chemicals in her body, Maria was unable to produce breast milk, resulting in additional expenses that she could not afford. Even though she was on maternity leave, she didn't receive enough financial support to survive. Her husband was not very happy about the child, and she understood that because she gave birth to a girl instead of a boy. She knew her men. They believed that girls were not worthy of existence, so they were not worthy of their father's attention either. She experienced it herself, so she knew that Boris had the same feelings. Boris was occasionally paying attention to his little girl, which left Maria feeling confused and unsure of what to think. Money was a major concern for them. They couldn't pay rent, and he couldn't provide for their livelihood. Their friends were helping with their babies' clothes and sharing food, but they didn't have any money either. As they had refugee status, they received food assistance from the church. Enough to live a modest life and count every bite. Sooner or later, her friends, one by one, left the country and went abroad. They were giving Maria and Boris advice on how to deal with immigration, but Boris didn't want to hear it. Maria didn't have a say. So eventually, all of their friends left, leaving Maria alone and helpless.

Lucy was constantly hungry, which caused her to cry day and night. Boris couldn't listen the crying, so he allegedly went to work. His clothes always smelled of cigarettes and alcohol. Maria used to ask him if he had a good time at work because he smelled like he had been at a nightclub. She always received a cold response, "Yes, it was fun." She couldn't bear to see her baby hungry, so she asked her neighbour if she could look after her baby while she went to clean a building on the other side of the city. A kind-hearted person had understanding, so she offered her help. Days after days, this neighbour helped her, but she gave her signals that Maria had to find another solution. In the good days, Boris used to help with the baby, and Maria was finally happy that she could provide a better life for them. Not having anything else on her mind but her baby, she came home after work one day. She entered her bedroom swiftly, grabbed her clothes, and departed just as quickly. Boris was with another girl in their bed. Shockingly, she discovered his cheating; silent in her disbelief, she left the room, and Boris ran after her into another room.

'Baby, this is not what it seems. Trust me; this is not like that at all.'

'All right, it's not.'

'Baby, trust me, this is not what it seems. This is not what you think it is.'

'How do you know what I think?'

'I know you think I cheat on you, but I don't. Trust me, this is not what it looks like.'

'What does it look like? Tell me, what did I just see right now.'

'She is just a friend. Trust me, it is nothing serious. We were just joking.'

'All right, it is nothing serious. It's not what I think. What else?'

'Look, baby, I know it's horrible that you saw that. Please, let's forget all about this.'

'Have you taken care of your child?'

'She is asleep. She didn't make any noise.'

Maria took her child in her arms and made a decision. She packed her clothes in a bag and left the house. It was warm on the bus. She didn't know where the bus was going. It was still daylight, but it would soon be dark. The bus driver reached the final stop and requested that she exit the bus. Lucy was crying, and the bus driver couldn't have any more patience. He didn't want to understand the mother's struggle. In one hand, Maria held her little baby, and in the other, she carried a bag. She was walking through an unfamiliar village. Some people were working in their gardens, some walking with their pets. She was thinking and feeling happy while she was on her mountain, taking care of her animals and grandparents, living a simple life.

'Your baby is crying a lot. Is the baby possibly sick?' - An old lady approached her from her garden over the fence. She had her hand on her hip, trying to alleviate her hip pain. She was limping. She had a scarf on her head and was wearing a woollen jumper. The thought crossed Maria's mind that she looked like her grandmother.

'She is just hungry.'

'Oh, dear. I heard that some mothers are unable to feed their babies. So sad. Have you tried using cow milk or goat milk? Some babies would drink this.'

'I can't afford to buy cow's milk, grandmother.'

'Oh, poor thing. Come to me. Please come. Let's feed the baby.' - She brought a glass of lukewarm milk to her.

'Try. Maybe she will take it.'

Lucy accepted the milk and calmed down. Outside was dark. Maria thanked and excused herself as she wanted to leave.

'There is no bus, my dear, until tomorrow morning. The last bus has left. Stay here with me tonight and leave tomorrow. What is your name? And, baby?'

'I am Maria. The baby is Lucia.'

'My mother's name was Maria, and I am Slava. What trouble has brought you here?'

'My husband.'

'Oh dear... What a pity... What a pity... So you don't have anyone to help you. No family? No friends?'

'No, mother, there is no one to help.'

'I have one cow, several chickens, two pigs, and a few ducks. Enough for me. I am alone here. I have neighbours, but they mind their own business. I have a small pension. I used to work as a cook in a school. I have been retired for a long time. My husband and I never had any children. He died a long time ago. I have health issues. I sometimes go to a doctor in the city, but they don't help. I will live as long as heaven allows. I work in the garden as much as I can. I had just finished my work when I saw you.'

'You live a simple life, mother. I wish I could.'

'Life in a city is never simple. There are a lot of bad people around. Are you a refugee? I feel so sad when I see all of that on television. Horrible. I was lucky. I lived in another time. People respected one another. We had work. We could take care of ourselves. Now, there are many people in need, unemployment is high, people are angry with each other, and criminals are causing destruction in the country. I guess you don't work?'

'No, Mother. I worked in a factory before the little one. I worked until last week of pregnancy, and then they sent me on maternity leave. I receive some money, but it is more symbolic than enough to sustain my living. I rent a place, and all of my money is spent paying the rent. My husband works but doesn't get any money. His employer earns a lot of money, but there is no law that can make him pay a salary. My husband went from one employer to another, and none of them paid him. One neighbour, who had children of her own, helped me with the baby, so I went to clean the corridors of buildings for a couple of hours every day. They paid me in cash. I was buying her special milk, but now she doesn't want it any more.'

'We can try it with cow's milk. My cow is very healthy. There was a sick boy in a house further down in a village. They had their cow, but he couldn't drink from it. His parents were buying the same milk that you were buying, but he didn't like it either. I suppose this milk is not suitable for them. So I gave him the milk from my cow, and he liked it. Stay for a couple of days with me, and if the baby likes the milk, come and take it with you.'

'Mother, I have nowhere to live. I left my husband. I cannot pay you for the milk.'

'Oh dear. This is a big evil. A big.'

'Mother, would you take care of my baby? I will find a job and pay you to take care of her. Would you please?' – Maria desperately begged the old lady while she shed heavy tears.

'Oh, dear. You seem very desperate. I have never had a baby. I had many brothers and sisters, all of them I raised, but I didn't have any of my own children. My husband and I couldn't have children. He wanted so much, but he was such a good soul that he didn't leave me because of it. He used to say, "Maybe it was my fault and not yours. I don't want to lose you. If we have one, I would be happy. But if we don't have any, this is our destiny." We wanted to adopt a child, but social workers told us that we could not because we were too old and our house was not good enough.'

'Mother, please, take my baby. I don't know what else to do. I beg you.'

'Dear, you can leave the baby with me, but please remember that this is your child. You are her mother, and she needs you. I can help you, but I don't know how long I will live. '

'I see mother. Plcase take my baby for a couple of weeks. I will find a job and give you some money. I will come regularly to visit her.'

'All right, dear. Leave her here. I will take care of her. You don't have to worry about her. I will take good care of her. You have to promise me that you will visit her as much as you can. Never forget that you are her mother.'

'I swear, Mother. I swear to God.'

She made a promise to this elderly lady, and she did her best to find work, a place to live, and to visit her regularly, as she was the light of her life. The baby was doing well. She gained weight, and started crawling. The old lady was very happy to have someone to live with, talk to, and occasionally have visitors. Maria always brought food and cloths for the baby and to the old lady gave her some money. As soon as she got paid, all the money disappeared. Maria was never hungrier than these days. She worked as hard as a slave to earn a living, and at the end she couldn't afford to buy food. She met her husband again, and he seemed unbothered that she had left their child with an unknown person. One day, she went to his employer and found out that he had left the job a long time ago. The employer ooked at her as if she were sick, as if she were mentally ill when she mentioned that he hadn't paid Boris his salary.

'I paid even more than he deserved. I paid him everything. I owe him something small, but he needs to come and pick it up himself instead of sending his wife. What a man!'

'So, you admit that you owe him?'

'Woman, he earned more at night than he deserved to be paid during the day. He earned more than I did by selling alcohol.'

'What do you mean he earned by nights more?'

'He was selling his girls to these foreigners? For big money. What? Don't tell me you didn't know that. The whole world knows about Big Boris. Whatever these foreigners needed, Boris was providing for them.'

'I don't believe that. You sick man. People work for you, and you don't pay them. And then you tell those stories. You sick man.'

'Am I sick? You are sick, you idiot. Every woman he has been with thought she was special to him, but he was selling them like a piece of meat. Do you know how many he brought me? You whore, stupid idiot. He is a pimp, a drug dealer, a criminal. He socialises with murderers, police officers, UN soldiers, and doctors who are involved in organ trafficking. He is involved in all bad, you stupid idiot. You don't know anything about your husband. What a freak.'

Just for a second, she blacked out. She grabbed the first bottle she could reach and smashed it against his window. She took another and another, throwing them in the man's direction. She didn't want to kill or harm him, but she wanted to punish him in some way. He grabbed her arm and threw her from the warehouse. Angry, embarrassed, hurt, and disappointed, she went to find her husband and confront him. She assumed that he was in a nightclub, the same place he used to take her out to. She was right; she found him there.

'You have been lying to me the whole time. I heard you are selling all these, what are you calling them, your friends!'

'This is a moment of truth, I guess, baby. Do you really want to hear the truth?'

'I want you to be a man and tell me.'

'You never wanted to see the real me. A real me! You thought I was a super human. I don't want to be a superhuman. I am a bad boy.'

'You gave me an indication you were a good person.'

'I am a good person. Can you say "I am not"? I married you. Is this what you wanted? Am I not a good man?'

'How can you work with prostitutes and criminals.?'

'Don't say that! They are not prostitutes. Not criminals, either.'

'Why are you doing that? Why?'

'Why? I made an offer after I saw there was a demand. If I didn't offer them to these idiots in uniform, someone else would have. I was hired to collect human hunters from bus stations and send them on to frontline. They were giving me money. They asked if they could hook up, and I introduced them to someone. Then another person came with the same demand. I just gave them what they wanted. Then, they wanted drugs. Here it is. They wanted children. No worries, I'll find you children. I don't care what they are doing with them. Whatever they asked, I gave it to them. They paid a good money, so why not?'

'You told me that you deliver drinks to coffee shops. I went to your employer.'

'What employer? He provided me with whatever I needed. Drugs, alcohol, paintings, gold…He got it from our soldiers who were robbing houses, and I sold it to UN officers. And yes, he owes me a lot of money.'

'Why did you marry me? Why did you bother?'

'Out of pity, my doll. I was trying to teach you how to please a man and to sell you to soldiers, but you were so into this church things that I felt pity for you. Do you know what priests do? Do you? Do you want to hear? No, of course, you don't want to hear. You think every man on earth is as good as you. Then I thought, "Let me give you what you want." The marriage is what you wanted, so here you are.'

'I was working as a slave, and you never paid rent, bought food, or provided for your daughter, even though you earned good money.'

'You wanted a man, so you paid for one. You wanted me, so you had to provide me with a good life. Not a life at all, but okay. I had a lot of fun with you. I hope you had fun with me as well.'

'You Satan. You don't ask for your child either.'

'It was your decision to have a baby. Do you know how many girls I have had my baby with? All of them got rid of it, but you wanted to keep it. So, you take care of it. I am not father material, after all. I live for my own pleasure, and if you don't like it, you can leave.'

'Why have a church wedding? What was its purpose? We could get married at the registrar's office.'

'So, I will be your only man. You cannot divorce me. You can't do anything, baby. Remember that. And yes, remember, I have a lot of friends in the police, in politics, wherever you want. Be as nice as you always were, and keep quiet. I know where your precious little light is.'

Maria's simple nature, mild and submissive character, and kind words usually made people trust her, although they would often laugh at her as well. She was telling the hard, raw truth, but perhaps in a simple and humorous manner, which made people laugh. This was something she used to attract people and avoid conflicts and arguments, but it also drew human vultures who thought she was stupid, primitive, and ignorant. No, she wasn't at all. She needed love like any other person on Earth. She knew that Boris was with her for reasons other than love, but she couldn't believe that someone from her own country could be so wicked and evil. Except for her paternal grandparents and her parents, no one on earth would deliberately harm her. She had accepted all the misery in her life, so she would accept this one, too. Being stoic, she continued to challenge her life and destiny.

While her baby was with a new grandmother, she could focus on surviving difficult jobs and being a burden to her acquaintances. She found a shared home, and being surrounded by many unfamiliar people, she felt more confident in modern life. No, she didn't think about going to pubs and nightclubs. She used every available moment and opportunity to visit her child. It was going well for a couple of months, and she was thinking that it would get even better soon. She will find a solution, and when her baby reaches school age, she will have her back. She never thought that her bad luck would continue so soon after grandmother Slava had a stroke, and social services placed her in a care home. After a couple of months, she passed away there, and suddenly, all of her cousins and nephews gathered to claim her property. She had a dilapidated, humid, two-room old house with a small bathroom, a small chicken house, a small stable for her old cow, and a small garden. She was not acknowledged by her family when she needed them, but when she died, tears suddenly appeared in their eyes. The baby she was taking care of was not of their blood, so she was chased away like a little puppy on the street.

For the first few days, little Lucy cried incessantly, pushing her mother away; she wanted her grandmother, Slava. Maria was going crazy with her flatmates. They didn't understand why the baby was so nervous and anxious, and they didn't want to understand. She wasn't theirs. They didn't give her much choice, so they asked the landlord to evict her from her room. Not nice to do this, heartless people. The mother took her baby and went to a female priory, asking for accommodation. They accommodated her for a couple of days but eventually asked her to leave as they were no longer able to assist her. She went to Caritas. She didn't find understanding in that place either, but they gave her the choice to leave her child with them. So she did.

She gave her child away again, thinking that since she was a Christian and this place belonged to a Christian Church, this place must be a place of God. It would be better to stay there than in a State orphanage. She heard all kinds of things, from children being forced into sex slavery with UN soldiers, to being sold into slavery around the world and eventually disappearing or being killed. No, Caritas Home was a better solution. They had compassionate hearts and would never do such a thing. The least of what she could imagine was when she was asked by nuns to give up her child. They interrogated her every time she visited Lucy. They seemed very polite and friendly, asking about her life, her struggles, the people she is with, the places she is visiting, her family, and her husband...

'Look, Maria, this is her only chance to survive! We cannot take care of her. She will be better off without you. Other people will take better care of her. You will bring her down. She will become a prostitute because of you. You are a fallen woman. A man didn't want you. He left you. He doesn't care about his child. We contacted him, and he told us to do whatever we wanted with the child. He doesn't care.'

'But I care. I am her mother.'

'Why are you then here if you care? Hm? Why?'

'I struggle to survive. But I will get a better-paid job, and once I get it, I will take her back.'

'When? Do you think you are a queen? You are illiterate. You are a cleaner. You will never have a salary that can cover all of your needs. Let her go. It is for her own good. You will have more children. You will forget about this one. Trust us. We will place Lucy in good hands. They are a God-fearing couple who want to adopt this child. We have already shown them, and they are now waiting for your signature. If you sign the papers today, she will be with them today.'

'But I will not see her anymore in my life. I can't let her go. I gave birth to her. I want to see her walk, laugh, and speak. I can't let her go. I will take care of her.'

'Maria, if you let this chance pass, you will regret it for life. These people are wealthy. They donated a large sum of money to Caritas. You cannot afford to have her. You cannot buy food or clothes or even have accommodation. You cannot educate her. No one will help you. You cannot handle all of this. You should've thought before she came to life.'

'What are you saying? That I am an immoral woman. I was married. I still am. I haven't been with my husband, actually with no one, before the marriage. How come I am the fallen woman?'

'Your husband doesn't want you any more. It must be for a reason. I spoke to him and he seemed to be a good Christian man. He suggested to give the child away as none of you can take care of her. He said, that you are mentally unstable and always give away your child. As a matter of fact, he already signed the papers. I just wanted to seek your approval for my clear conscience. It is a done deal.'

'But how can you do this? How can you be so cruel? Don't you think that I had no choice? I didn't give up on her. I still looked after her, but it was more convenient to be with an old lady than with me.'

'Do you see? You have already admitted that you gave her away because it was more convenient to do so. Anyway, it is a done deal. I was thinking of bringing Lucy to you, but now I have changed my mind. From tomorrow, you don't have to come here anymore because she will not be here.'

'But you can't do that!! I am her mother! I have certain rights. Lucy is my child! I want to see her!'

'No!! You are a bad Christian, a bad mother, and a fallen woman. Your husband gave you away.'

'You have no honour! You are taking my child without my permission! I am taking my child right now! Give her back to me!'

'No!! What you have to do now is leave this place without saying a single word. Like an honourable woman, which you are not.'

'No, I am not leaving! I want my child! Lucy!!! Lucy!!!'

'Sister, call the others! We need their help to chase away this beast!'

She was thrown onto the street, screaming and crying, and left in front of their door. Maria was devastated, uncontrollable, crying, and screaming, "Give my baby back." The door opened, and one of the nuns threw a bucket of cold water on her.

'Get lost from here, or I will call the police!'

'Call the police! Call! I want to tell them that you kidnapped my child!'

The police came, and without asking the nuns about the incident, she was taken to the police station. They didn't want to listen to her; they trusted honourable nuns. They didn't care. She was charged with disturbing public order and peace. She spent one week in prison, and then she was kicked out with a threat to leave nuns in peace. She was completely broken. She had no money, no friends, no family, and no one kind and caring to help her in these difficult moments. She didn't want to hate. No one. She didn't want to hate her husband, her flatmates, or nuns. She didn't want to carry this burden in her heart. She believed in God, and she believed that He would take care of her.

A solution to her misery came from the priest who had served in her valley village parish before the war. Now, as a refugee priest, he was serving his parish in a church on the state border. She asked her flatmates to lend her some money for a ticket to the church. The priest looked at her with pity after hearing what happened. He was partly responsible for her misery from the beginning, and seeing how his actions had affected her life and future made him reflect. He knew someone who owned a restaurant in Germany. Since she was from Bosnia, she had the necessary permission to stay and work there as a refugee. He promised to find information about Lucy while she was in Germany.

With these thoughts in her mind, hope in her heart, and a little money in her pocket that the priest gave her, believing that she would find someone who could rescue her from misery, she left Croatia by bus and headed to Munich. The restaurant was owned by a Bosnian family who left their home in the early 1960s. An old widow, with three adult daughters and one adult son, all of whom were married and had teenage children, regarded Maria as an intruder. The old woman didn't pretend to like her. Maria was of a lower social status compared to this elderly woman and her family. She spoke the German language; her children and grandchildren were Germans; they all owned big and luxurious Mercedes; they rented a large restaurant. Maria was no match compared to them. She didn't speak the language. She didn't wear German clothes. If she were good, she would have found a job in Croatia; this is what they were telling her from the beginning.

The restaurant where Maria worked was very big. The family worked hard, but they expected Maria to work even harder. She worked twenty hours a day, seven days a week. They didn't want her for these four hours, so they let her rest a bit despite they thought she didn't deserve it. She had a tough life on her mountain, but she never worked as hard anywhere else. They had another assistant from Cro- atia who worked for them from time to time, but for some reason she was better treated. As the village attracted tourists, the restaurant anticipated an increase in guests and workload. There was a German lady who worked as a waitress, and for some reason, this lady loved these two women. She used to ride a motorcycle to work. Maria and her colleague looked at her with admiration. She is a woman riding a bike. Wow! This symbolised female freedom. The German lady was a young, blonde, beautiful, sophisticated, very friendly, and intelligent lady. For the first time, Maria wished to be like someone else, sophisticated, free, and intelligent like her. Bit by bit, word by word, Maria was learning the German language with Ursula's help. They liked each other despite the language barrier, always laughed, making jokes, and helping each other. The family didn't like Maria engaging in conversation with the German waitress. They always screamed that she was wasting her time and not doing her job, washing dishes and cleaning floors. Words of belittlement, words of rage, words of making her feel guilty for everything made Maria even smaller, but every time she saw Ursula, hope warmed her heart. She was thinking in a time of solitude, a foreign lady, educated, funny, and loveable, accepted and respected her for being a kind human. She was treated kindly with respect by an unknown woman who didn't need to be kind to her while her own people treated her as she was unworthy human being.

When she arrived at the restaurant, she was promised that they would legalise her stay. She was told that she could request asylum. However, as this was not possible, the family lied to her, telling her that they had done it in her name and that she needed to be patient and wait. In the meantime, she was locked in the attic of the restaurant and was forbidden to leave the building. She needed air. Every time she approached the exit, the family would scream at her to go back inside, fearing that someone might spot her.

'So what if they see me? I know I am not attractive, but I don't think I will scare anyone... I think.'

'The whole village knows us. They don't know you. They are coming to the restaurant because they know us. They believe in us. If they think that someone else is working in this restaurant, they will stop coming here.'

'Will they think I'm going to poison them? I don't cook. You are a chef. I am only an assistant.'

'But they don't know that. They might think you are a chef.'

'Oh, my goodness. And this is why I can't go out and breathe?'

'Breathe in! And what do you want outside, after all? Are you looking for a man? What? Are you trying to find a German husband here?'

"Listen to her? Is there a man behind this door?!" - Maria was looking at them in disbelief.

'Yes, all the girls I brought from Croatia and Bosnia came here to find husbands. You need to understand that I brought you here to work for us, not to find a husband!'

"Oh, crazy family! Girls are coming to work in restaurants to look for husbands. Idiots!!"

'I heard that you are married after all and that your husband chased you away. Is this why you are looking for men? Don't you dare interfere in my son's marriage! I will kill you if I catch you talking to him. He will not leave his wife for you.'

"God, give me patience with these savages, primitive beings! I lived in a primitive village, but we weren't as primitive-minded as these idiots. Did Germany make them such lunatics? I came to Germany in search of a husband! Be patient! Be patient!"

She was patient. And obedient. And calm. She worked as much as they wanted, doing what they wanted and how they wanted. The restaurant was huge. It could easily accommodate two hundred guests. It was a huge, typical German old-style building that needed extra care and cleaning. It was too much for one person. One month has passed. Then, second. Then third. She didn't receive any money from them. She needed women's hygiene products, additional clothes, and sometimes even food. She was starving as they counted her every bite. They brought her everything she asked for, making a big fuss to let her know how expensive they were and that they would deduct the cost from her wages. But she didn't receive any wages. The last time they mentioned this, she unexpectedly replied, which they thought was disrespectful of her.

'She is asking for money! Imagine, she is asking for money! Ungrateful! She is such a poor worker. Lazy! We have to work for her. We need to remind her of what she needs to do, but she does everything wrong. Imagine! Last week, at midnight, I told her to finish cleaning the kitchen. She finished at four in the morning. What did she do until morning?! Lazy idiot! And then she slept. She woke up at seven. She had to get up at six. Stupid girl. She has probably never worked in her life. And she is asking for money. She has to pay us for her staying here. We feed her and provide her with accommodation. We pay for her. And she is asking for money now. What does she need money for? To go out.'

'Look, I am not being disrespectful, but we agreed that you would pay me for my work, as well as provide food and accommodation. I am locked as a slave. I work twenty hours a day because you only cook and serve. All the preparation I am doing.'

'No, no. We are also buying food.'

'But then, I am placing all the food in refrigerators and freezers. Do you think that one person can accomplish all of that in a short amount of time? Do you think that one person can work so much?'

'If you hurry, and do not talk so much, you will spend less time working and have time to sleep.'

'So, I have to work and sleep? Nothing else.'

'What else do you want?'

'I want to see the village where I am. I want to go for a walk.'

'When do you want to work?'

'I am also a Christian. You make me work on Sundays as well. While you all go to church, I have to prepare food for cooking.'

'We have to earn money. This is not Balkan. You have to work in Germany. Nothing will come from heaven. You have to participate as well. In order to earn money, you have to work.'

'What am I doing here other than working? Why can my colleagues go home? Why they can have a day off?'

'We are open seven days a week. I don't need them as much as I need you.'

'They receive payment for their work. Why don't I get any?'

'Ok! How much money do you want?'

'All you owe me. We agreed on seven hundred fifty per month plus food and accommodation. You owe me for three months, and you will give me two thousand two hundred fifty marks.'

'Look at her! She wants all of her money. Ok. I will give you money. - The old woman went into the bar and took money from her daughter's wallet.'

'Here is your money. You will get five hundred. We didn't earn more today.'

'But you owe me more. When will I get the rest?'

'When we earn money.'

"This is madness! I worked for three months, and now they are earning? What did they do for these three months? They worked for charity?!" – 'I will remind you tomorrow and every day after until I receive my money.'

'Your money? Nothing here is yours, you bitch!'

'You are being disrespectful as a Christian.' "Calling me a bitch! These people are primitive idiots. When I get all my money, I am out of here."

Every day, she asked for money. Sometimes, she received spare change in small bills, while other times, it was thrown in her face. On occasion, she was denied with screaming, and she was even threatened with the police being called on her for supposedly bullying them.

Maria was becoming increasingly determined to leave them, even though their responsibilities towards her were increasing every day. In the end, she got two-thirds of the debt.

'Look, if I don't receive my payment, I will report you to the police for not compensating me for my work.'

'Is that so? Go! Go now, this moment. Get out of here.' – They opened the door and kicked her out. But suddenly, they realised that this was the front door and that someone might see her, so they pulled her back in.

'You see what you are doing to us. We are Christians. We do not do that. Get back to your duties!'

Maria was shocked. What just happened? Since she left her village and the nightmare of war, no one treated her as a human being. She was treated as feeble-minded, naive, stupid, ignorant, lazy, and primitive and was subjected to mocking and harassment.

Maria finished her late-night shift, constantly being watched with hatred in their eyes, as they knew she would no longer tolerate them. They didn't know what she would do, so they had to get rid of her. But how? In a few days, she found herself locked inside the restaurant, with all the doors closely monitored. They had a milder approach to her. One day, they called her to come with them to buy food. She was naive but not overly naive. She knew something was happening, but she played along. The money they gave her was kept in Maria's underwear, just in case she will need them. She sat for the first time with their precious son in the big, expensive Mercedes. She noticed that this was his expensive toy and how proud he was. With them was his sister, who constantly spoke to him in German, thinking that Maria would not understand. They travelled for a couple of hours in an unknown direction. Then they stopped and asked Maria to join them at a big shopping centre.

'This shopping centre is a big place. This kind of place doesn't exist in Bosnia. You know, you can buy everything you need in one place. You can spend all your money and stay here the entire day.'

'Oh, really? Good to know.'

'Yes, you see, we will go to the toilet first, and then we will go shopping. I suggest using the toilet as it was a long trip.'

Maria joined the girl in the restroom, and when she finished, she waited outside for her to exit. Fifteen minutes passed, and she didn't come out. She walked out into the corridor, her eyes fixed on the direction of the toilet. But no, she didn't see her. It had been thirty minutes, then forty-five minutes, and Maria was still waiting in the same place. People were passing by. The place was enormous. She thought that maybe they were looking for her. But one and a half hours passed, and she was still waiting for them in front of the toilet. Then she decided to get out and look for their car. But the car wasn't there. At first, she thought maybe she didn't see the right car, so she went looking at every Mercedes that was parked there. Someone noticed her looking suspicious, so they called the police. Two policemen arrived at the parking lot and began speaking to her. She didn't understand them, and they couldn't communicate with her. They tried to find out where she was from and which language she spoke. So they started talking by hand.

'Ich! Deutsch. Sie (pointed at her)'

'Bosnia. Ich Bosnia.'

'Reisepass?'

'No, pass.'

'Come.'

She ended up in the police station, so soon that she was not even able to understand what was happening, sitting in front of a kind but firm police officers. Soon a translator arrived.

'They are saying that you don't have a passport with you.'

'That's right, I don't have it with me.'

'You know, you need to have a passport with you all the time. How did you come in to Germany? How long are you have you been here?'

'I have been here in Germany for approximately 6 months. I came to a Bosnian family to work in their restaurant. They asked me to give them my passport to legalise my stay here. They never gave it back. I asked them, but they said it that it was with you.'

'Did you work here?'

'Yes, I have worked here at the restaurant.'

'Did they pay you?'

'Yes, they did pay me something?'

'Can you provide us with details about where you worked? Which place and the name of the restaurant.?'

Maria was obedient and provided as many details as she could re-member. She had been sitting on the chair for several hours, and the night was approaching. She was thinking about where she would sleep tonight.

'Maria, we have checked your immigration status. You are illegal here. There was no application for asylum here, and certainly not for a work permit. Are you aware that you are living here illegally?'

'I'm sorry, I don't understand. How can this be? They took my passport. They said they have had to apply for a work permit. They told me that the process hadn't finished. Could you please check again? I am not a criminal.'

'We will check again unless you provided us with the wrong name.'

'No, I haven't. I swear to God, this is my actual name.'

'We have to initiate legal proceedings against you. You will be detained until the verdict is reached.'

'But why?'

'This is how it is.'

'What will happen to me?'

'You may be sent back to Croatia as Bosnia is still a risky place.'

'What about the restaurant owners? I told you everything.'

'We will check with them. We have already asked our colleagues to speak with them. But since we have no evidence of your employment there, and if they fail to verify your identity, we are unable to take any action against them. I believe in your story, but unfortunately, human trafficking is prevalent here. Especially since you come from a war zone, you are just a hunted prey for criminals.'

In a few days, she was extradited and sent back to Croatia. Handcuffed like the worst criminal with her escort, entered for the first time in an aeroplane. She used to think, in her better days, that it would be nice to see aeroplanes with her own eyes or even fly. Modestly, she desired to leave and explore an unfamiliar country, so here she was. Her wish came true. Croatian police took her into custody when she arrived. Her identity was proven, but since she was not criminally charged, she could be released. Social services intervened and arranged for her to be placed back into the immigration barracks. At least she wasn't thrown onto the streets. She had shelter and food. She has seen the world, shopping centre, foreign nature, flown by aeroplane, and now she is a world woman. This is how she comforts herself.

It took a couple of days to recover from the shock. When she woke from the misery, the first thing she did was to go back to her parish and talk to the priest. But the priest didn't want to talk to her. She started shouting, blaming the priest for what had happened to her. She screamed at him, calling him names and cursing at him.

'Do not behave like this; someone will hear you.'

'Let them hear me. Let them know what you did.'

'I did something for you. I tried to help you. But you escaped from them.'

'I escaped? They abandoned me at a shopping mall.'

'They said you left them at the shopping mall. You were angry because they didn't allow you to go out by yourself. They were protecting you.'

'By working twenty hours for them. They didn't pay me.'

'They said they paid everything to you.'

'No, they only paid me for two months. They didn't pay me for the other four months.'

'Then go back and ask them for your money. I trust that my cousin was telling me the truth.'

'Your cousin? It was your cousin who I worked for? Of course, you trust them, but I am a liar.'

'Get out of this sacred house, Maria. You are a disgrace! No wonder why your husband left and gave your child to a stranger.'

'What?!! Say this again!'

'Get out, Maria. God is punishing you for being a wicked person.'

'Am I a wicked person? What are you saying, Father?'

'Get out of here. I don't want to see you here in this church anymore. You are just like your mother. Get out. No one wants you because you are a bad person. Even parents gave up on you. Leave!'

Did God just give up on her? Was she slapped in the face? She was expelled from God's house. The last person who knew her from her childhood fired her. He shot her right in the heart. She felt pain in her chest, and it left her breathless. She expected an unknown person to hurt her, but her priest... How? Why? Was she really a wicked person? In such a short time period, she went through hell. Everyone had abandoned her. Everyone pointed at her. Everyone was pushing and pulling her soul out of her body. Her faith vanished. She shed tears, but the heaviness on her chest didn't leave. Her mind deserted her as her thoughts raced, demanding new questions without any answers. Days later, she was still lost in her thoughts, feeling trapped. Although she was physically alive, the old Maria was slowly fading away. Her mind was consumed with thoughts of revenge, but a tiny voice soothed her with hope and a promise. She will live again.

In order to escape the refugee centre, her eyes caught a small newspaper ad asking for a woman to take care of an old couple. Maria saw an opportunity in this ad, and after a short call, she was invited to go and live with them. For some reason, they liked her, and perhaps they saw potential in her. The husband was incredibly nice to Maria. He didn't ask her much, but he showed incredible human compassion when he heard her life story. Both of them have been teachers for a long time. Coming from a poor family, the socialist regime gave them the opportunity to educate themselves. They had a son who was highly educated. He was a biologist and couldn't find a promising career in his home town. The war situation helped him leave the country together with his family and immigrate to Canada. It was too far from home. The old couple supported his decision, hoping that he would have a better future. But their decision meant that they will sacrifice their happiness and be alone for the rest of their lives. They had to look after themselves. They didn't need much, but as they got older, even small things became too heavy for them. Maria seemed like a decent person whom they trusted with their property and lives.

She lived with this couple in a tall residential building, surrounded with other buildings in a green park, in a decent three-bedroom flat. She was cooking and cleaning for them, caring for them as if they were her parents. As weeks passed, the old gentleman became seriously ill. In a couple of months, he died. Doctors couldn't save him. The woman, without thinking beforehand, applied to a care home. The demand for accommodation was high, but the supply was insufficient. She had to wait for several years to be placed in one of them. After the funeral, their son offered to compensate Maria if she stayed with his mother a bit longer. The old lady seemed happy that she would not be alone in her old days and that she would be taken care of. In the first few months, everything was alright for both of them. They lived happily, and for the first time, Maria felt good about herself. The old lady initiated, supported, and helped her start her high school education. Maria was an intelligent human being and a hard worker. The old lady, perhaps feeling young herself, was determined not to accept "no" as an answer. Even though Maria gave her a million reasons not to go to school in her mid-twenties, the old lady was persistent.

'It is never too late for education. You see, I am learning Esperanto now. I will probably never speak it well, but I want to learn this. I will also learn about computers. My son is suggesting that if I learn how to use a personal computer, I will be able to communicate with him through video calls. Better cannot be.'

'How am I going to go to school again? Everyone will laugh at me. I can't do that.'

'This is a night school for adults. I am sure you will not see young boys and girls there. Everyone will work, and when they finish their tasks, they will attend classes.'

'But, how am I going to go for four years? It is too long.'

'No, you will only study for two years, but during that time, you will be required to pass exams covering four years of material. I am sure the program will be adapted to the student's age. I am sure you will not have sports, music, or art...'

'How am I going to pay for tuition? It is too expensive.'

'We will ask refugee and social institutions for help, and if necessary, I will also provide assistance.'

'How am I going to learn English, maths, and other subjects?'

'Not a problem at all. Come on. I am a teacher, and if the old guy were alive, he would enjoy giving you lessons. Don't worry, just sign these papers, and you can start tomorrow.'

Being a student gave Maria a fear she had never experienced before. She didn't have trust in her own worth. Her self-confidence was incredibly low. In the beginning, she tried to escape her study chores for home duties, but the old teacher was incredibly persistent in sending her back to school. Little by little, class after class, day by day, her self-confidence was building up as she consistently received good marks. The old lady was happy to see that her efforts were bringing results. She trusted her. A good team of two organised their daily lives in a military style. They knew when they had to attend classes, meet friends, learn English, practise Math, cook, and when to go out. The old lady was Maria's adoptive mother and gave her so much love and affection that she had missed all her life. She restored Maria's trust in people, self-confidence, and skills she never knew she had. In a short time, she learned to drive a car, speak fluent English, and, with some difficulty, German. She also became proficient in using computers and acquired such manners that no one would have ever thought she lived in an abandoned mountain village far from civilisation. Little makeup and modest fashion made her look like a completely different person. She changed not only her appearance but also the way she spoke, her behaviour, and her trust in people. Her simple mind became brilliant, and her respect for humans turned into humans respecting her. She was taught that her soul and mind were precious jewels that should be kept hidden deep within her body and that all she had to offer the world were words that people wanted to hear. She should keep her opinion to herself. She should not imitate other people if she wants to be accepted and respected. It was tough for her to accept the new Maria. Sometimes, she would look at herself in the mirror and ask, "Who is that person?" What does she want, and where should she go? Many times, she had the opinion that she was becoming someone else.

'I don't like pretending to be someone I'm not. I am who I am, and this is what I will be.'

'Maria, the world is visual. People will treat you based on your appearance and your behaviour. If you lift your chin, you will show self-confidence. You don't have to wear a mini skirt, but if you wear a smart dress, it will make a difference. Please try. If you speak like a bear, you will be treated like an animal. If you speak like an intellectual, you will be treated like a scientist. That's it. If you listen to folk music, you may be perceived as a primitive peasant, but if you listen to classical music, you may be seen as a sophisticated individual. No one cares what quality do you have, but how you present yourself.'

'But I don't like this music. What is that? How can someone like violins and pianos? And the dance? What is wrong with the way I dance? My grandmother taught me this. This is how we used to dance in our village.'

'And that is fine with your village. One day, you will return there and dance in the main square with your fellow villagers. I have different plans for you. I would love to see you wearing a princess gown, gracefully dancing a waltz in a ballroom. I would like to see you with your diploma in your hands. I would like to see people respecting you for your professional knowledge, skills and intellect. The more knowledge and skills you possess, the greater the opportunities will come your way in life. You will learn to love other things. Am I wrong to wish this for you?'

'No, mother, you are not. Thank you. You are right.'

'I love how you call me "mother." I love hearing this again. Come on, say it again. Oh, I love you, my little flower.'

Two years passed in the blink of an eye. Maria obtained her high school degree and diploma. It was celebrated with a trip to the coast. It was the first time Maria saw the blue Adriatic Sea and its crystal-clear water. One more skill to add to her curriculum was sea swimming. She entered the water gracefully, resembling a green frog, and emerged with the elegance of a mermaid. Even though her thirties were rapidly approaching, she looked as happy as a bunny jumping in the grass. She never had a childhood; she missed out on her teenage years and grew up very early. However, the present time gave her a feeling of lost time. In her past life, she didn't have choices, and the future was unknown. The present time compensated for all that she missed but secretly desired. For the first time in her life, she dared to dream, make plans, and make decisions between choices. All of this happened with a great deal of effort from the old lady and her family.

Even though this family was not her biological family, it was her chosen family. All she got from them was not given by force but by their free will and good faith. They haven't been religious. They have been labelled as communists and have missed out on their pastimes, various events, opportunities, and systems. They have openly criticised communism as well as the leaders who brought the once most prominent country in the world to disaster and the rule of criminals. The old lady was saying that history will reveal the truth. The good will prevail over evil in the end. She was looking at how everything they had built for future generations was destroyed by that generation in a second. She wasn't happy. In the beginning, she thought that the system would improve and communism would be replaced with a better system where all people would be equal and have equal opportunities. She hoped for a social system without corrupt leaders who steal national wealth and send it abroad, along with their children. She was becoming depressed each day when looking at the news. She was growing tired of life. People have changed a lot. She couldn't openly speak about what bothered her. She had to change her personality as well. She never felt fear in the old system, but in the new system, she had to be afraid of people who listened and talked to her. The depression she felt caused her illness, and soon she became unrecognisable. It was time to be institutionalised. In her moments of clarity, she asked Maria:

'Promise me that you will continue to educate yourself. Promise me, please.'

'Mother, I've had enough. I can't study any more.'

'Please, go and educate yourself. No amount of money on this earth can compensate for the value you gain by educating yourself. You will be your own boss. You will be free. No one will be able to take that away from you. Do that for me as a memory of myself.'

'Mother, I need to pay tuition. This time, I cannot ask for your help. It is very expensive.'

'I have some savings. Use it for your education.'

'No, mother. I cannot use your savings. All these years, you gave me money and spent it all on me. I have to take care of you now.'

'Maybe my son can help us.'

'No, it is not possible. I have to look for a job, but I am afraid of what will happen to you. We'll speak to your son so he can help you make a decision.'

'You are the daughter I always wanted. You can decide for me.'

'No, mother. Not this time. Your son has to decide.'

So he decided. She had to be placed in a care home. With a heavy heart, Maria packed her suitcases. The care home was only half an hour away, but the thought of not living with her, supporting her, and listening to her made her very sad.

'I will go to the care home, but please take care of our home. I am giving you this apartment so that you will have a place to live.'

'Yes, mother, as you wish. I will take care of it.'

Her wishes couldn't be fulfilled. Care home fees were so high that savings were depleted very quickly. The pension was not sufficient, and her son was struggling to pay the fees on time. Maria made the decision to sell their home, and her son approved of it. The old lady was not aware of this; otherwise, she wouldn't have wanted to stay in a care home.

Maria found a job soon after placing the old lady in a care home. It was a job in administration and sales. The company needed some- one who was skilled in computer usage, fluent in English and had good communication skills. Maria was another person at that time. She knew that she could do the job, and she did it well. After work, she always visited her old lady. There were four elderly ladies in the room, so when she visited them, she was helping all of them. Soon, she became familiar with all the staff and established good relation- ships. Things were going well until the director called her to pay the fees. Maria didn't hesitate and paid all the fees. She continued doing that every month. Her salary wasn't large enough to cover all fees and bills. Even though she and her son decided to sell the house, she was contemplating how to go about it. She hesitated to start the sales pro- cess. She had to talk to the director and find a solution. The solution was simple: Maria will continue to pay her fees as before. The director didn't care much about her struggles. After several months of his reign, another director came. This time, Maria was able to connect with this person on a deep level, so they were able to find a solution. They of- fered her a job in an administration that paid better, allowing her to cover her fees and home bills, and she could keep the home. She was so happy about the offer that she misheard the amount of her salary. When she signed her contract and saw the amount, she wondered why she was hired. The director was the old lady's student, to whom she can thank for her successful career. She wanted to help her former teacher and her protégé. When Maria took the position, she was offered the opportunity to study on their behalf as well. Again, she was confused but soon realised that the company had tax relief for educating employees. They utilised tax allowances to reduce their tax burden by providing employees with free education and non-refundable loans. Maria didn't think twice. Finally, she got everything sorted.

Chapter 3

Alexander Conrad was born as the first child of parents Elsa and Eric Herbert Conrad in Switzerland. He was a privileged child born into a financially stable family. His ancestors haven't been as lucky as he was, but evidently, luck has worked in his favour. His mother, Elsa, was born as a Donauschwaben in Croatia under very unusual circumstances and in an inconvenient location. Her grandfather, being a German in a place under the control of the Third Reich, had no option but to join the local SS units. It was expected that his son would also join the units. What was in their minds and hearts at that time, only they knew it. Were they afraid of punishment if they did not participate in the global war circus? Were they supporting the idea that only one race dominates the world? Who knows? Their decision had a deep impact on generations after them; Alexander too. Did they get their hands dirty? Did they have blood on their hands? Have they been monsters in the war machinery or just simple observers who monitored whether the war idea was followed? In the twilight of war madness, this wasn't important. It was important who won and who lost. Grandfather committed suicide because he didn't see any other solution at the end of the lost war. He didn't want to escape to Germany. It was a foreign country to him. His home was the place where he wanted to die. A single bullet granted his wish. Her father wanted to live. Despite his decision to escape with his pregnant wife, he was unsuccessful. He was immediately caught and hanged in the main square as a symbol of the defeat of an ideology. He was left on the pole for several days so that other citizens could see him. His wife was taken to jail and prosecuted. She didn't participate in the war machinery, but as the wife of a defeated army officer, she was considered guilty. She was sentenced to jail for the next fifteen years.

She gave birth to a healthy child, a girl with blue eyes. Führer would say, a pure Aryan girl. They both lived in the jail for a couple of years, in a place where the defeated army once had imprisoned members of the victorious army. Ghosts of tortured and murdered souls were sharing their stories with the living, regardless of whether the living wanted to listen or had regrets. The importance of their stories was irrelevant. Most of the prisoners were women. Their husbands were Nazis or fascists who were killed at the end of the war and had no chance of escaping. They died in the same manner as their victims. Women were left to bear the blame and shame for being with and supporting them. They knew that they had no chance of surviving in the place where they lived after being released. They have witnessed horrible scenes and endured hard times during which human dignity was violated by a perverse group of individuals. They couldn't escape, they couldn't disagree, and they couldn't disobey. They tried to save their own lives at the expense of others' lives. Leaders, as always, managed to escape punishment for their deeds, but ordinary people, as always, had to foot the bill. Elsa's mother was one of them. She didn't hate anyone. She grew up with her neighbours without asking for their background, but she also couldn't find a solution to escape unfortunate circumstances. Her husband paid for his decision with his life as well. Her regrets did not help her daughter's future either. She had plans, of course, but life in the prison wasn't helpful. Lack of food, malnutrition, constant mental pressure by guards, and horrible living conditions in cold, overcrowded cells in winter and hot in summer couldn't help her remain hopeful.

As the child was growing, prison authorities decided to separate the mother from the child and place her in an orphanage. There were many orphans after the war, so leaders had to be very careful with sharing information. It was a sensitive issue. They had to place children from opposing armies, children whose parents had killed each other, together. How would a child of a fascist murderer be accepted equally as a victim child whose parents were killed by fascists? A system had to protect all children, regardless of what happened in the war. So, the only idea they came up with was to change their surnames and keep their identity secret until they left the institution. If they had any living relatives who could discover their true identity, the system was very harsh on them. Teachers also had to be very sensitive and understand that a child shouldn't bear the guilt of their parents. However, being human meant that teachers were selective in their approach to upbringing. Elsa was growing up with low self-esteem, as she believed she was a naughty child. She was always blamed for everything. She thought she was not a good person, so she felt the need to improve herself. She always put in extra effort, behaved excellently, learned more than other children, and strived to be the best of the best, just to be recognised and treated like other children. Among her companions, she found comfort in the presence of other children, innocent as she was. She didn't understand that some of them might have been children of her parents' enemies. It didn't matter to them. They understood that their parents were killed in the war and there was no one who could take care of them. The system also had a program of pride. All of them have been Tito's pioneers, wearing a red scarf around their necks and a blue cap with a yellow star on it. They proudly marched in their blue skirts and white shirts on every holiday, unburdened by their family history. They have been promising citizens of the country with rapid uprising and a good living standard. People had dreams, desires, and hopes that the future would bring better days. Even though the wounds had been deep and fresh, people on the winning side tried to ignore the bad memories.

Politics always had victims, and the system of that time also had victims. The structure of prisoners was changing with time. No one will know whether Elsa's mother, a war prisoner, died a natural death or was poisoned. However, shortly after Elsa left her, she passed away. Years later, when Elsa attempted to uncover the truth, she discovered information about her mother's time spent in that location. An autopsy was never conducted, and her grave was never found. Elsa had doubts that she had been poisoned. Even if her suspicions were correct, it wouldn't bring her parents back.

Her new parents became her mother's sister and her uncle. When the war broke out, her father took her uncle Ivan in the car and drove to Switzerland. They have been best friends despite one being German and the other being Jewish. Their wives had been half Germans, but all of them grew up as Croats. They grew up as friends, playing the same games, hanging out together in the same places, and sharing the same childhood memories. Just before the war, they both decided to marry sisters. Elsa's mother was a nurse, and her aunt was one of the first female doctors to study in Switzerland. It was their parents' wish to educate their children. Elsa's father was a machine engineer, and her uncle was a banker. He came from a family who owed a bank, but he was the only child, and his parents died very early. He didn't have any relatives who could take care of him, so he grew up in the house next to Elsa's grandparents, as they were his neighbours. It was her grandfather's order to send Uncle Ivan to Switzerland, as he thought it would be very bad for him to stay at home. They took care of his house and all his property during the war, but when they died, the state took possession of the house. It became the home of many families due to its size.

Elsa didn't know who she was or what was behind her stay in the orphanage. One day, she was called by the principal and introduced to a beautiful, modern, and good-looking lady who was presented to her as Aunt Lilly. It was a shock to her. She thought she didn't have anyone in her life, but suddenly, a living relative appeared in front of her. Of course, Elsa denied her aunty. Despite objections, pleas, begging, and negotiations, she was sent to live with her. New experiences such as train riding, foreign languages, and different architecture preoccupied her disturbed mind. She travelled for approximately two days to reach their beautiful Swiss country house. Surrounded by mountains and the sound of gurgling water, she was trying to rebuild herself. She loved the country she came from, and after a brief period of indignation, she continued to live as a member of her Aunt Lilly and Uncle Ivan's family.

Elsa was a citizen of Yugoslavia and held a passport from that country. She spoke the Croatian language at home and identified herself as both a Croat and a Yugoslav. Despite their difficult circumstances, Aunt and Uncle loved that country dearly. All of them spoke the same language at home, unencumbered by the war and the past. Aunty was involved in the work of the Red Cross, and during the war, she was connected with the Partisans and the Communist Party. This earned the trust and respect of leaders, so she was never blacklisted or questioned for her brother-in-law and sister. She couldn't help her brother-in-law survive due to post-war turbulence, but her name definitely helped her sister survive and Elsa to be born. It helped Elsa to reunite with them and have a Yugoslav passport, which provided them with the freedom to travel across the world and the protection of host institutions.

While Elsa was growing up, she didn't inquire much about her parents because she received all the parental love she needed from her loved ones. Maybe subconsciously, she was afraid of what she might hear. However, as she entered her teenage years, she began to wonder about her mother's appearance, where her parents had met, what her mother's eyes looked like, and whether her father was kind. Lilly and Ivan were not fond of these questions, but they had no option but to provide answers. They always measured their words and were cautious about what they would say.

Elsa naturally chose to attend medical school. She had to continue the family tradition, and this was a part of her ancestor's wishes. For an unknown reason, perhaps while she was looking at corpses, she began to wonder where her parents were buried. She got an answer that no one knew. It was a war. They were killed, and their bodies were buried somewhere. She wanted to know who killed them, when they were killed, and all the details. She pressured her aunt to ask questions at the Red Cross. Aunt was replying that there were many victims and it was not possible to know about every one of them. The stubborn child was not happy with the answer. She wanted to know. She used a situation where three of them argued in seeking answers, so she took her passport and left for Yugoslavia. She had enough information that she could use to investigate what had happened. It wasn't her first time visiting Yugoslavia, and she spoke the language. She thought it was right and enough to ask questions and receive answers. She went looking for monuments in their hometown, where the names of victims were written, but she couldn't find any with the names of her parents on them. She went to their meeting place in a restaurant in the centre of town, hoping she might find someone from that time. When she received her passport for the first time, she discovered her true surname, so she started questioning people mentioning her true surname. Lilly explained to her that the orphanage didn't know her true identity, so they gave her one they thought might be correct. When she was searching for her parents' graves, she used their actual names. She asked for directions and received them until she asked the wrong person. Actually, he was the right person who knew both of her parents, but he didn't want to tell her the truth. Instead, he called the police on her, asking them to take her away. She was surprised to find herself in a police station, being treated as a criminal.

'Look, little one, you are asking the wrong questions. Why did you come here?'

'I came to find my parents' grave. Is this a crime?'

'Maybe you will discover the truth you don't want to hear.'

'They are dead! I cannot bring them to life. All I want is to have a place where I can bring a flower occasionally. Is this a bad idea?'

'Many people don't have a place where they can put a flower from time to time, either.'

'How come I can find the names of villagers and partisans on monuments, but nothing that indicates where my father died?'

'You don't want to know that.'

'Yes, I want to know.'

'Really... Then look at this.' (He brought a picture of a hanged man in front of her face). 'Do you see the uniform? Do you know how many people he killed? Do you know that his victims still remember him, and yet you go around asking for your father? You are lucky no one killed you yet. Have you received your answer now? Do you need more answers? He was on the other side.'

'What about my mother?'

'You were born in a prison. She was imprisoned after the war. Just because your Aunt Lilly helped us, she wasn't executed. We didn't want to be like them, killing women and children, so we let you be born. We took care of you, didn't we?'

'Is she still alive?'

'No, she got sick. Officers couldn't help her. She died after you went to the orphanage.'

'Where are their graves? I want to know.'

'I don't care what you want, little girl. Be smart and leave the town. Go back to Germany or wherever you currently reside.'

'Is there a place, please, uncle?'

'There is no burial place for people like them. We bury these kinds of people in unmarked places so that time forgets them.'

'Please, Uncle, don't be cruel.'

'Me, cruel? Do you know how many people died because of your cruel soldiers? Go and ask if there is a family whose members have not been butchered. Go to concentration camps if you dare. We have all of these pictures. We witnessed massacres with our own eyes. I am a living witness. I saw all of it. I know who your father and mother were. I know... We are still discovering dead bodies after almost twenty years. Do you want to leave flowers there as well? Go to Jasenovac! Go to Gradiška! Go there! When you cross the river, re-member that bodies are floating there every day. There were more floating bodies than wishes in the river. I was witnessing my family being murdered. I was listening to their screams. I was listening to how people, like your father, give orders to kill old people, women, children… Do you think that I wouldn't like to leave flowers on their graves? Go home, little one! Go home, and don't make me regret I let you live!'

'Am I guilty of my father's deeds? Why am I being punished for what he did?'

'You are still alive. Are you being punished? No, you are not. We have given you a life to live, so live it!'

'All I want to know is where he was buried. I think you know where it is.'

'You don't listen!! Go home! Or I will put you in jail!'

Elsa thought she was going to die the day she was escorted to the Yugoslavian border by an officer in civilian clothes. She was sitting in a train compartment, travelling towards Austria, with an older gentleman who alternated between glancing at her and reading his newspapers. She promised herself that she would take revenge on all of them. She was crying, screaming, swearing, and silently questioning herself without uttering a single word. She had free hands, but the compartment was locked with a key. The officer brought a lot of food and drinks with him, offering them to her to eat whenever she wanted. She was stubbornly proud. She decided to ignore his offer. Obviously, this wasn't his first case, so he didn't pay much attention to her attitude. He didn't wear a weapon, but you could see that nothing could break him down.

'You know, I have a daughter a bit younger than you. She is also stubborn. She thinks she can punish me if she is arrogant towards me. She can't hurt me. Do you know why? Because I am older than her and I understand her. She can't understand me because she is not my age. But it is fine. She is going to grow up, and she will understand my actions.'

'Why should I care about your daughter? And why don't we just wait until you hand me over to someone else?'

'I will hand you over to your guardians in Zurich. You know that.'

'Why don't you just kill me? Like my parents.'

'I wouldn't go there, little one. I don't know who your parents were, and to be honest, I do not care. All I care about is bringing you safely back to your home.'

'This country was once my home.'

'And it still is.'

'How can this country be my country when you send me away?'

'Young people your age end up in jail for less. You are a privileged one, so instead, we are sending you away.'

'My uncle and aunt, I suppose...'

'I suggest that you calm down, live your life to the fullest, keep your mouth shut, mind your own business, and everything will be fine.'

'I shouldn't ask about my parents either.'

'I was a communist during the war. I didn't initially participate much in partisan actions. I am also German, from the same place as your parents. At first, I was forced to dress as a Hitler Youth member. However, when I discovered the truth behind this national euphoria, I realised that I wanted to be on the right side, not just on the side of the strongest. My family decided to get involved and asked if we could be contacted by someone who is a member of the Communist Party. We wanted to help. When I was contacted, they asked me if I could play the role of a loyal German to the Nazi party. I was challenged, tested, and given such tasks just to earn trust. I was captured by SS troops and shot. It was a shame how one German could go against another German. The history will never write this. I was shot and thrown into the river. I was still alive, barely, when someone pulled me from the river and helped me to recover. I had been hiding in a flour casket for over six months, and after a brave villager risked his life to find a partisan, I was safely transported to free territory. You would be disgusted by what one human can do to another. Despite having to execute another living being and being shot by my own people, I do not regret fighting for freedom. It was worth all the effort.'

'So, what are you then? A German, you definitely are not.'

'I am a human being, and I will remain as such. My ancestors were born in Germany. We spoke the German language and were Catholic Christians. We came to Croatia, which is now a part of Yugoslavia. We learned another language, lived and worked peacefully with other nations. No one questioned my nationality or my loyalty. One inhuman being came to power, and the people became beasts. They should have seen the truth. They should have chosen the right side. But no, they were scared. Someone came, put a gun to their forehead, and they went with them, obeying their orders. They thought they would survive if they were on the side of the "stronger" by having superior war machinery. But when they lost, they had to pay the price for their actions. They chose the wrong side. That's it.'

'My parents didn't kill anyone.'

'It doesn't matter if they did or not. They were on the side that lost a war. I chose the side that won the war. Do you think your parents would forgive me if we lost the war? No, they wouldn't. They would have killed me because I wasn't on their side.'

'You have to fight for justice. You had to find someone who would claim that they have had not done anything wrong to anyone.'

'Well, at the end of the war, there was a huge chaos, full of misleading information and mistakes. Fascists were promised absolution and asylum if they surrendered. They surrendered and were sent to the border. They were promised that Britain would take them. But English and American leaders took back their promise and ordered us to execute our own people. "Deal with your own people, they said."... It is something I didn't participate in, but actions made me ashamed of... If we were not being ordered to deal with our fascists, we wouldn't kill anyone. It was a political decision and a condition for us to be left alone. Otherwise, they would have thrown us to the Russians as they did to others. The last thing I said, you should remember, but do not talk about it to anyone. Have you heard me?! Our history will not remember the shame we brought upon our people.'

'Who would listen to me anyway?'

'I am giving you advice as a father. Mind your own business, keep a low profile, choose your company wisely, align yourself with the right side, and strive to survive. Be smart.'

'What are you saying? I have to forget what happened to my family. I should never come back to my country. Should I not speak my own language? What are you saying?'

'I am suggesting that you should go home, continue studying, find a boyfriend, get married, have children, and live your life. Of course, you will not forget your parents and what happened. It is not possible to do that. I am asking you to find peace within yourself. It was a war, and they were victims of war. When you find peace within your soul, come back home. No one will send you away. No one will point at you, and you will not be victimised. Do not forget that you belong to this country. Be proud of where you come from. Be proud of your ancestors. Be proud of the people you come from.'

'Oh, it's so easy to say. Forgive and forget.'

'You are very young; you think with your heart. When you get older, you will reach this stage where you will gain perspective from all sides and find the answers you seek.'

As a stormy wind, hungry for revenge, with a confused mind and overwhelming emotions, all she wanted was to hurt someone. People who loved her beyond imagination became her target. The happiness they felt when she returned safely turned into misery.

'Why didn't you tell me?! Why? Why didn't you tell me that my parents were murderers?!! Why did you keep this information away from me?!' – she was screaming at them with all the power of her voice.

'We didn't want to trouble you. It was a war.'

'Yes, it was a war. They killed people!!'

'We don't know that. Your father would never do that. He was my best friend. He wouldn't harm anyone.' - Her uncle tried to calm the situation.

'Oh no, Uncle! This was not true. He was killing people. This is why he was punished!'

'Don't talk this way, Elsa. Do not say such things. It was a war. He couldn't escape the war. He had to join SS units. He didn't have a choice.'

'Apparently, they could choose. Why did other Germans choose to become partisans and communists? If they chose that, I wouldn't be ashamed now.'

'He didn't have a choice, Elsa. Believe me when I say that. He didn't have a choice. Your grandfather didn't have a choice either.'

'But they killed people! They also killed a large number of Jews. Not only Croats and Serbs, but they also killed Jews too!'

'They haven't been involved in concentration camps, Elsa. Please stop using these words.'

'How do you know? If you had stayed there, maybe he would have killed you, too.'

'No, he wouldn't. They wouldn't. I knew them. They wouldn't do that. They saved my life. They were unable to harm their own people.'

'Obviously, they could, and they did. Why would he end up hanged if he didn't, Uncle?'

'It was a war. In war, these things happen! People die.'

'Yes, he chose the stronger side. Is this how he became a Nazi? Not because he believed in this ideology? Maybe he sent you here to Switzerland because he couldn't bear to see you. Maybe he wanted to take your money, your house… maybe he just couldn't look at you any more.'

'Oh, Elsa, please do not say that. I grew up in their house. They were my family. They wouldn't harm anyone.'

'Maybe they shouldn't have sent you here?! Maybe they shouldn't let you go?! Maybe you told partisans to kill them? Maybe you wanted their wealth. Maybe my father should've killed you, taken your money, and come home. He would've been alive now. Or, maybe you wanted me as you couldn't have children. Yes, definitely, this is it! You said that my father killed people so that partisans would kill him. This is why I wasn't punished. This is why I was taken away from my father and mother. Just to be brought here. Maybe you are not my family either. Maybe you are not my Aunt and Uncle.'

'Elsa, do not speak any more! You are hurting your Uncle. We were treating you as our own daughter. You can't talk like this to your Uncle. Have some respect for him.'

'Respect!? You deserve all of this. You are alive, and my parents are not. You had the power to save them if you wanted, but you didn't. You are a murderess as well. I hate you!! I hate you!! May you find the same destiny as my parents?'

'Ok, Elsa, we understand that you are angry with us. Just calm down! Calm down, please.'

'No, I want! You are guilty of my parents' death. You were connected to communists. You were also guilty of what happened there! If you wanted to help, you would've helped. You could've stopped this mass execution at the end of the war. I am sure you knew all that would happen. You passed messages to communists. You knew that all fascists would be executed! You knew that, and you didn't do anything to prevent that or save my family.'

'How do you know about it?! Who told you that?!'

'It doesn't matter who told me. You had the power to help people at the end of the war. You could've helped them! All leaders survived. All of them are hiding somewhere now. You let them survive, but you crucified my family. You are not my family! I don't want to hear anything from you! – Elsa left the house of her Aunt and Uncle in the same way as she got in, like the wind.'

'Elsa, please don't go! Elsa, please come back, don't go! Come down, girl. We couldn't do anything! Trust us! – Aunt was screaming in tears after her.'

'Let her calm down. Let her go. She will be fine. Give her time. She is badly hurt. It is understandable. She will be fine, dear. When she calms down, we'll speak to her.' – Uncle was calming his wife, pulling her back from the street into the house. Both of them were shaking in disbelief at this huge conflict. Elsa just accused them of causing the death of their entire family, their beloved sister and the friend. She accused them of causing the death of their loved ones. It was so painful that, for a moment, it seemed as if she had killed their souls.

Elsa entered the house of her best friend Lilly with a swift and graceful stride, like a gust of wind.

'My parents were killed, Lilly. My father was executed by hanging in the main square. He was a Nazi. I saw a picture. This makes sense now. I know why a teacher harassed and physically abused me. Not because I was naughty, but because I was the daughter of a Nazi soldier.'

'A Nazi? Were your parents Nazis?'

'Apparently, yes!'

'Get out of my house! Mum, the daughter of a Nazi, stepped into our house! Mum! Come quickly!'

'What are you doing, Lily? You are my best friend. Why are you acting like this?'

'I am a Serb. Your parents killed my entire family. You didn't leave anyone alive. Murderers! Get out of my house. Get out! Mum! Her parents were Nazis!'

Lili's mother came storming in, wielding a stick and began beating Elsa.

'Out Satan! Out! Get out, or I will beat you to death!' - The punches were not as painful as her words. They dragged her by her hair on the street and continued beating and whinging until she started bleeding. – 'Get out of our sight, Satan! If we see you next time, we will kill you!'

Her world died in just a second. She wanted to hear the truth, but it ended up shattering her soul. Her tears didn't help; her soul was bleeding. Her crying and screaming didn't help either; her world just died, too. People were passing by on the street. Some of them laughed, some ignored her, and some felt pity. However, not a single person offered their helping hand. Rain was pouring over her body, washing blood from her skin and mingling with her heavy tears. Elsa got up and straightened her posture. "I am alive! I am alive! You will not kill me! You will not take away my dignity!"

Everybody gets help from their guardian angel in difficult moments, and Elsa is no exception. Her guardian angel was Yana, her uncle's servant. She came from behind, covering her wet body with her jumper, and pulled her towards her house.

'Come, dear. Come with me.'

'Leave me alone, Aunty. Let me go.' – She cried.

'You are not well, my dear. Come with me. When you get better, you will go on your way.'

'I am ashamed, Aunty. My parents killed your family as well. I know all about your past. I am sorry, Aunty. Really. I don't deserve to live. Please, let me go.'

'You will go, my dear. Don't worry. Let me assist you until you recover, and then you can leave.'

'I am ashamed. How can I ask for help from you? Now I know who I am.'

'I know who you are, too. You are a lovely young lady who will survive these hard times and continue living.'

'Aren't you angry with me? Now you know who I am, too.'

'I knew who you were all along. Your aunt and uncle told me. They didn't want me to feel bad living with them if I wasn't fine with you.'

'You have always been so kind to me. How could you stand this, knowing that I am the child of a murderer?'

'My entire family was murdered before my eyes. I was stabbed several times, but I survived. With the assistance of a German officer. After this group of Ustasha slaughtered the entire village, they paused to assess the outcome of their actions. One of them noticed my movements and ordered a soldier to evacuate the village, leaving the bodies to be discovered. He said that this should serve as a lesson to other villagers. When everyone had departed, he commanded his soldiers in the car to proceed. He rode a bicycle. I heard that they were advising him not to stay alone because it wasn't safe, but he insisted that they leave. When they left, he took me into the house and bandaged my wounds. We stayed near the bodies all night, waiting for the partisans. They came during the night and found him and me. They took him and me with themselves after burying the bodies.'

'What happened to him after that?'

'He became a partisan. He took care of me the whole time, and we separated once he was certain that I was fine.'

'Is he still alive?'

'No, dear. I was so in love with him. I said, "If I survive the war, I will marry him." I was searching for him but found out that he had been killed in action. I was so sad. I said to myself, "If he doesn't propose to me, I will propose to him." But now, he is no longer alive... I don't want anyone any more.'

'Have you been a partisan? How did you end up here?'

'I was a child partisan. I couldn't participate in the action; they wouldn't allow me. They thought I was too emotional and that I would cause a disaster, so they ordered me to be in an ambulance and take care of the wounded. But after the war, I saw many things I didn't like. You couldn't speak freely. Many people disappeared simply because local leaders did not like them. I was working in an office when one of the communist leaders started talking about someone in a position he wanted to be in. He then proceeded to snitch and report that the person had said something inappropriate. He was so proud that he caused misery to another human.'

'What happened to the man who was accused of being anti-communist?'

'He went to prison together with his wife. Their children were taken from them. Who knows how they live now or if he works? I don't know. The world is completely insane. I thought, maybe someone would snitch on me as well, and I would end up in prison, too. So, I took this opportunity to leave the country.'

'You are always so calm and nice. How do you manage this?'

'It's not so easy. A lot of things happened in my life. My father was an alcoholic. I hated him, wishing for his death. When my father died at the hands of my neighbour, I felt hatred towards the neighbour and loved my father. I loved my Croatian Ustashas. I thought it would be nice to join them, but I was too young. They killed my entire family and all the villagers. They stabbed me just for fun. I hated Nazis but was saved by one of them. I joined the Partisans, but I witnessed their cruelty when they retaliated. They were just as cruel as fascists. People do not consider what is right and wrong when their ego speaks, and their soul remains hidden. It is very hard to be human when you serve inhumanely. People put on uniforms to exert power over others, but they fail to realise that true power lies in self-control, in the ability to manage one's own ego. People are joining armies for financial reasons as well. This is blood money. This money will not bring you happiness or a stable life. When you earn money in a disgraceful way, you will take away your luck. Then, you have victims. They see with their own eyes that they will be harmed, yet they deliberately act stupidly and move towards their own disaster. Nothing is black and white on this earth. There are no inherently good or bad people on earth. We are all capable of both good and bad. We choose to be good or bad, victims or victors. Sometimes, our actions are flawless, but we fail to speak up when we should, causing harm to others. Sometimes, we say hurtful words to someone who we love the most, causing harm to their soul. However, these words may have a positive impact on their future. I met bad people doing good and good people doing bad things. I was raised as a Catholic Christian and witnessed instances where priests slaughtering other people just because they were not fascists. I witnessed mothers taking the lives of other mothers' children. I saw people like me, who are war victims, helping their enemies. You choose what you want to be. You choose your thoughts. You choose your emotions. People often believe that by putting on a uniform, they will automatically do something good. They will fight for a cause, whichever it is. They think that whatever they do could be justified and that it will go unpunished. But actually, they serve individuals who can escape if they are in danger, change their appearance, and make you take the blame for everything. They do not understand that they are servants to their masters. They also do not understand that their master depends on them and that they cannot push their agenda without their service. They can say, "I will do anything for money!" And they can have all the money in the world. They can also have all the power in the world. How they are going to live afterwards is another question. Is the fear they will experience for the rest of their life worth the money they earned from their masters in the shadows? Sooner or later, all devils want to live like angels.'

'I wish I could be like you. I am feeling frustrated with people at the moment.'

'Why do you want this burden on your soul? Will you change your destiny, your future, if you hate? Do you think you will be weak if you let heaven deal with them?'

'I don't know. I know. I hate all of them now. I feel like I want to die right now.'

'Maybe you should give life a chance. Maybe you should live because your parents haven't been given this chance. They didn't have a chance, but maybe you will have a chance to become what you want to be. Maybe you will bring beautiful humans to earth.'

'How can you be so nice to people after everything that has happened to you? Have you never wished for revenge?'

'Yes, I wished for, and I got it.'

'How? When?'

'Ah, this is tough. At the end of the war, during these two to three months, the communists called upon those who sought revenge against their enemies to gather at the border and seek retribution. I was only seventeen. A bit younger than you now. I was filled with hatred and a thirst for revenge. I knew who killed my family. They were from another village. We used to see each other at the church gathering on Sundays. I knew them all, and they knew me. I was looking in the face of every fascist. I saw how my fellows searched in the group for their enemies. They took them for their hands or pushed them by guns towards shallow pitches and shot them. Sometimes, they stabbed them with bayonets until they died. Sometimes, they just shot them. Sometimes, they used long knives. Sometimes, they beat them to death. Sometimes, they jumped on their backs to break every bone in their bodies. I found my enemy, too. In the middle of a group, he looked me in the face, thinking I wouldn't have the guts to kill him. Firstly, I stabbed him. I think I stabbed him a hundred times while he was lying on the ground. I didn't want to kill him immediately. I was avoiding his heart. The blood was all over me. Then, I took a long knife and began cutting his legs and arms. I wanted him to be afraid of me. I wanted him to see how much he hurt me. At first, he didn't shriek at all. Then he couldn't handle the pain, so he started screaming. I didn't hear his voice. All I could hear was my adrenaline. I was hitting and hitting and hitting… Then, one of my commanders, who was behind my back, touched my arm and asked if I wished to finish my work more quickly because there were others who were waiting for the same destiny. I finished him. Then I finished others too… I was only seventeen…'

'What? Wow! I would never say ... How did it feel to do that?'

'I didn't have any feeling at that moment. I only had a rush in my head. It looked like I had slaughtered chickens, pigs, or cattle. They were not humans to me. I despised them so much... But after we eliminated them all, we returned to our barracks and caught sight of our uniforms... Their body parts and blood were splattered all over us... We couldn't help but laugh at how some of them had behaved. Some of them cried, asking to be saved for the sake of their children. Some of them played the role of heroes, while others pleaded to be finished as soon as possible. After taking a shower and changing clothes, we began singing and dancing around the fire. We thought we did a good thing. We thought this was how it should be... But after a couple of days, we received orders to keep our mouths shut and not to tell anyone that we had participated in this shameful execution... It took a couple of months until we realised what we had done. We started losing our sanity. Some of us have committed suicide. Most of us have had to live with remorse and shame. I tried to live a normal life, but I couldn't. After a few years, an opportunity to work abroad presented itself, and I seized it. I think our party didn't believe that I would leave the cause and the Communist Party, so they let me go. When I settled down, I started going to church. I regained my faith.'

'Is it finished now? Have you found peace of mind and soul?'

'No, dear. I will never find peace of mind and soul. Not even faith in God will help me any more. I died the moment my family died. Everything afterwards only prolonged my pain. I no longer consider myself a human being.'

'But you are a human being. You are a very good person. You took care of me. You cared about Aunty and Uncle.'

'No, dear. Every time I looked at you, I felt ashamed. When you first arrived, your aunt told me who you were and asked if I would have enough power and strength to act as a normal human being; if I could take you as my medicine, as my cure. I realised that we have all been victims of disturbed individuals. Your grandfather, father, mother, uncle, aunt, my German saviour, my family, neighbours who killed my family and I never had a chance to be normal human beings. We have all been actors in someone's twisted imagination. For years and years, I lived with hatred. I hated everyone and everything. Until I understood that wars don't happen because we hate other languages, nations, or religions, but because we are manipulated in every aspect of our understandings, I couldn't find a reason to live.'

'But someone else attacked you, and you were just defending yourself.'

'In the war, the most important thing is who initiated and who concluded the conflict. All that happens in war makes people equal. Both sides are equally bad. Both sides share guilt. What is most important is how well you understand the propaganda from the start and whether you will be able to live without regret after the war. I don't believe that your family was bad when they put on the black uniform. I don't believe they had a choice because they wanted to survive by aligning themselves with the stronger side. Imagine what would have happened if people had immediately realised that they were being manipulated by political and military propaganda and had stripped evil individuals of their power. Just imagine... Imagine a world without these few groups of Satanists. Imagine living your life without manipulation and harm. What would have become of you, the world, and these evil individuals?'

'Should I forget and forgive them?'

'You can live your life in a way that no one, absolutely no one, has power over you. Your power is within you. Do not take the side of the strongest, but rather the honest. Do not align yourself with bad people, but rather with good people. Do not be ignorant and uneducated, as you will become an easy target for manipulation. Knowledge is freedom. Educate yourself in every field and question everything that is served to you. Keep this little spark of your soul deep within yourself. Do not show that you have a heart or a soul. They are after this.'

Elsa did survive the first impact of getting the truth out. She was very ashamed that she questioned the love of her uncle and aunt, but her pride talked to her ego. All the words spoken were so painful in her memory. She couldn't simply pretend that nothing had been said. She knew they were her true family. She saw pictures of her parents. She understood that they didn't have the power to help her parents, but people said such cruel words to her that she now felt ashamed she passed the hate forward. She couldn't pretend that she hadn't accused her loved ones. The words Yana spoke had the deepest impact on her, and she respected the suggestion that she cool down and continue with her life.

An elderly gentleman recently became widowed and required the assistance of a woman to help him carry on with his life. He didn't question Elsa as long as she was good at housework. He noticed that she liked to read books whenever it was possible. He deliberately let her do as much as she wanted, acting as if he didn't need anything from her. His young son, Eric, would come from time to time to visit him. He had just gotten married and had a young son. His wife didn't like to travel, so she said. He had a feeling she didn't like to travel to him as he was very strict and discerning. For some reason, he didn't like her. He never admitted that to her or his son. She needed someone who would admire her and say things she wanted to hear. Even though he never said a bad word to her, he also didn't say a good word either. She was avoiding him, always excused by her parenting (despite having a nanny), a headache, or other duties. He hadn't seen his grandson in 6 years. That was alright because he was afraid he might get sick if he travelled by an aeroplane or a car. It was a long way. He couldn't travel to him due to his health condition as well. He loved looking at his photos and was very proud of how he was growing. He was also eager to hear about the kind of child he was becoming. He was able to communicate with him on the phone, so this was satisfying enough.

He noticed that his son visits him almost every month. At first, he thought it was because he was afraid for him, but he noticed that he was looking in Elsa's direction rather than at him. The old gentleman was a bit confused with discovering. He didn't want his son to cheat on his wife, but also not to cheat on this girl either. He didn't want his son to leave his wife because of his grandson. However, he knew that Elsa might be a better partner for his son, so he was hoping that his son would consider taking that step. It was a kind of mixed feelings and desire.

'I appreciate your time, and thank you for accepting this meeting, Herr Conrad.'

'I accepted your meeting, Herr Stern, out of curiosity. You have been very secretive in your letter. I can only offer you alcohol, if you please. My servant is off today, so I won't be able to offer you anything else '

'No, thank you, Herr Conrad. I will not take up much of your time. I came here to say that you have something of mine.'

'What might that be?'

'Elsa.'

'Elsa? How can this be? You look like a very successful business-man. She is my servant.'

'I don't have much time, so I will be direct. She is the daughter of my best friend, who was killed in the war. I am Jewish, and he was German. I was raised by his family, as my parents passed away when I was very young. His father was my godfather, and I was raised as one of his. When the war broke out, my friend helped me come here.

He sold everything he could and gave me the money to start a business here. You know, we married sisters, so we became a family. He was killed after the war, and his wife was imprisoned. Elsa was born in prison and was subsequently separated from her mother in order to provide her with better living conditions. Her mother died in prison. My wife and I do not have any children. We decided to bring her here and raise her as our own daughter. We kept the secret that her father was in the Nazi troops and was executed. We also didn't say anything about her mother. We wanted to save her from the truth. We thought we were doing good , but obviously, she doesn't think the same way. She found out the truth by herself and blamed us for keeping the secret from her. She accused us of not being her family. I think she thinks we don't love her, but we do very much. My wife cries every day. She is getting sick. I can't sleep because I'm worried about both of them. I want both to be happy. I want Elsa to have a future. I think she blames herself for being alive while her parents are not. I couldn't save him. We couldn't save them. I am not a god. No one would have listened to me. I am just a simple man. I have no power to save anyone. Maybe I will save her. Who knows? Maybe?'

'Please do not be upset. I am sure everything will be alright. Young people think we are guilty of everything. They think we have the power to change their lives. But we can't.'

'I wish I could have found the right time and situation to tell her the truth, but I haven't. She is very angry with us. She didn't call or visit us for several months. If our servant hadn't told us that she knew where she was, we wouldn't have found her. We notified the police, and they began searching for her. They found her at her university a couple of weeks ago. She didn't want to tell them where she lived.

When I told my wife this, she was happy to realise that she was alive. All we want to know is that she is alive.'

'She is safe here too.'

'I want her to be happy. This is all I want. This is all we want for her.'

'How can I help you?'

'I want you to send her back to the university. Her mother was a nurse. My wife is a doctor. I want her to continue her grandparents' dream. Both of them wanted their daughters to be educated. To be highly educated is a source of pride for women of that region. This should be my legacy and a way to pay respect to the people who raised me.'

'I am fine with that. If she wants to continue studying, I can help with that.'

'No, no, you don't understand me. I will pay for her education and cover all of her expenses. However, if she understands that I am pay-ing for it, she will stop studying. I will also pay for an additional serv-ant to assist you.'

'Money is not a worry for me. I want to help you, too. And to her, as well.'

'I put my trust in you. And faith.'

Soon, these two gentlemen became close friends and shared infor-mation about Elsa during their secret meetings. Elsa was sent back to finish her studies and also work part-time at the house of Herr Conrad.

She had no idea that she was the reason for a new friendship. However, she was aware that she had become the subject of young Eric's interest. She was cautious around him. She didn't want to get into trouble with his wife and be a reason for their separation. She was aware that the old gentleman didn't like his wife. He encouraged Elsa to go out at night with Eric. At first, she thought Eric was only being kind because she was taking care of his father. However, when he expressed his romantic feelings, Elsa made the decision to be fair and end this "friendship". She gave him an ultimatum: either he stops seeing her, or she will leave his father.

After several months of not seeing Elsa, Eric decided to leave London and return to Zurich. Somehow, it was expected, as Eric was not happy with his relationship, and the difference in characters became the main reason for splitting. Elsa initially felt very bad. She thought she was the cause of Eric's divorce. Seeing how miserable and angry he was, she decided to concentrate on her studies, care for the old man, and stay out of his sight. Eric gave himself time to recover by immersing himself in his work. The house was very big, and their garden was also spacious, so it wasn't difficult to avoid seeing each other.

Two years after his divorce, they started dating. After a short period of engagement, they got married in a Registrar's office. Alexander was on his way. It was a very busy period for Elsa. She was getting married, expecting a baby, and finishing her studies, so she didn't notice that she was being followed day and night. She didn't notice that her aunt and uncle were always there during the most important period of her life. They didn't want to cause any distractions or stress her out, so they always stayed close enough to be a part of the most important moments in her life but far enough not to be noticed.

The day Alexander was born, Elsa felt very sad for being all alone. She knew that mothers were always by their daughters' side in this very important moment. She was all alone. Her husband was by her side, but she didn't want him there. She needed her mother, and the only mother she knew was her aunt. Moments, as long as a century, passed by as she cried for her mother. She got up from her hospital bed and went to a call box.

'Aunty, I need you. Please come to me. I need you. You are my mother. I am in labour, I need you. I cannot bring a child into this life without my mother.'

'Oh, my sunshine, I will be there in a moment.'

Aunt Lilly was frantically driving to the hospital to see her niece. The moment she caught Elsa's hand, Alexander entered this world. Being born into a privileged family meant that he didn't experience any situations that could hinder his emotional and mental development. He had teachers of all sorts. His parents wanted him to learn languages, so they hired nannies who spoke native language. If they wanted him to learn skills, he had highly educated teachers who helped him develop all the skills a child needed. They believed in the importance of education so that he would develop as a good and normal human being. When he travelled around the world, he had an entourage of people who satisfied all his needs. He was a little prince from a fairy tale. Even though he had a good start which indicated that he would grow up as a good human, this was not assurance that he will not change his character due to different circumstances. It was not assurance that he might not develop dark secret desires or misbehave.

His mother had career obligations to fulfil, and his father had to take care of the family business. He was working in the pharmaceutical industry. They also started a business in private hospital treatments, so they bought properties and converted them into hospitals. Their clientele consisted mainly of individuals with significant financial resources. Elsa's uncle decided to abandon his career as a banker, selling his shares in banks and giving the proceeds to Elsa and her husband for investment in hospitals. Elsa gave birth to two more children, a daughter and a son. She gave her best to be a good mother, but being torn between her career and motherhood meant that she would suffer in all areas. She loved her children, she cared for them, but she didn't have the time to be a mother who could educate her children. She needed to pass her wisdom onto her children, something so crucial to a human beings, but she failed. Her husband was also busy with his business. He loved Elsa, and in a moment of solitude, he understood that they were parting ways as a couple and as a family. Children were given to others for education. Aunt Lilly and Yana were always there to help as well. It was their wisdom and life experience that passed onto them, whether good or bad. Elsa and Eric haven't been much involved in the upbringing of their children. Alexander was almost seven years old when Elsa and Eric decided to bring their children along with them to their jobs after realising that children are not connected with them. They decided to share an office space in one of their properties so they could see each other and their children more often.

The full schedule of their lives became even more hectic when Elsa decided to go regularly to church. She wanted to be a Roman Catholic, just like her ancestors. Her aunt was not very keen on religion. She thought that religion keeps its members under strong control and takes away genuine faith. However, Elsa thought that as she lacked religious studies, it would be more beneficial if children learned about faith at an early age. Eric was raised as a Protestant. He didn't mind if Elsa wanted to be a Roman Catholic, but he was surprised when she made the decision to baptise Alexander in the Catholic church, believing that the father, as the master of the house, should bring this decision. He didn't like that she made a decision on her own and organised everything by herself, ignoring him totally. Elsa, being a woman, won. When other children were born, Eric was determined that they should be baptised in a Protestant church. This time, Elsa realised how Eric could be a strong leader. Elsa was not a submissive person, but she knew her limits. Just because they were baptised in different churches, the family had arguments about which church they should go to. To avoid conflict and arguments, they decided to attend the Roman Catholic Church on one Sunday and the Protestant church on another Sunday. When the children were growing up, Elsa was more stubborn and asked Eric to enrol them in a school where religious studies were a significant subject. For the first time, Eric raised his voice at Elsa and ordered her to stop with this nonsense. He will not allow her to brainwash his children. Again, she won.

Alexander was a well-behaved child, at least until he discovered his ego. His half-brother visited his father and other siblings every winter. He was a frequent victim of mockery as he always returned to the UK with at least one broken bone. Officially, George had both parents, but in reality, he grew up alone. He had to learn every survival trick by himself. His mother was preoccupied with her life of gambling and drinking, indulging in a hedonistic lifestyle, while his father took care of another family. Maybe George hated his siblings, who had a normal life. Maybe he was just having fun in a peculiar way; who knows? Alexander loved him, and his visits were attracted to the blood bond, so putting him in dangerous situations hadn't been taken in a negative way. While he was underage, all of these funny situations were monitored. However, when Alexander changed schools at the age of fifteen, these funny situations were becoming very serious.

The first conflict Alexander had with his parents happened when he asked if he could go to the cinema and watch a film that his parents thought was not suitable for children. There has been explicit content that they thought he shouldn't be exposed to at this age. However, his friends and George were speaking about a film, and they mocked him for not seeing it. So he decided to go to the cinema without his parents' permission. He skipped the training and escaped from his chauffeur. The chauffeur immediately reported to his parents. His father thought this was outrageous, leaving the hard part to the mother to deal with. She kept talking and talking, unable to stop with her "what ifs" and complaints about Alexander's behaviour.

'You are acting like Hitler!'– A word said to his mother changed his life's direction and relationship with his parents forever unable to understand the meaning at that time and withdraw his deed. The next thing he remembered, was a hard slap in his face.

'Hitler?! Are you comparing me to Hitler?!'– One slap after another, his mother couldn't stop until her husband intervened and pushed her aside. She couldn't stop beating her son.

'Son, out of all the words you could have said, you choose this one? You don't know what this meant to her.'

Being young and driven by hormones, with a bit of pride and stubbornness, he didn't want to admit that he had crossed the line and lost his mother's trust. He didn't understand what the word had caused in her. He thought it was just her overreacting to a silly name, but to her, it was like her own child mocked the death of her parents and belittled everything they went through because of that evil man. From that moment onwards, they just argued and fought. They lost mutual respect. The angrier she became with him, the more uncontrollable he became. The more she talked and tried to restrain him, the more he desired freedom. He didn't want to hear about his grandparents, their lives, or his mother's childhood.

Despite being very intelligent, his grades were lower than expected. He was frequently trying to escape from his chauffeurs, as they often argued, and sometimes he even physically abused them. They reached a point where no one wanted to work for this family. Eventually, his parents took over this duty and drove him to school but allowed him to walk home. It was a bad decision for him to join groups of troubled children. He was attending a school where all the students were rich children. All children were privileged, but some were troubled due to a lack of emotional and mental support from their parents. After talking with his father, George stepped in as a support for the young boy, but instead, he further confused his mind. Instead of going to school, at sixteen and seventeen, he was travelling across Europe, attending various parties, meeting people he shouldn't have met, going to places a young boy shouldn't go to, and engaging in activities a young boy shouldn't have done. He thought he was enjoying his life. He thought, "This is freedom." After a while, Eric had had enough, so he asked George to leave Alexander alone and return to the UK George understood that they had completely lost control. Alexander thought that all he was doing was enjoying his freedom by escaping parental control. Of course, not thinking clear enough out of selfishness, this enjoyment was at the expense of his parents' money. People in his surroundings understood that he was able to provide them with benefits, so they loved being around him taking advantage of him. He felt special, loved, respected, and like a member of a fun gang. Sometimes, he was a troublemaker and other times, he was a leader of the pack. His parents tolerated him, believing that this was just a temporary phase, something new teenagers do. They thought that time would work in their favour, changing him once he finished with all the naughtiness he was engaging in. They made excuses for themselves as well as for him. But he didn't stop. The culmination of his drinking, drug abuse, violence, and association with the wrong crowd occurred when he took a car and struck a pedestrian. He ended up in a police station facing charges. He was still a minor, and his family meant a lot to the locals. Police wanted to speak to his parents before making a final decision. His father was tired of him. His mother adored Alexander, but he was exhausting her to the point where she couldn't take care of other children. They gave up on him, leaving him to destroy his life, so when a policeman offered them an escape route, they willingly accepted the proposal.

'Son, this is it. I can't do this any more. You crossed the line a long time ago. For a couple of years now, we have not been able to find peace. You broke every rule we had. We didn't raise you that way. We completely lost control over you. We don't know what to do with you any more.'

'Control! You said it, Dad. All you care about is controlling me.'

'You lost control over yourself, child. You disappear for weeks, drink excessively, do drugs, party with unknown adults, and engage in fights at nightclubs. You are violent towards everyone. You have completely lost control, son.'

'Now you are telling me that you have been better in at my age...
I am your son. Look at George. He is the same, and you don't care.
Why are you hating me so much just for having a little bit of fun?'

'We can no longer do that. You could have killed an innocent person.'

'Well, he is guilty himself. He came out of nowhere. He didn't
watch where he was going.'

'You stole my car!'

'Technically, this is not stealing. You are my father, and therefore
this car is also mine.'

'You don't understand! You could have become a murderer. You
could end up in jail.'

'But you are my father, and you will help me stay out of jail. Right,
Dad!'

'No! I signed papers stating that you will join the army.'

'Ha-ha. That will only be a couple of months, and this will be fun.'

'No. This will not take a couple of months. You will attend military school and remain in their service until you complete it.'

'Yeah, well, whatever. When am I going? At least you won't be on
my back.'

After a couple of months, Alexander realised that he had experienced all the fun before he had put on a uniform. In the beginning, he
thought he could live life on his own terms, but his officers were not

his parents, siblings, or servants. In the short breaks he had, his thoughts went in the direction of his mother. She was his guide, but she let him go. The first time she let him go, he was lost. He thought he was escaping her control and that she was holding him back from living his life. His life, not hers. He thought he was fighting to live his own dreams, not hers. Being outside of her guidance, he realised that she was overprotective, and he didn't comprehend that she wanted him to be safe. He understood that she didn't want him to experience the same suffering she had. He lost it. Indeed, he lost both her and himself together. He was homesick. He wanted to reunite with his family, but his pride prevented him from taking the first step. He desired so much to hear someone calling him back. He was left among strangers who didn't care much about him. And if he left the army, where should he go? He had a particular lifestyle. He wasn't ignorant about life. He didn't have any qualifications or skills to support himself, and the world can be harsh towards gentle and honest individuals. He could be a criminal, but the life of a criminal is full of suffering, violence, and constraints. He didn't want to go back to his family crawling, either. He didn't have any solution, so the only place where he could stay was the army. It is not the best environment, but it is not the worst either. He understood that the best way to avoid oppression and aggression from officers was to obey rules and use his intelligence. He didn't lack intelligence, and over the past few years, he had the opportunity to learn communication skills and character analysis. This was a very useful skill.

***

After two years had passed, his father showed up at the barracks doorstep. Alexander thought that his family had given up on him because they hadn't sent him a single letter. No phone calls were received, but one day his father appeared. At first, he didn't want to see him. However, knowing how stubborn and persistent he can be, he reluctantly showed up in the visitation room. His father looked older and more serious.

'I was struggling to come over. I wasn't sure if you would like to see us, to see me. But I tried.'

'But you came over. How are you, Dad?'

'I am fine. We are all fine. Your siblings are growing up. We struggle with life, that's all. One member is missing.'

'How's Mum? Did she not come to visit me?'

'No, she didn't come. For several months now, she has been urging me to come over. To visit you.'

'Why are you having difficulty contacting me? You haven't done anything wrong.'

'Mum and I have a deep regret, a remorse that doesn't give us peace. We wanted to come over many times. We wrote countless letters to you but didn't send them. We didn't want to anger you.'

'I am not angry, Dad. I am not angry at either of you at all. I am truly sorry this happened. I really lost control of myself. Tell Mum it's alright to come over whenever you want. And, by the way, Anabel is sending me letters from time to time. I know all about you.'

'Oh, does she? A little rascal... Well, this is sibling's love, I guess. How do you live here? Do you want to come out?'

'No, Dad. I am fine here. I want to complete my studies and become an officer. Maybe this is my future. Army!? Who would have thought that I could become a soldier? I never imagined myself in uniform, like my ancestors. I hope I will never find myself in a situation where I would end my life hanging on a pole, like a flag…'

'Please never mention this! Please! This is not a joke.'

'I know, Dad. I know. Maybe I will choose my side wisely this time.'

Alexander's military training and studies to become an officer were at the end. His mother and siblings were able to visit him whenever he was permitted to have guests, and whenever he had free time, he would go home. His mum found peace with him. She was more careful with words. She didn't like seeing his uniform, you could see how sad she was, but she kept quiet. It reminded her of her late father she has never met him and his destiny. She didn't push her luck with her child, either, by telling him "ifs" sentences. She controlled herself and the words that came out of her mouth. It seemed that this worked for all of them, so finally, they were able to enjoy moments of peace and harmony.

After the training, just about the time when he had to decide about his future career, an opportunity arose when the war in Yugoslavia broke out. He was looking at television actions that he wanted to see with his own eyes. He spoke the language and was familiar with the culture, yet he was not sentimentally involved or had any personal interest in choosing a side. He was a perfect match for the position of Military observer. His supervisors wanted to know what was going on in the far neighbourhood, and being neutral, they had to find a way how to be involved but not officially participate. The answer came through the Pontifical Vatican Swiss army. His mother grew anxious upon learning about his decision. He was looking at her face while she was watching the television news. Even though she didn't know anyone there and was occasionaly visiting this country on vacation with her family, she loved this country to bits. The origin of her identity was there. The language she spoke to her children was from that country. The history of her existence and the graves of her ancestors was there. She grew up in another country. She loved her second home country very much because it provided her with a future, a good life, a family, and a new home. She had two home countries, but she shed tears more for the one she didn't live in. She was spiritually and emotionally more connected with the country she was born in even though she didn't live there for most of her life. Even in such dreadful circumstances, hating the country where she was born would have felt like abandoning herself. The images that appeared before her were extremely distressing, and she struggled to find inner peace. She was confused about what was happening there. She had conflicting emotions. She was expected to hate one side and love another, but she was unsure of which one. She didn't understand who the villain in this story was. When she learned that Alexander would be involved in observing military actions, she felt anxious and scared. She never thought that someone from her family would participate again in a war. She was proud that the country she was living in was neutral in every military and political aspect. She didn't know if she should be worried for her son's life, too, as he could be a victim. Her entire life came to a halt when he packed his bag, and the situation became unbearable. It was too real for her.

This was an exciting period in the young man's life. The first flight to the office in Rome and then to the border with Austria became ecstatic. Finally, he will be a real soldier and participate in real action. This is what he thought. However, the uniform he was wearing and the insignia on it showed that he was supposed to be only an observer and nothing more, but being young and foolish, this didn't mean a thing to him. He was a bit surprised and disappointed to learn that nothing significant was happening in the city where the Swiss embassy was. He was expecting more action. The building was empty anyway, as were other embassies. Churches were actively assisting refugees by providing them with shelter and support. Convoys of military and food donations were flowing into the country despite heavy embargo. He didn't expect to see full shops working as normal and weapons of all sorts flowing as free as the embargo didn't exist. He saw famous journalists posing in front of UN headquarters, frantically speaking about military actions as they were looking at it with their own eyes, telling the world that they spoke from their experience only the truth, while the truth was that they feared for their lives in a free town where military actions didn't exist. They have never been on the frontline even for a second, but the whole "truth" came from public relations, given to them, and they interpreted it as they pleased. He shared a table among all these military observers and famous journalists who were keen to work on different cases. He relied solely on his colleagues' information, which turned out to be unreliable and untruthful. He joined the gang without questioning or doubting until he realized what is going on. All the news was communicated through state officials instead of on-field reporters, but journalists, military observers, and others formed their desired perceptions and reported to their supervisors accordingly. As a result, the ambiguous proceedings made him visualise a bone being thrown at hundreds of hungry dogs. "This is not observing! This is not getting the naked truth!" - Alexander was thinking as he woke up.

As he was a very sociable person with good communication skills, always prepared to joke and make fun, he conducted his first interview on the streets of the big city. He went to local pubs, meeting young men and girls in uniforms. It took him a while to gain their trust. He was hearing stories of people carrying two golden bullets with their names on them and wondered if he would do the same in a time of need. They were telling him that one bullet was for them if they were about to be caught. They didn't want to be tortured and slaughtered if they had to die. The second bullet was for the president if they survived the war, as he was responsible for the war they were sent to. Many of them whom he had met never came back to the coffee shops where they had met. Then, he tried to discreetly interview refugees in churches who were coming for food aid. He was meeting different people every day, searching for the truth. He was listening to incredible stories every day, which made him suspicious about foreigners participating in this mess. The information he obtained was insufficient to report important details to his supervisors despite his effort. The only thing where he could get real stuff was to go on the field. He mentioned this to his supervisors in both the Vatican and Switzerland, but they rejected his idea. His persistence and diplomatic negotiation made them re-think their decision.

'You have sent me for observation to give you the truth, and I cannot say that what I am giving you is the truth. I am not a journalist who waits in the office for a pigeon with a message so that I can spread false information to the public and politicians, leading to incorrect decisions. If you want the truth, then support my idea to go on the frontline.'

"Beware of what you wish for," wise people would say, their words echoing in his mind. He loved military action films, secretly imagined himself holding a heavy gun, shooting at villains, and miraculously dodging hundreds of bullets. However, the reality is different. You don't hear your thoughts; your heart doesn't beat; all you know is a rush of adrenaline when you hear an explosion. There are no heroes when you see how a bullet passes the body at arm's length near you. You don't think it could've been me. You hide, shout, scream... and you survive. You hate the moon on the dark night or the sun on the summer sky, as it will make you run, hide or die. You love rain as you can get some sleep and rest. You don't think of the smell, of body parts under your boots, of gender or age of victims. You don't care whether they have been good or bad while they were alive. You feel nothing for the screams of living humans beneath the boots of executioners, who order their victims to stay still while they take their lives. You have no feelings when you look at lifeless bodies, still warm, still moving in a pool of warm blood. You have no feelings when you look at executors with bloody clothes, with a bloody knife dripping with fresh blood, tired of killing their victims. They were swearing at them as they gave them a hard time to finish their jobs. It was their job!? The killing was the job of a soldier fighting for the interests of the elite sitting comfortably in their modern, huge offices, annoyed that they have to hear about incompetent servants and missing their children's birthday parties. These soldiers tried their best to serve their generals who were busy partying on their enemies' yachts. The same authority figures were exploiting the poor victims' wealth while holidaying with their families on the enemy's side. Two sides were fighting on the field while their commanders from both sides were sitting naked in luxurious yachts somewhere far away from the war, enjoying expensive drinks and food and laughing with officers who were supposed to be their adversaries. They confidently issued orders to their soldiers from the safety of free territory. While simple soldiers were dying and killing each other, commanders were enjoying the fruits of their "slaves," making plans with enemies about further military actions. Trust in leaders is a weapon aimed at yourself.

In war, there are no clear distinctions between the good and bad sides. Everyone fought for "freedom". Everyone fought for their "family". Everyone was just "responding to a provocation, defending themselves". Everyone was just trying to "survive". It didn't matter who was lying on the ground in a pool of blood. It didn't matter whose house was burning. "You will burn my house, and when I get the chance, I will burn your house" was a common motto. Revenge mattered; it was a guide. "You killed my friend, and I will kill your friend. It doesn't matter whether you are young, old, a child, a man or a woman, rich, poor…Kill, steal, slaughter, burn, humiliate, torture, rape, and exploit as much as possible. It doesn't matter if I know you or if we had a past friendship or sibling relationship. I will kill you because you are not on my side. You are not of my nationality, of my religion, of my part of the world. I will do everything my sick mind tells me. I will do without questioning whatever it was expected from my officers to do. It doesn't matter if doing so is unethical, illegal, unconventional, immoral, or inhuman. I have a hidden agenda to feed my selfish and egoistic desires to take your life, and I will do everything in my capacity to fulfil them." This was a war motto.

Alexander was shocked at first to learn how people think while pursuing military objectives. He was shocked at what a human could do to another fellow human. He was shocked to hear how they justified their decisions, where ethics, morality, honesty, honour, and promise had no value. The lowest humans' desires and needs were fulfilled to the fullest. A human life didn't matter. He never thought he would call for God's protection and pray to survive, but in bad times, he remembered his name. The worst thing was that he was alone. He had trust issues. He couldn't speak to anyone. He was a silent participant in the worst human degradation, and he couldn't do anything. In short periods of silence, he remembered his grandfather. He understood what he was going through. But Alexander had a choice. He was not a soldier of any opposed army. He was just an observer. His connections and character opened the most sealed doors and brought him to the places of nightmare only a few of them could see. "So, this is what the hell looks like?! This is what demons look like!? This is what they do?!" Years later, when he remembered where he was, he wondered how he could be everywhere where the worst actions had taken place. He was looking with his own eyes at executions, burnings of entire villages, human enslavement, rape, concentration camps, tortures, and he stayed alive. He was on every side. He was supposed to be only on the side of Catholic Christians, but Orthodox Christians and Muslims called him on their side, too, to be an observer. He was supposed to be neutral in his reports, and all he wanted was the truth. But to gain the trust of savages meant to fall on the level of savages as well. He could take alcohol and drugs without affecting his consciousness or actions. He knew his limits and the consequences of exceeding them. Perhaps this was the key to his success. He was sometimes happy that they gave him access to the action course and did not call him when actions were over. He wanted to see everything with his own eyes. From time to time, he had to remind himself what was right and what was wrong, to be objective and neutral. He started enjoying war games as others did after a while, being a human he was caught in this wicked game too. He was increasingly consumed by this nightmare. After a year and a half of participating in the war as an observer, he was losing himself, but a spark of an unseemly girl's eye, walking in a convoy of refugees, brought him to reality. Just for a second, he saw this thin, short-haired girl, who looked more like a boy, with poor clothes on her, nothing special about her, looking for a second in his direction. He heard the voice in himself: "Beware of what you are doing. I will not forgive you." Second after, he heard his name and a soldier called him.

'Alex, namesake, look who I found for you. Here is your bride! – A soldier with the same name, who became his "friend" for the name's sake, pulled an old woman in a national dress out of the convoy, showing him how ugly and old she was, making fun of an old woman who barely walked.

'No, not for me. Thank you. I am still in celibacy.'

'Come on, be a real man, priest. You should have some fun, my friend. God is on vacation.'

'Not for me, thank you. You can take her for yourself.'

'Who, me? I wouldn't spit on her. Look at her… You don't want her, huh? Ok.' – He pulled the trigger and shot the old woman in front of all the people walking by. No one responded to this. No refugees, no his comrades, no his officers, no UN soldiers, no observers… Like she wasn't a human. No reaction at all. They were continuing walking not interested in what had just happened. At the same time, a word crossed his mind: "I lost already! God forgive me!"

***

After almost six years of war observation, military actions were almost finalised. Alexander was well-known on all sides. If anyone had ever visited the Balkans, they would have had the opportunity to meet and greet him. He was everywhere, and everyone knew him. No one could understand his true nature. It was unclear whether he was a good or a bad person. He was omnipresent and omniscient. Not so many people knew what he was doing there among them, but they used him to get information. He also utilised these connections to achieve his desires. He refrained from judging others. He didn't preach, he didn't point, he didn't snitch, but he knew everything. He knew what "good people" do when they can and what they do when they can't. He knew that all of them were equally bad as these three enemies who were fighting. He knew about national treasure theft, organ harvesting, human enslavers, protected animal stealing, buying cheap stolen gold, illegal border crossing, top secret information trade, kidnapping, trading babies, kidnapping girls for global prostitution… He knew everything, and still, he could sit peacefully with them, eat, and drink as if they were his best friends. Sometimes, he would be tested to determine if he was a spy and a potential danger to them. Other times, they would try to tempt him with the intention of recruiting him into their groups. Whatever the reason was to speak to him, all of them had a huge benefit. Sometimes, he was doing dirty work for them, gaining their trust and joining their groups; sometimes, he was just an observer keeping secret . He had been devoid of emotions for a significant period of time and did not feel their absence. He was an emotionless human machine until a little girl named Stella entered his life.

'Hey, Alex, could I have a moment with you?'

'Yes, of course! How can I assist you?'

'I have a living package. Are you interested?'

'What do you have? A bear? You took all the bears out of the mountain. Horses? None left. Girls? You can handle them by yourself.'

'No, little people.'

'Why me?'

'Well, it's kind of related to you.'

'How is this possible? I didn't make any babies while I was here. I can't tell this for you. You are spreading your genetics around the globe.'

'No, it is not mine.'

'OK. I am listening.'

'A couple is collecting children for the global market. They told me that the church gave them a child who was not supposed to be there.'

'How come?'

'The girl was cleaned (read raped) in a concentration camp and kept to give a birth but let her go before the baby was born. She came here and gave up on the baby. She was not welcomed in children's homes , so they gave the child to the couple.'

'For adoption?'

'No man, for adoption?! These children are for the market. You know, people who like children.'

'You mean, these couples are selling children to paedophiles.'

'Well, not only to paedophiles,. People are purchasing children for various reasons. Some of them like to eat young meat. Some to play with them. I heard some of them are kept and treated like pets. Some of them are used for pharmaceutical treatment.'

'So, what do you want from me?'

'Well, I used to work with them. Some individuals have entered the industry and are threatening us to cease our operations in this area, or they will report us to the authorities.'

'So what? The authorities are working with you.'

'Well, they are a "kind of higher authority". They requested additional funds in exchange for allowing us to work on their territory. We cannot afford that.'

'I still do not understand what you are asking of me.'

'You have your channels and contacts if you are able to discreetly transport the package to a certain place.'

'I can't compromise my connections and relationships. I have never worked with live packages.'

'We can split the money. It is crucial to deliver the package to this address.'

'How much money are we talking about?'

'I sold the package for 25,000 marks. I can give you ten thousands.'

'I have to see the package first.'

A large house in an exclusive neighbourhood, surrounded by diplomatic institutions, concealed a significant secret. Alexander saw many young girls tending to infants while lying on the floor. They appeared to be waiting for someone. All eyes turned towards him as he entered with the human smuggler. A baby cried in the corner of the room. She was petite. She looked like she was hungry and scared, but out of fear, she immediately stopped crying. She was only wearing diapers and had no clothes nearby. Alexander sat near her, and for some reason, this little blue-eyed baby got up and pinched his arm, trying to balance her walk. He sat her opposite of him and looked at her. He saw the same spark as he saw in the eyes of a random girl who made him think of his actions. He desired this spark. It felt as though a spark was guiding him through his personal hell. This little girl had the same look and the same energy coming out of her eyes that, for a moment, he didn't know where he was and who he was.

'Did you already sell the package?'

'Yes, I told you, I sold it. I got advance payment.'

'For twenty-five thousand marks?'

'What if I give you fifty thousand marks?'

'Hey, man. This package is not worth the price. I can kill for fifty marks, and you are giving me fifty thousand. Why would you take her?'

'I can do what you do. But I have better buyers.'

'Hay man, you probably have. Ok, deal. I can keep her until tomorrow. Is this enough for you until tomorrow? I can't have her for longer.'

'Ok, tomorrow it is. Don't try to cross me; I can easily find you wherever you go.'

'Well, I can wait for you until tomorrow. If you cross me, then I will get rid of her in other ways.'

Alex had no trouble finding a large sum of money in just one day. He already had prepared money in case he needed to escape from hell. He didn't know why he was doing that. He was unsure of what to do with the child, but he felt compelled to take her. The child was stuck in his mind, and he gained his peace only when he got her in his arms. He was surprised to see her legal documents, but he doubted their authenticity. In less than 24 hours, with the assistance of his connections, she was brought to his apartment in Switzerland. The child became anxious and started crying due to the stress and travel in the car boot. She was drugged while she was travelling, but afterwards she didn't stop crying. Alexander had younger siblings, and caring for children wasn't so strange for him, but this time was a bit different. He got this child illegally, and it could compromise him for life. He made a decision to take her, but now, when she finally came into his life, he doubted his decision.

'Bring this child immediately here!' – His mother screamed at him when he told her.

'From all the wrong things you did, this is a culmination, son!' – His father screamed, too.

'Mum, dad, you are sitting in this beautiful, spacious, modern house, thinking you know it all. I can sense that you still have doubts about me. You still think I am not capable of making the right decision. Will you give me a chance to explain the situation?'

'Alexander, is this your child? Are you telling me that you have made a child with someone there?'

'No, mum, this is not my child.'

'This is crazy. Where did this child come from? You just came from Croatia. Did someone give it to you?'

'Oh, mum, so many questions. Take a deep breath!'

'We are all listening to you, son. Now speak!'

'Mum! Dad! The world is truly cruel. All the information and footage you shared with me about the war cannot compare to what I have personally witnessed. The value of a human life was fifty German marks. Did you know that people paid fifty marks to shoot another human? This war turned into a human-hunting playground. If someone was permitted to use a knife to kill, they were required to pay a hundred marks. The price depended on the severity of the killing. Imagine the world we live in. You mentioned that one person was a villain while the other was defending their life and family. In this war, everyone played the role of both villain and defender, attacking and defending simultaneously. A brother went on brother. A woman murdered her husband due to opposite nationality. How did she not ask about his nationality before marrying him? One brother killed another because they supported different nationalities based on their parents nationality. I can comprehend this notion of national vampirism. I have heard that the Balkans can be a bit crazy, but I always believed that Westerners were more civilised and had nothing to be ashamed of. While the Balkans were engaged in conflict, Westerners took advantage of the situation to exploit their resources. Nothing was sacred to them. Again, I would understand if they took goods, gold, pictures, and national treasures…but they were killing, buying, and kidnapping humans. There were concentration camps just for organ harvesting, and doctors participated in these things. Doctors, mum! Doctors, like you! They were saving one patient's life who paid them a fortune while killing another human being, caught like an animal on safari. I would understand if they were adopting children who were legally parentless, but they kidnapped children for their own perverse desires. Girls as young as five years old were raped. They were killed for amusement. There is no perversion in the human head that I haven't seen with my own eyes. I cannot identify any individual as a good, normal human being. Do you know what would've happened to this child if I didn't bring her here? She would've been raped, killed, and eaten! All this would've happened here. Do you understand this!? Do you?! Mum! Dad! She would've been eaten like a piece of animal meat!'

'Oh, my God! What are you saying, my child?'

'I am saying, mum, I've seen such things I cannot explain to you in words.'

'What are institutions doing there? What are western institutions doing there?'

'Mum, western institutions are doing that. Civilian institutions are balancing the situation, but if any of them had power, as little power as they had, they were joining these wicked things. It was a mess. I was looking at hell with my own eyes. There are no other demons but humans, mum. All of them wanted a piece of the cake. All who could make money participated in this wickedness. In the end, innocent humans paid the price. All of them were corrupt. Maybe at the beginning, it was an offensive-defensive game, but afterwards, all parties were just killing and harming each other for money and power.'

'So you saved the baby's life? – Anabel just entered the room with her fiancé and their youngest brother.'

'You can say that. Yes.'

'What now? Are you going to keep the baby, or are you going to hand it over to social institutions?'

'No, I am not giving her to anyone. I will keep her. But I need your help.'

'How are we going to legalise her here, son? - Mum was concerned.'

'I don't know. You tell me what are my options?'

'You can go to social services and inform them that one of your girls brought a child, claiming it is yours.' - His little brother made fun of him.

' No, I will go and tell you made it with someone. And now, I have to take care of it. You idiot!'

'I could say that a woman brought the child in to a hospital and left it.' – His mother provided an option.

'No, mum, they would take the child. – Anabel added.'

'We cannot compromise ourselves with lies.' – Father interfered.

'We can say that I gave birth to the child. So the child can be in my name.' - Anabel said.

'No, they would ask for a blood test and examination. They would see you didn't give birth to the child.'

'Mum, you can do something about the blood test. You have the power. Do we not own the hospital?'

'I don't think it would be possible to do such things.'

'This country is not immune of to illegal things. These things happen here, too.'

'Yes, but I don't want to compromise the whole family for the sake of your brother's stupidity.'

'Mum, you are judging me again. Haven't I just told you why I brought her here?'

'How on earth did you bring her here after all? Did you put her in a box and shoot her over the border? You put her in a letter, and the mailman delivered it to your address.' - Little brother taunted him again.

'Someone brought her here. She appeared to have papers. These individuals brought numerous children and falsely claimed them as refugee children.'

'Do you have papers?'

'The name mentioned may not be the actual name. Here you have it.'

'Lucia Tomić…'

'We cannot keep this name as it is. We need to change it.'

'You know what. Stop making plans. I will contact someone at the Vatican and ask for help. – his father abruptly ended the conversation.'

'Dad, someone has to be in charge of her.'

'Your brother, of course.'

'No dad, look at her. She is a gift from heaven. We are getting married and plan to adopt a child. He will never be a good father. Look at him! I will look after her.'

'You!! You are still not married. You haven't finished school yet. No job either. How will you care for a baby?'

'The child needs both parents, and this may help resolve our problems if we adopt the child.'

'Okay, if that's the case, you will marry my sister and legally adopt the child. We will remain silent and pretend that this child is yours. I will consult with a priest who can help me legalise her arrival here.

You will sign the required documents, and everything will be resolved.' - What was said, was done.

Days passed. Then weeks… then months… Stella was growing. She took her first steps soon after adoption. Then, pronounced her first clear word. She started running and making people fall in love with her. She brought happy days to her family. She was a doll, a family pet, an entertainer, and a subject to worry. But she loved her uncle Alexander the most of all. She never felt unloved or unaccepted by anyone, but her uncle's love made her feel like a special human being. She was lessening all his troubles and was looking forward to healing his emotional wounds. This little being was the cure for his damaged soul and life. He lost his compass and lived a directionless life.

After leaving the army, he decided to join the family business. He went on to educate himself further and made new friends and connections. But it wasn't possible to leave old ones behind. He was not drawn to war games, but rather, he was unable to break free from the influence of his "dark friends." He believed he had no obligations to them, but they disagreed. He couldn't escape from their circle, and more and more people from that circle, who were new to him but familiar to the others, approached him. The language they used was highly symbolic and ambiguous. You had to decipher the meaning behind their words, determining whether they were a threat or a plea for help. He was trapped in a vicious cycle of darkness and negative energy. His eyes witnessed the cruelty of humans towards the weak, driven by wickedness, perversion, money, and power. He could never understand why he kept involving himself in these circles. Was he drawn to wickedness or power? Was he drawn to the benefits or the protection offered by the so-called brotherhood of a dark secret society? Was he brainwashed into thinking that what he was doing was correct? Did he satisfy his perverse desires? Was he simply curious and too weak to leave this society? He was asking himself why he was there. He questioned the existence of God when he witnessed the wickedness of humans. He was asking himself who he should serve if he needed to serve. He never received the answers he was seeking. He was a mere leaf adrift in a stormy sea. Some of his so-called friends experienced the power of joining these groups, and he felt drowned in earthly waste. His business flourished; his pocket was full of money, but he felt he didn't have the feelings he should have had. No tear, no scream, no begging, nothing could shake him or wake him up. Stella was the sole person capable of animating him. She was the only person who he believed was worth his life. She was his North Star.

Years passed by. As his family aged, he also grew older. He hasn't got married yet despite having several serious relationships. He had no desire for a family. Deep down in his soul, he believed he was unworthy of a normal life. He fulfilled all of his low and high desires. He shattered many hearts, but his own heart remained unbroken. He desired someone to break his heart, but laughing, he was saying he didn't possess one. Somehow he managed to balance his life and made a wise choice in seeking out someone who could provide him with simple thoughts and recharge his spiritual energy. He was torn between aligning with the good guys and the bad guys, often switching sides depending on his mood. While he felt weak in the presence of the honest and good guys, he felt confident and empowered when he was with the bad ones. The constant fluctuation in energy levels was making him tired. He had seen it all, been everywhere, met everyone, and done everything... there was nothing left for him to accomplish. There was no more to experience. Nothing excited him any more.

'Why don't you get married? This will uplift your spirit.' – His childhood friends provided guidance when they met him at a cosy restaurant near a lake. – 'Find someone for God's sake. Stop searching. Stop chasing women. Make some babies.'

'I can't find the right woman.'

'Are you looking in the right place for her?'

'I have had a strange feeling my entire life. Every time I approach a woman, I get this feeling that maybe she could be the one. I am unsure of what I am looking for. It is not physical. It is not emotional. It is a kind of spiritual need. It is not something I can easily explain. You mentioned that your wife is your half. This is exactly what I am looking for. My significant other. Someone who completes me in every way.'

'My friend, when you find the one for yourself, please find one for me too.'

Alexander's life had been a resounding success in every aspect since his meeting with friends. His business expanded. His social circle also expanded. He continued to live life to the fullest, enjoying every minute of his existence. He was considered a living legend by everyone who knew him. He never made a wrong decision, was always surrounded by beautiful women, drove the best and most expensive cars, and lived in luxurious homes around the world. He was content with the only life he knew. He neither missed nor regretted anything. He chose a wife for himself, as everyone expected this, worthy of his social status. She blessed him with two beautiful children. They had a similar upbringing to him, attending private schools and being surrounded by servants, teachers, and guards. He was delighted upon receiving them. He fulfilled all their desires. Money was not a concern for him. All he needed was a phone to fulfil all his family's needs. It looked like he was living a life everyone is hoping for, but deep down in his soul he was waiting for something he didn't understand.

Despite his fairy tale, his soul continued to yearn. He didn't understand why he was constantly searching and waiting for something or someone. As he grew older, he became increasingly hyperactive as he didn't have more time. He pushed himself to the limit. He was constantly travelling, meeting people, and working on various projects. In the end, his family realised that as long as he provided for their material needs, they didn't really need him. Eventually, his wife exploited every opportunity available to her and ended up in a relationship with a younger competitor while still married. Alexander failed to provide the excitement she desired, so she sought it out on her own. He wasn't very upset about it as he didn't care much for her. Moreover, when his wife asked for additional support so she could financially assist her new boyfriend, he didn't object. He didn't have a sentimental bond with his wife, so her actions couldn't upset him or threaten him in any way. His children had been settled in private schools and lived independent lives, doing as they pleased. You could say they had been disconnected as a family without realizing that.

Chapter 4

'Uncle! She is requesting a bank statement. She is asking so many questions. What should I do?'

'Where is Thomas?'

'Well, he passed away unexpectedly. He had an accident and died a couple of weeks ago. I received this information about ten days ago when a new accountant began requesting information. What should I do?'

'Why don't you meet the new accountant? Start from there. Stella, please be cautious with your responses.'

A tall, 26-year-old girl with blue eyes looked a bit like a tomboy, full of energy and ambition, and was determined to make her uncle proud. Uncle George, who resided in England, passed away several months ago. He fought hard against his illness, but unfortunately, he was unable to overcome it. Alexander was the first to offer his help, as he knew that he needed someone by his side. Other family members joined immediately, but they all had their own families and business schedules to follow, leaving Stella to handle the most challenging situations. Stella, like many privileged youngsters, enrolled in a prestigious school in England with a hyped name and questionable quality. These schools are often seen as clubs for future leaders. Her belief in her maturity and education led her to believe she could handle the management of a complex group of companies, which her uncle George had been overseeing. She quickly realised that she lacked the necessary skills and decided to seek help from outsourcing. She struggled with basic tasks and made poor hiring decisions. She hired an increasing number of people to perform simple tasks resulting in chaos. Finally, she made the decision to outsource the finance department to a private practise and hire an accountant who would refrain from asking too many questions. She thought she was fine until another accountant started asking questions. She knew that not all of their projects were legal, but they still managed to survive. She knew that her uncle Alexander would not be as gentle as her uncle George. She wanted to conceal her failures while also being close to her uncle. She loved him more than her parents and siblings but he was also her superior who expected high performance quality.

'Maria, this is Stella. She is a secretary of the company you are making accounts for.'

Maria looked at Stella in disbelief. She shook her hands, but just for a moment, she lost herself. She was very familiar to her. She was fatigued and unwell, hindering her ability to maintain a professional demeanour. Her boss introduced Stella to her, and as he laughed and acted foolishly in front of the beautiful girl, Maria couldn't help but watch her. She was so familiar to her. She looked at her boss, a sixty-five-year-old, overweight man, sitting in shorts with bare feet at a cluttered desk filled with dirty papers, boxes, and folders. She couldn't help but think how inappropriate the situation and the place were.

'I am afraid I am not much of help. You know, the company was owned by my uncle. I am not familiar with the company's finances as it belonged to my uncle. I really don't know much about finances. I had some people who were responsible for managing the company, but they have since departed. I am unsure of how to acquire the statements you have asked for. Can you finalise accounts with what you have?'

'We should acquire them. This is something we need to have. Otherwise, the accounts will be incorrect, and we cannot be held responsible for the reports.' – Maria's boss didn't allow her to talk.

'But, Maria, you said, if I cannot find them, you will be able to finalise them.'

'No, Stella, you understood that wrong. I said, the due date is tight, and we can finalise the accounts as they are to avoid a penalty, but we need to have them so we can amend accounts afterwards.'

'So, do we still have time then?'

'No, we have not. You have to find the a way how to get them.'

'Okay, fine. But I don't know anything about finances. Can you help me? I am not a named person in the bank, so no one in the bank wants to talk to me. Can you request the bank to send them to you?'

'No, Stella, we are not doing that. It is not our responsibility to assist with that matter, and Maria is unable to provide assistance. Please contact the bank and request the name be changed to yours. And you need to do it quickly. Before submitting accounts to Revenue, it is necessary to pay for our services.'

'We always communicated with Thomas because he was always helpful. We are currently lost.'

'We can accommodate your request, but there will be an additional charge for the extra work.'

'Money is not a concern; simply state the amount.'

'I can provide a quote.'

'OK. Can Maria come to our office in the future and take everything she needs? Or perhaps she can work from our office to avoid taking papers home.'

'Maria, you need to go to their office tomorrow and resolve this situation. Have you understood this?'

'Yes, Harry, I understand what you're saying, but how can I get there? I need two hours to drive there.'

'So what? Two hours is nothing. We will pay mileage to you.'

'It is not the mileage in question. I will spend four hours driving. I have to get up three hours earlier and come home late. How long do you expect me to be there?'

'Eight hours, of course. Take your laptop and leave. You don't need to be in the office tomorrow.'

Maria sighed deeply. Why doesn't she have luck in her life? Why does she always end up with the toughest jobs, the lowest pay, and in the most troubled companies? She left Croatia some five years ago in despair, hoping for a better future. Her last job was in the accounting department of a hospital. God has a really strange sense of humour. One day, she got a new boss. The boss was the wife of her ex-husband. She was mentally torturing her, and just for a moment, she lost control.

She was looking at her ex-husband every day and how caring and loving he was to his current wife. He was nothing alike they were together. Maria's boss was familiar with her and went out of their way to inflict additional suffering. One day, she was told by her, "If you were a good person and not a primitive peasant as you are, your husband wouldn't sell your daughter, but he was ashamed of you, and he didn't want to see you and her existing in this life, so he gave her away, as far away possibly". She took her savings, passport, and some of her clothes and left the country. She had an acquaintance living in London who called her to visit her, and after a few weeks of living with her, she decided to stay forever.

She had experienced discrimination throughout her life, but she had learned to accept the situation as it was. She was a quiet person, always avoiding conflicts and arguments, and for that, she was always looked at as a mentally undeveloped and primitive person. Actually, she was a very deep and intelligent person, always looking five steps ahead. After years of experience, she realised that shallow individuals are the ones who hold power in the world, and they will not comprehend her message. She was misunderstood by most people, so she stopped sharing her knowledge and philosophy with others. When she was younger, she attempted to capture people's attention by self-deprecating humour, telling jokes, and subsequently agreeing with others' opinions and actions. As she aged, she became less interested in others and began to choose her companions more selectively. Being an introvert, this wasn't very difficult for her.

In just a few days, she found herself stuck in traffic, and what used to be a two-hour commute turned into a gruelling four-hour journey in one direction. The task she was supposed to complete within one or two weeks became a mission impossible. She was tired, and this is what she said to her boss. But thinking only of his own benefit and exerting power over her life, he compelled her to continue travelling and working remotely.

'Maria, you seem dissatisfied with us Maria. Are we making you unhappy? - Stella asked her one day after seeing her without energy sitting over a pile of papers.'

'No, Stella. I am just very tired. It took me three hours to arrive. I will need some two hours back.'

'Oh, so much? I didn't know that. How did it take me an hour to get to your office?'

'Yes, but my commute to the office takes one hour. The office is in between my home and this place. Is it not possible for me to take documents and complete my work in the office?'

'Oh, no, it's not possible. I need them here. What about system backup?'

'Our systems are not compatible. Can we access it online?'

'No, I am afraid it's not possible. We have no technical possibilities. If it is too challenging for you, I can request Harry to assign someone else to assist me.'

Harry didn't seem to consider the challenge of Maria travelling three hours to reach the client. He didn't understand why Maria was requesting special treatment and rejecting the clients' demands. Being a foreigner in a difficult financial situation, she didn't have a choice; she had to travel or leave her job. She forced a smile and buried herself in paperwork. To speed up the job, she would work long hours and sleep in her car in a parking lot. Accidentally, Stella noticed that Maria was changing her clothes in their company's toilet, so she approached her to understand the situation.

'Maria, how is travelling today?'

'It was fine, Stella. It is fine.'

'You know, I was thinking, we have a hostel for our employees here. Would you like to remain there until you complete the task?'

'Oh, yes, I would like to. I was considering staying at a hotel, but it is more than I can afford.'

'It is not very posh, you know. Maybe you wouldn't like it at all.'

'Is it clean?'

'Of course, it is clean. We can arrange a meal in a nearby restaurant if you wish.'

'Oh, yes. I would appreciate it. Thank you.'

'Oh, there's no need to be so grateful. I apologise for not considering this earlier. Sometimes, I struggle to understand the needs of others. I noticed that you changed your clothes, which made me think that you haven't slept at all.'

'I have; you don't have to worry.'

'Would you like to join me for lunch? I would like to see how I can help you more.'

'You know, my uncle Alex always says that I live in clouds and that he left me to be there. He says, that sometimes I have to jump down to see how common people live, and what bothers them.' – Stella said over the lunch in a typical English restaurant.

'Why would you do that, Stella?'

'Well, he says, that I have everything. I have a loving family, and private schooling; I have travelled the world. I don't know what real life is. He says that he fears that this situation may change if my luck changes, and I may struggle to handle all the problems. I understand I lived like a princess, but I never had a chance to meet people outside of my circle.'

'There are two types of people in the world. One is facing all the difficulties of surviving, working for top people, and top people.'

'I guess I am a "top person".'

'Yes, you are.'

'Is this bad?'

'Think this way,: ninety-nine people are under the one who is on top. If there is synergy among all individuals, it can lead to the formation of a strong pyramid. Otherwise, it would be only a ruin, a pile of shattered bricks. In a ruin, there is no a single brick that forms a top.'

'How can I make a synergy?'

'Well, your uncle is right. You need to experience a less privileged life, interact with different people, and gain an understanding of who we are, how we live, and why we are in this situation.'

'You know, when I came here in the UK, my uncle George gave me his car to drive. The car was a Maserati, but it was a British car. I didn't know how to drive it so I damaged the car. My uncle was so angry at me as it was his best car. So he called my uncle Alex and told me off. My uncle came here immediately, and we went to buy me a car. You know what he bought me. It was and old little Ford. It was a fifteen-years-old car. "You can do whatever you want with it," he said to me. My parents never got to know that otherwise, they would ask me to get home immediately.'

'You are fortunate. I got my first car at the age of forty. This is my second car in my life, and I am more than fifty years old.'

'Oh no! Why?'

'I couldn't afford it. I obtained my driver's license at the age of twenty-five, I believe. I drove an old car that was given to me for a couple of years. The car fell apart from itself, and when it couldn't pass MOT, I just threw it away. I couldn't afford to purchase another one.'

'Maria, where do you come from?'

'Oh, my life is very strange, my dear. I always say from the top of a Mountain, somewhere in the clouds. I am of mixed origin. My ancestors originated from north eastern Europe. They were refugees escaping from wars. They have established roots by marrying locals. I was born in Bosnia. When the war broke out, I escaped to Croatia. I was called Croat, and Croatia was my country despite being born in Bosnia. Once upon a time, all these small republics were Yugoslavia, you don't know that. Today, nationality is determined based on religion. I was a Roman Catholic.'

'You were a Catholic. You are not any more?'

'No, dear. I don't believe God exists any more. I no longer practise religion. It took me a while to understand that religion is not for me.'

'How? Why? I mean, we go regularly to church, but I am not very religious, to be honest. I don't find this very appalling. Religion is a topic that interests everyone. One is a Christian, another a Muslim. There are numerous religions. I attend church because my friends and family go. It is simply a habit.'

'You said it. It is a social habit. It is something someone else brought onto me. I continue to have disagreements with God, but I have made the decision to no longer attend church. I can pray in my house if I feel the need. I don't need to seek approval from others. I don't need anyone to say that I am a good person because I go to a church or how bad I am because I don't go. I don't need to be told that I believe in a right or wrong God.'

'So, what is a God for you?'

'A creator! An ultimate power. Beginning and end of everything. God is a genderless, colourless, in a dimension and frequency humans do not understand yet. We think God is good despite facing absence of God's presence but then we doubt when we don't receive mercy. Someone told us if we are good and live according to "God's teaching" we will receive his mercy, but then again, despite thinking God knows everything and he is everywhere, we do things opposite to religious teachings. I have a feeling, this teaching is here to make us blind on injustice we are facing from ruling elite.'

'Oh, my God! These words are my Uncle Alex's words. This is exactly what he is saying. He says, that humans are fighting over the name of their beliefs, of philosophy, or power that a religion brings, while everyone says God is one. On the other way, no one can give a definition of God. He says, when he asked what God is, all of them said, God is love. If it is love, why do they kill people in the name of love?'

'He is likely a very deep person.'

'Sometimes, I think he is. Then I think he is the most shallow person in the world'

'What about your family? Are they religious?'

'No, they are not. My father is a Muslim. My mother is a Protestant. We celebrate both religious festivals. But this is only for tradition's sake. We are not religious. My youngest sister has begun wearing a head covering while dating an Orthodox Christian, how strange. I don't know why? I believe her friends are the reason, or maybe her boyfriend. Every time she fights with him, she is covering her head, like she wants to show him something. My mum says this is only temporarily, and my father is furious. I think, she is like this just to annoy my father. I don't know.'

'If your father is a Muslim, why does she want to annoy him by respecting his religion? Or her boyfriend, who wouldn't care less for head covering.'

'Both my parents are doctors. They don't believe in religious dogma. They desire our freedom. They encourage us to think critically and not be manipulated by others or anything else. They expect us to behave as free individuals, not to act in a primitive manner. Maybe is her boyfriend who is challenging her. He like to tease her.'

'Do you think a religion can make you primitive?'

'No, no, I didn't say that. Religion can hinder personal growth and development as a human being. It is full of interdictions. Don't do this, don't do that. My uncle Alex says, you lose the natural direction of what is right and what is wrong. Instead, you know what is right and what is wrong only because it was told you so. You see, he is right,; animals do not go to church, but still know what is right and what is wrong, and we say we are evolved beings. We live and die because we were taught what to do and what is right and wrong.'

'Do you believe we have evolved enough to recognise the truth and understand the concept of mind manipulation? I always believed that the church would teach me the right way to live and guide me in shaping my life.'

'So, did you learn how to live?'

'No, people will teach you. Interest is a teacher of life. Benefits will direct your behaviour.'

Maria lay down in bed, attempting to relax and sleep. She had a lot on her mind. The words of her boss lingered in her mind, keeping her from sleeping after a night shift at the shop. Whenever she was unemployed, she asked the agency to get her a night shift in retail while she was looking for another job.

"Maria, take your bag and go home. I don't want to see you here in our office. I am dissatisfied with the quality of your work. It took you 3 weeks to finish the accounts of five companies. Five for God's sake. You are completely incapable of performing this job. You are supposed to finish all five companies in three days. It took you three weeks. And again, all totally wrong. I am fed up with the errors you keep making. I am tired of constantly fixing your mistakes. I am telling you what to do, and you deliberately disobey me.'

Maria was awakened by a knock on the door and the ringing of the bell. "Maybe if I pretend to sleep, they will go away". But no, the visitor was persistent. "Maybe it is the landlord. He has the key; why doesn't he just enter?"

'Good afternoon Maria. Oh, I am sorry. I hope I didn't wake you up.'

'Good afternoon Stella. Actually, I was trying to get some sleep. I just finished my night shift and in a few hours, I will have to go back again. I haven't slept at all. Please come in. How did you locate me?'

'I asked your boss for your phone number, and he told me that you just left them. He informed me that he does not have your contact information. I sensed that something had happened, so I wanted to check on you.'

'I haven't just left them. He fired me. It took a long time to finish the work, and he wasn't very happy with the time I had spent on work. He also didn't like my work.'

'Oh no. I was taking your time as well. I apologise for not considering your schedule. I have caused you significant harm.'

'That's fine, Stella. I will find something else. But you didn't tell me how you found me.'

'Oh, I have connections. I found you based on your car plates. I hope you are not angry with me. I wanted to keep in touch with you.'

'It is fine, Stella. I'm glad you found me.'

'Actually, I wanted to offer you a job. I need to have someone capable of dealing with all companies. I had bookkeepers and accountants, and this is the result of their efforts. They pretended to know how to handle the situation, but instead, they created chaos. When you arrived, I could already see improvement. I don't want my Uncle Alex to see the mess because he is very pedantic, and if he does see it, he will replace me with someone else. Would you please consider this role?'

'I am far away from the company. I am unable to travel daily.'

'You are renting this place anyway. You can find a place near the company.'

'OK, Stella, I can take the offer, but in the meantime, I need to go to work. I still need to make a deposit for the new rent.'

'I can give you for a deposit, and you will give me back eventually.'

'No, I can't do that. Give me a month. I will work night shifts, terminate the rental agreement, and search for housing close to the company.'

'Ok, just to be sure that you will come to work with me, I will start night shifts as well. So tell me where I should ask for them.'

'But you can't get shifts if they don't need you.'

'Don't worry. So, should I come with you today?'

On To Maria's surprise, Stella joined her that night. Even to a bigger surprise, she joined her every time she went to work. She simply refused to look away. She must have been very eager to hire her for the company. Maria eventually understood that Stella was not as innocent as she wanted to present herself. Yes, she held the official position of secretary in the company, but these companies are part of her family's portfolio. A lot of people depended on her, her work, and her decision. Maria was more than capable of running all these companies, and it was as simple as driving a car. She didn't understand why Stella wanted her. She could find someone else, but eventually, she realised it was the a mutual energy that connected them together. Maria once again experienced her maternal instincts towards someone else, and Stella clearly felt secure in her presence. When she saw her for the first time, it reminded her of a photo that her grandmother had on her wall. The photo depicts her mother as a young girl. Stella resembled her. She heard that everyone has a doppelgänger, so perhaps she is the reincarnation of her grandmother. Despite the age difference, they made a strong bond.

'Stella, where are you? I am calling you because I am worried. I expect you to be awake and present at work during your scheduled hours. Have we agreed that you would take care of this? Haven't we not? I am calling the company, and no one knows where you are. Do you think someone will work if you do not supervise employees? Call me immediately!'

'Hello, Uncle Alex. Sorry for that. I am currently working. I just need a few more days. I will get back in a week's time.'

'In which part of the globe are you? You should tell me when you are not in the company.'

'I am in the UK, uncle. I regularly communicate with managers, and everything is going well. I also reply on to my emails.'

'Why aren't you in the company?'

'I work. You advised me to work as a regular employee to gain an understanding of the nature of work and what responsibilities are. If I have to give orders, I need to know what receiving orders are.'

'You're joking. What are you doing, Stella?'

'I took some night shifts at a superstore. I will complete the work next week.'

'You can't be serious. But if you are, I can give you credit for that. Who gave you this idea?'

'No one. I watched a documentary on TV. I decided to give it a try. No one here knows me, so I am safe and sound. Work is manual, so I need a bit of muscle. I am uncertain about the pay. It is quite challenging, considering the difficulty of the work. I met some interesting people here. Some of them are friendly, while others ignore me. Some individuals pretend to work, but in reality, they are lazy. Some individuals are extremely diligent, working night shifts while also attending college during the day. I witnessed a pregnant woman who was only a few weeks away from giving birth, yet she was lifting heavy boxes while young people around her sat and stared at their phones.'

'Is it difficult for you? You have never tried that.'

'No, Uncle, I really enjoy it. I interact with people beyond my usual circle. Maria always reminds me to dress warmly when I go into the freezer, even though I often forget to wear gloves or a thick jacket. If there was no a jacket, she would go into the freezer and remove the boxes. She wouldn't let me do it instead.'

'You have already met some friends. Good for you. How long will this experiment of yours last? We need to know your location and ensure your safety. I heard that you're also not coming home. Where do you sleep?'

'Maria offered me a place to stay so I don't have to travel.'

'How can you sleep in someone else's house, Stella? You should not do that. How can you trust Maria? Something might happen if she discovered your true identity.'

'Don't worry, Uncle. I am capable of looking after myself. Maria, an accountant, recently handled our accounts. She was fired from her previous job and is currently employed at this location. I asked her to join us because I felt responsible for her losing her job. She said she would, but she needs to find another place to live. She will finalise her rental agreement and then join us.'

'Oh, Stella. What are you currently involved in? If she got fired, she is probably useless. Otherwise, she could've kept her job. Can you please return? Please don't ask me to leave the project at this time. I need to trust you. If you do not return home and report to the company within a week, I will come there.'

Fearing her uncle, she decided to push Maria to her side. She called her friend, who then called her father. Her father then contacted his friend to arrange Maria's night shifts. In this way, Stella would remain uninvolved, and Maria would be unaware of the events. Maria had no choice but to be carried away by the water.

After a few weeks, Maria had settled into her new apartment and started her new job. When she initially came to do her accounts, she found herself sitting in a small building a bit far away from the mansion. All she saw was the house staff. She wondered what the mansion looked like, but she never had the opportunity to go inside. She considered it inappropriate to invade someone's privacy. As a new employee, she found herself in a traditional English office, which was not quite to her liking. The office was on the other way from the mansion and near to their industrial estate. She had a better understanding of the situation in these companies and was surprised to see that ten people were required to do a job that could be done by one person in her home country. Many of them simply pretended to work. They were merely numbers on a piece of paper. They talked a lot; they were skilled at talking but not effective at all. She sat in front of her computer, studying numbers. Some unusual transactions caught her attention. She began seeking answers, hoping to keep it private and quiet. However, the questions exploded in her face. The question was passed from one person to another, but it returned to questioning her. Then she asked another question, and the same thing occurred. It looked like an echo in a twilight zone. She stopped asking questions after a while. She decided to find answers on her own. She knew she should-n't openly show that she had Stella on her side, so she tried to be discreet. She knew that a foolish mind could generate harmful thoughts and cause significant damage. She began compiling a list of questions to ask Stella the next time they met.

'Stella, I need to know the identities of the individuals you are making payments to.'

'Oh, Maria, you have no idea how much I despise questions. We are currently in the gym, so let's exercise. Why not consult your colleagues in the finance department? They are making payments.'

'There appears to be a disruption in communication and mutual understanding. I am unable to receive any responses.'

'Ok, give me the list. Let me check... Ah, yes, why don't you join me for lunch tomorrow...'

'I can come to lunch, of course, but you can let me know now.'

'No, they will tell you by themselves. It will be intriguing to witness your reaction.'

'You are very secretive. Will I meet a charming prince riding a white horse?'

'I have to warn you. I like you very much, and I would like to be your lifelong friend. If you cannot be loyal to me or my family or me, it's best not to ask any questions.'

'Huh? You are intriguing me now. And worrying me.'

'Just imagine hearing something you don't want to hear.'

'Oh, dear. Listening is easy. What you choose to do with it is another matter.'

'All I ask is for you to be open-minded and give me and us a chance.'

She expected to see something spectacular when she stepped into the mansion, but it exceeded her expectations. A harmonious blend of old and new creates a space that honours the past while providing modern comfort for future generations to enjoy. All historic houses had a lingering scent of the past, a reminder of times long gone. This was a unique experience. The old wallpapers were removed and replaced with new modern patterns. The interior was modernised to maintain its original style while improving functionality. The heavy, dark-coloured curtains were replaced with lighter, transparent curtains in softer colours. Small rooms with multiple doors were demolished to create more spacious rooms. Every corner was vying for attention. The colours on the wallpapers enhanced pictures of anonymous individuals, often without conveying genuine emotions. Maria looked at them and thought that they seemed emotionless, unlike her. Sculptures of all sizes were waiting for her to pass by, anticipating her scream or at least a sigh. She was thinking about the perfection of someone's work as she looked at them. Who knows what thoughts went through the sculptor's mind as they transformed raw, hard stone into a magnificent work of art? Have they been happy about receiving money for their livelihood, or have they been happy because the peace matched their expectations? Have they envisioned the location and future viewers of the sculpture? Humans may come and go, but their work endures.

'Ah, you're finally here! I can tell that you are pleased with what you are seeing. I also have a fondness for this house. My uncle purchased it without inquiring about the identities of these individuals. It is beautiful, isn't it?'

'Yes, it is indeed beautiful. I always enjoy visiting old houses. I can sense the presence of ancient spirits. However, this exceeds my expectations. I appreciate the blend of traditional and modern elements.'

'I think my uncle spent a real fortune to make it like home, despite not having a real family. I think it was more of a project for him.'

'Couldn't he enjoy the fruits of his labour in the end?'

'Unfortunately, he couldn't. He fell ill and departed prematurely.'

'Is this what you wanted to show me? Is this house the source of expenses that I need to include in my reports?'

'Hmm, yes and no... Let's have dinner.'

A pleasant conversation between a young boss and an older employee seemed as if they had met before and were now catching up. They have not noticed that some of their moves are identical. They giggled in the same way, had the same logic, shared the same points of view, and even had moles in the same spots. They walked with the same posture, standing tall with their backs straight and chins held high. When they said something funny, everyone laughed at them. Sometimes, they made serious statements, but people still laughed, not taking them seriously. Eventually, they turned their disadvantage into an advantage. They both had open faces, ready to take every joke directed at them. They would turn the joke into a pleasant conversation, effectively deterring people from bothering them any further. None of them have been in control of the situation, but somehow, they managed to achieve their desired outcomes or avoid punishment. No one could be angry with them when they turned people away, and no one could refuse when they asked for a favour. But no one took them seriously when they wanted to be taken seriously. No one realised that beneath their exteriors, both of them were silently pleading for help. Even in their moments of sadness, they still appeared comical. Both of them had attractive bodies and faces, but they were unable to form meaningful relationships. Maria abandoned her longing for companionship after facing multiple rejections, while Stella continued to hold onto her dream of finding her prince.

It was late afternoon when they both decided to take a walk in the garden. Stella wanted to show Maria a beautiful garden and deer after she told her that she had grown up among bears and wolves. Both were laughing, chasing deer escaping from two crazy fools. Their path went in a different direction. It was a beautiful, warm day, and Stella didn't want to let her new friend go home. She had a lot in common, and she felt she had found a common soul. The difference in age didn't matter as they were both women with the same common sense, if they had it at all, or so they thought.

In the far distance of the vast estate, Maria noticed a Greek temple not too far from the house. She ran in that direction when a few drops of rain began to fall. Stella shouted for them to go back, but Maria was eager to see the pillars and statues, so she ran quickly in that direction. Stella ran after her, unable to prevent it. It was too late; Maria uncovered the secret. She was out of breath. Women and children gazed towards them. The fear on their faces caused them to cling to their chaperones. All of them had deep facial scars, severe burns on their arms, some were missing limbs, or walked with prosthetic legs. The chaperones pushed the children behind them, preventing them from being seen and giving them a false sense of protection. Maria was taken aback. Instinctively she knew something was not right here and she had to escape from this situation very quickly. She found herself face to face with "human bears" and realised she had witnessed something forbidden. Maybe Stella set her up crossed her mind. Maybe she had to witness this in order to become involved in a situation she didn't want to be a part of. But being Maria was not difficult, and her humorous personality helped her navigate the situation. She made comical gestures with her head and arms, mimicking a chirping bird as she ran among the children. The kids screamed and scattered in the opposite direction. She was running in the wrong direction again, away from the mansion instead of towards it. Stella shouted at her to stop, but Maria, like a wounded animal, was desperately trying to escape from what she had just witnessed. Finally, Stella grabbed her arm and halted her.

'You haven't seen anything! OK? They are simply children that we care for in a nursery. OK? We care for them when their parents are away. All right? It is not what you think! They all are all okay, right?'

'What are you talking about, Stella? I don't understand. Was something wrong?'

'No Maria, everything is fine. I know that it may seem unusual to see children in the woods. It is nearly dark.'

'Well, children or bears? What is the difference?'

'No, bears, Maria. Children were housed in the nearby mansion and accompanied by teachers. OK? Nothing unusual here.'

'I really do not understand you. Our teacher used to send us to the mountains to search for flowers and admire the beauty of nature. Not that we haven't seen nature before. It was irrelevant whether it was snowing or raining. It was simply wandering in nature. I am just saying.'

'Well, yes, children have to experience nature.'

'Of course, my dear! This is what I am saying! They need to experience nature. Whether it's sunny, raining, or snowing. I didn't have winter shoes when it was raining, and I had winter boots when it was a hot sunny day. It didn't matter. When our teachers instructed us to walk, we followed their directions and walked in the specified direction. I am now all wet, so let's hurry to my car. Where is it? In which direction?'

Stella couldn't argue with Maria because she understood that Maria was mocking her. The worried expression on Maria's face indicated that she needed to leave the estate immediately. It shouldn't waste her time. Stella caught her arm as she ran towards the mansion, this time in the right direction. When she finally reached the car and tried to get in, Stella was pleading.

'Please don't leave! Stay a moment. Your clothes are wet. Please come inside and change it.'

'Thank you, Stella, but I won't get sick. Don't worry. I will be home shortly.'

'I feel very bad. Please don't go. Stay with me a little longer. I feel lonely, and you were good company. I don't want to let you go. Please stay.'

'My dear. I can't stay. I have a dog to walk and a cat to feed.'

'Oh, come on. You have neither a dog nor a cat. This is just an excuse. Was it so bad with me? I thought you enjoyed today.'

'It was a lovely day, but it is dark now, and I really have to leave.'

'Please don't go. I want to introduce someone to you.'

'Whoever you want to introduce me to can wait until tomorrow. I really have to go now.'

Stella was more aggressive, while Maria was more determined to leave. She held onto Maria's arm and gently pushed away from the car towards the mansion. But Maria gently pushed her back.

'Look, Maria, the main gate is closed, and our gatekeeper has left home. I don't have any keys to open. You can't leave.'

'You know, people are saying that we have thick heads, thicker than a wall. I always wanted to test this belief. It doesn't matter if they are closed; I will open them with my head. Do you want to see?'

'No, no, there is no need. I want you to stay. Even the door is closed.'

'No worries, Stella. I will open them up if you let me go.'

'But I really need you to stay.'

'Why do you need me to stay? I don't understand.'

'I want you to meet someone. Someone special to me.'

Just for a second, Maria felt sick. She felt a strong, dark, and heavy energy as if a shadow was creeping up behind her.

'Who is it that you want me to meet? Is it a prince? Your prince on a white horse? Please ask him to wait until tomorrow.'

'No, no prince. I want you to meet my uncle. He really wants to meet you.'

'Your uncle? What? Your dead uncle wants to meet me?'

She didn't hear a reply. Her body fell onto the wet ground, and her mind experienced a blackout.

Who knows how long she had been unconscious, but regaining consciousness confused her a bit. She had high blood pressure issues and required medication. Stress, the food she ate, and her emotions worked against her. She felt that someone was in the room, but she was scared to open her eyes. When she decided to open her eyes, she saw only a shadow sitting in a large, comfortable chair, a bit far from her. She needed her glasses. Is that a ghost sitting there?

'Your glasses are next to you, on the right. - the shadow was approaching. - 'Good evening.'

'I have to leave. Can you please escort me to the door?'

'I thought you would be our guest tonight.'

'No, sorry. Let me leave. I have to leave. Now! Immediately. I don't want to be rude, but I told Stella that I have to leave.'

'I can drive you home. I don't think you should be driving when you are not feeling well.'

'No, sorry. I need to leave. Please show me the way to the door.'

She didn't want to look at the shadow, not because of fear, but because she felt something very strange near it - something new connected to old that she couldn't explain. She didn't know whether it was fear, excitement, or a new feeling that made her uncomfortable.

'All right, Maria. This way. Do you want someone else to drive you home?'

'No! I will drive myself home. I need to go!'

She was walking towards her car, almost running. She needed to leave. Once she left the main gate behind her and drove onto the main road, she made the decision not to go home but to head towards her friend's house in North West London. It was late at night, almost midnight, when she called her friend to open the door.

'Did something happen, sister? Please come in quickly. Come in. Let me hug and kiss you. Come, sit down. I will call my husband to join us.'

'No, Sofia, don't wake him up. In a couple of hours, he will go to work. He needs sleep. You go to sleep, too. You will also go to work.'

'I have time, my love. I will go to work in the afternoon. Let's eat and talk. What happened? What brought you here in the middle of the night?'

'I was scared to go home. I think I saw something I didn't dare to see.'

'What was it?'

'I saw a group of children with some adult women and a man. They were extremely scared when they saw me. They acted as if I caught them doing something they shouldn't have been doing. You should see their eyes; they were wide open; and fear in their eyes... They were thin and pale, covered in scars, scratches, and open wounds on their faces. Like they were beaten and tortured. I can't actually explain how they looked, but they appeared strange to me. Something was not right there.'

'My dear, we come from different cultures. Our children are our world. We would give our bodies and souls for our children, but not every parent here would care for their children. When I think about it more, not all parents in our town were good either. I mean… what does it mean when you say they looked strange to you? Some children are skinny.'

'It started raining, and it was drizzling. They were walking in the woods, in line, touching the shoulders of the child in front like being blind, wearing tattered clothes. They didn't speak to each other. They didn't jump, scream, or make any sound... as if they were ghosts. They weren't; they looked alive. Just scared...'

'I can't believe that after all we went through in the war, you still believe in ghosts.'

'It's not a matter of whether I believe in ghosts or not, but rather that I have a strange feeling about what happened. Then Stella was so insistent on staying with them tonight. She was giving me indication that something strange I might see or experience. Why? She said she wanted me to meet her uncle. Her uncle was dead.'

'Well, maybe she has another uncle.'

'Maybe she has. But why should he meet me? Why did she call me at all? She is a wealthy child. Why would she invite an employee to her home, which is not just a home but rather a palace, and introduce her to an even wealthier uncle? Is this not something to think about?'

'Well, the last thing is something to think about. Rich people only socialise with other wealthy individuals, and they speak to the poor only when they need something from us. Is this something that scared you and led you to come to us?'

'Yes, it is just a strange feeling that something is not right.'

'Maria? What brings you here in the middle of the night?' - Goran was worried when he heard Maria's voice.

'Nothing, my brother. I am sorry for waking you up. I was very loud. Go to sleep. For a couple of hours, you have to go to work.'

'It doesn't matter. There must be something wrong since you came at this hour.'

'I went to have lunch with my young boss. She called me to show me her house. I couldn't refuse her. This was not a home. It was a grand palace situated in the centre of an expansive estate, surrounded by a thick wood. There were many houses there, but you couldn't notice their gates. If she hadn't picked me up in the centre of the village after two hours of unsuccessful wandering on these narrow roads, I wouldn't have been able to find the gate. It was all fine until we went to her park. We were walking and walking until I saw a Greek temple and wanted to see what was there. There were some Greek statues. When I approached, I saw children, men, and women standing and chanting. When they saw me, they were so scared, as if I had caught them doing something wrong. They were so scared... I can't explain how they looked. And then, what confused me even more, was Stella's behaviour. Her behaviour scared me a lot. I wouldn't think much if she hadn't started convincing me that everything was normal. What was normal? She then asked me to stay with her for the entire night. We are not friends. Why would I stay overnight at her house? She said, the gate was closed, and the gatekeeper has had left. Then she said that her uncle wanted to meet me. Her uncle died several years ago. Who should I meet and why?'

'Something is wrong here, sister. Calm down. Sleep. Stay here to-morrow. Sofia will leave for work in the afternoon, and I will come home. Children will be here, too. I will invite some friends to come over as well. You don't have to be afraid. We will protect you. Do you understand? You don't have to be afraid of anyone. Nothing will hap-pen to you.'

'Thank you, brother. I sincerely apologise for disturbing your peace. I didn't want this to happen.'

'When you are alone and don't have a family, you can choose to adopt another family. But a man without a family is unprotected and vulnerable. So, we are a family now, and you don't have to be scared. OK?'

It had been several days since Maria's visit, and the more she thought about it, the more uncomfortable she felt about returning to her old job and old life. Her friends, along with their companions who came to comfort Maria, persuaded her to leave the old job and start all over. They even started looking for another job and accommodation for her. She felt fortunate and secure among them, so she made the decision to quit her job. It was only a few weeks later that she found another place to live. Her phone was ringing from time to time, but she didn't want to respond. It was the end of the story for her. Little did she know that her story had just begun.

Maybe she was a naive person, or maybe she just didn't want to think clearly, but one day, on her way to the local shops, her path crossed with a young man who approached her in her language. First, confusion changed to fear and anger. She understood that she needed to be very careful about her next steps.

'Aunty, you need to see the man whom you are refusing to meet.'

'Young man, I don't need to meet anyone.'

'I think you do.'

'What if I don't want to meet him?'

'Then I have to speak to you again.'

'If I still don't want to meet him again, what will happen?'

'In this case, I will continue to visit you until I persuade you.'

'If you don't see me, you can't persuade me.'

'Aunty, I know all about you. I know where you live, who you meet, and who you speak with. I know everything you do, and when you do it. I will definitely see you somewhere. I suggest that you spare our time and effort and meet the person.'

'So, why is he sending you? Why isn't he here instead of you?'

'Aunty, do you think he ever walks in places like this? Do you think we are worthy of his time? If I am not in front of you, someone else will be, but you will not see him begging or trying to convince you by talking to him. I will give you some friendly advice: please go and see him.'

At first, her stubbornness and pride were preventing her from making a decision. However, after careful thinking, she decided to meet him. The young man approached her again in a few days with information. She was thinking about whether it was wise to tell her friends, but she was unsure of how it would impact them if they tried to dissuade her from meeting him. She loved them. She cared about them. She didn't want anything bad to happen, no matter what decision she made. In the end, she decided to meet this "uncle".

The meeting took place in a luxurious hotel in London. The famous hotel brand didn't impress her, knowing that behind the scenes, there are stories that are not so posh. Her acquaintances used to work there, proud that they had become members of a famous hotel brand. After some time, they were relieved to escape the horror of being trapped in modern slavery. The interior was satisfying when she entered and introduced herself to the receptionist. She was somewhat disappointed when they directed her to a partition in a large room. She was hoping to catch a glimpse of this renowned hotel, even though the purpose of her visit was not as pleasant.

'Here I am, Mister Uncle. You made me come over to see you. What can I thank you for your interest in me?' – She sat on a soft chair, resembling a sack of potatoes, without looking at the man who was waiting for her.

'Mister Uncle?... Good afternoon, Maria. I hope you are well.'

Their eyes finally met. The silence killed the time. The brain abandoned thoughts. The body stopped the heart from beating. Emotions died. Past didn't exist. Two living creatures facing each other, two perfect opposites, two strangers, were hit by an unknown frequency of universal energy. Peace, heavenly peace, surrounded them, giving them comfort they hadn't experienced in this life. Who knows how long they have been in this state and what happened for them to regain consciousness? "She is the one!" "He is the one!" "He is the one?"

'Have I died?' - Maria spoke first.

'Have I met you somewhere in the past?'

'No, Uncle, I don't think so.'

'My name is not Uncle. My name is Alexander Conrad.'

'You are not Stella's uncle. I thought so. It would be very strange for him to rise from his grave. She said he was dead.'

'I see! Now I understand your behaviour that night. You thought I was a ghost?'

'Yes, kind of.'

'Well, my brother passed away some time ago. That was his house. However, Stella has, or had, three uncles. I am one of them. I have a younger brother as well. She is my sister's daughter. She has a few siblings and a few cousins as well. So, no, you haven't seen a ghost. It was simply a misunderstanding.'

'I guess it was. This was not the reason to use intimidation as a means to bring me here and explain things I didn't want to know.'

'Have I somehow intimidated you?'

'Not you directly. The young man from my region did.'

'I apologise for that. When I give an order, I expect it to be carried out.'

'So, you are a general, and all the servants are your soldiers.'

'I suppose this is how things work in my world.'

'I was not happy that I was forced to meet you. I don't know why I had to meet you at all.'

'You suddenly disappeared from our lives. Why did you quit your job, never returned to your home, and changed your address? Have we caused you distress?'

'No, you haven't. I am an impulsive person, I don't think before-hand. I make decisions suddenly.'

'Stella says, maybe you have the wrong idea about what is happening in the mansion.'

'What is happening in the mansion?'

'You tell me!'

'Look, I haven't seen anything that you have to be worried about.'

'You have seen a replica of a Greek temple in the garden. Why should anyone worry?'

'Exactly. Now you know what I think. I can go home now. Is this alright with you?'

'No. It is not alright. I want to get to know you better, so I have an offer for you.'

'I am afraid there is nothing you can offer me that would interest me.'

'What about the truth?'

'The truth?'

'Yes. You have something I need, and I offer something you might want.'

'I am listening.'

'I offer you the truth about your daughter.'

'I don't have a daughter.'

'Yes, you do.'

'She is dead! I was a bad mother. I couldn't take care of her. I don't believe she is alive. I believe she died a long time ago... What is it that you think I can give you?'

'The Truth for a Truth.'

'I have nothing to offer you, and I don't need the truth about my little one from you.'

'I heard you are from Bosnia. You were in a concentration camp. You lost a child. You have managed to overcome your weaknesses and create a life worthy of respect. I want to learn how a victim can become a victor. This is what I want to understand.'

'Are you a psychologist?'

'No, I am an engineer. I have hobbies. This is one of them. I want to learn about human behaviour.'

'And you think I am a victor? And not a victim any more?'

'The majority of people are stuck in their problems. They start drinking and become homeless when they experience less distress than you did. They never return to a normal life. I want to know how a person can forget what they have experienced and continue living a normal life. What happened that helped you overcome your weaknesses for the benefit of your success? I think if you hadn't faced all these challenges, you would have lived a simple life as a peasant in the mountains of Bosnia.'

'Wow, is a simple peasant life not normal for you? What does a normal life mean to you? What does a normal person mean to you? Is a soldier, who kills another human for financial gain and believes they are fighting for their nation's freedom, considered a normal person? Is a priest, who practises paedophilia at one moment and then sets up ethical rules for society, considered a normal person? Is it normal for a doctor to refuse to treat a person despite knowing that they can cure the patient? Is it normal to consider someone who witnesses injustice being done to another person and does nothing, a normal person? Is a politician a normal person? Is it a poor man, normal? Is a rich man living a lavish life, who doesn't know the meaning of sacred, considered a normal person? Who sets the norms in society? Obedient? Disobedient? I don't know. If you can tell me what a normal person is and what a normal life entails, maybe I could provide you with some answers. But I don't believe I will give you the correct answer.'

'I don't know the answers to your questions. All I know is that your life continued on an upward slope after your tragedy. I want to learn how you did it.'

'Simple. I didn't need a pharmakos in the backyard to find peace of mind and achieve success. I didn't care about people's opinions about my worthiness. I stopped following so-called leaders and started leading myself towards the place I wanted to be. I stopped being a sheep with a shepherd and became a black sheep who led herself. I started listening to myself and stopped listening to others. It is as simple as that.'

'If you are not a member of a pack, you are prey. Didn't you seek refuge with your community members for protection when you believed that both Stella and I posed a threat to you? I don't believe any of your friends haven't given you advice on the situation you were currently in. I can't believe you didn't care about them.'

'They have advised me, of course. And I listened, of course.'

'Then your theory, or your secret, is not true. You don't listen to yourself, and you care too much about other people's opinions. You see, this is what I meant. I want to know what made you this way.'

'...To be honest, I am also interested in this. But still, you have nothing to offer me, so I won't waste my time with you.'

'I said, I can give you the truth about your daughter.'

'As I said, she is dead.'

'What if I told you that she is not dead? She is very much alive.'

'What am I going to do with this information? Should I approach her and anticipate appreciation for giving her away? For not being able to take care of her. For not being able to protect her. For not being able to find her. What am I going to do with this information?'

'Are you not curious about how she lived her entire life?'

'I don't believe she had a good life if she was alive. I know she had a hard life. I was guilty of bringing her into this world. I should have been a nun.'

'You have lost faith in humanity and Christianity.'

'No. I have faith in humanity, but not in religious leaders. They are just manipulators. They are perfect deceivers. My grandfather used to say, "If someone convinces you that a stone was touched by God, therefore it is a creation of God, you will bow and pray to the stone because it will be the closest thing to your creator." Someone may say that you are not worthy of being God's creation, but rather a sinner. Therefore, you must pray for forgiveness in order to be blessed and forgiven by God. Others will say that you are a creation of God and, therefore, a divine creation. You are equal to God, so you don't need to bow and pray. You have everything, yet you still obey another human who is considered God. The human mind is an incredibly faulty

216

machine. Anyone can guide you. Everyone can make you trust. Do you know what truth is?'

'I don't. I am trying to find what is good, what is bad, what is wrong, and what is right.'

'You are a rich person. Why do you need to know that? You have everything. Enjoy your life.'

'I had everything in my life. I was successful in everything. All that I wanted to see, know, and experience, I have accomplished. Yet, something is missing. Something tells me that you might be able to help me with this. Maybe I have nothing to offer you, nothing you wish for. I hope you might be interested in joining me on my quest for truth.'

'Alexander, go home. Sleep. Eat. Enjoy your life. Let me live my life. I wish you all the best.' – Maria got up quickly and left before she could see his facial expression. She didn't want to hear his voice, see his face, or feel his energy. She didn't want to be around him and re-member who she was and what she had experienced. She thought she had overcome all these feelings. She thought she was a strong person. Yet, he made her feel weak. She didn't like feeling weak. He didn't offer any logical explanation as to why he wanted to meet her. Yes, she recognised him after so many years. But this doesn't mean any-thing.

"Did she call me a child sacrificer?!...I can't believe this...I have a pharmakos in my back garden? This is unreal. Did she really mean that?" Alexander was thinking about his conversation with Maria. He had mixed feelings about the meeting and about her. She was incred-ibly brave to stand up to him. He was disgusted by her in an instant.

In a second, he was shocked and thrilled by her words. What bravery!! No one, no one, ever talked to him this way. Not even his family members, who have the most freedom, tell him everything to his face. Everything has a limit, but she crossed it. Unbelievable. Why did she come back into his life again? Her face has changed since he first saw her. She looked like a young boy with short hair and a very flat chest. Her face was not unattractive, but her overall appearance was so unappealing that no man wanted to look at her. However, for an unknown reason, the spark she had in her eyes made him remember her. Every time something was offered to him, something he shouldn't have been doing, the spark came to his mind that made him decide to refuse the offer. It was just a reminder that he was about to do something wrong. The spark gave him a big NO to the offers; stolen jewellery, stolen property, child trafficking, human hunting, and secret deeds…He was in these circles, unable to escape from these people. He had to be very clever to manipulate situations without getting his hands dirty. It was an art, a true skill, to play with dirt and stay clean. Maria's eye spark gave him guidance and fear. From time to time, he would wonder, but he would immediately conclude that she was dead. It would be pointless for him to look after her, especially since they never had a conversation or were introduced to each other. He never had any regrets because he was merely a silent witness to the human tragedy. He never thought he was doing something wrong by observing and taking no action. He never had any emotions about the whole situation. For him, this was a duty that he had to perform. He never asked himself why he accepted this duty. But seeing her alive under normal circumstances, he began doubting his life and existence. She survived incredible situations and the cruelty of other humans, yet she lived a life worthy of respect. She was a beautiful human being, full of compassion, understanding, and respect for others. She could be humble at times and proud of others. She pretended to be less, hiding her true abilities. He pretended to be more by showing off his dominant character. He thought he knew himself. He thought he was the master of the universe and that no one was equal to him. But here she was, showing him how worthless he was. It took her only a few moments to show him how small he was actually.

'Uncle, did you meet her? Did she tell you what happened? Did she tell you about the incident in the garden?'

'Yes, Stella, I met her.'

'Did she tell anyone? Are we safe?'

'She told her friends. How could you be so careless and naive?'

'I thought she would not speak to anyone. She will keep this a secret.'

'Why would you think that? Have I told you to keep this secret?'

'What are we going to do now with her friends?'

'Let's kill them all, Stella. Should we? All who saw or know anything about this! Or maybe we shouldn't do anything, ha, Stella?'

'I am so sorry, Uncle. I really didn't want this to happen. I am really sorry, Uncle. Please forgive me.' - fear in Stella's eyes was real while he was shouting at her.

'I don't know why I am so soft on you and so strict on my children. Why am I so trusting in you, yet you fail to do what you have been told? You should be better than this!'

'I know, Uncle. I am so sorry... What should I do about Maria? Should we let her go?'

'This ignorant, uneducated, and ugly woman. She is a worthless human being. How could you be friends with her?'

'Uncle, she is not uneducated, and not ugly either. As a woman, I would know that. She looks normal. And she is not a savage. Actually, she is a very kind and well-behaved person. I am sorry she punched your ego, but you have probably done something to upset her.'

'Oh, whatever...She is too dangerous now. I have to find a way to keep her close to me. I have to find a way to bring her by my side.'

It wasn't strange at all when the recruiter asked Maria about her skills. It was all done so professionally. Questions such as "Do you have any experience in asset and property management? Have you worked in this field before? Do you speak any foreign languages? Have you travelled, or do you have the desire to travel? Do you have a family that depends on you and your working hours?" are completely normal in the recruitment process. She signed a perfectly legal agreement. The only thing that made her suspicious was all the benefits they gave her. As it was very important for her not to refuse the offer. However, as she was thinking, she needed a job. She knew what she had to do and was fine with what was expected from her. She was somewhat panicked because she had to work with affluent individuals who possessed large egos, expecting her to be humiliated yet grateful that she was in their presence. She knew that the people she would be working with would not help her if she needed assistance due to their corrupt mindset while working under such circumstances. Hoping that she was wrong, in her opinion, was what brought her on a boat that day. She had been working independently for a couple of months now in various offices, locations, and countries. Her job involved managing properties and assets, which required her to physically locate, allocate, re-value, and assess them. The list was huge, and it wasn't an easy job. It looked nice when the ticket was booked for a place and hotel that looked gorgeous in the picture. It looked nice when she arrived, but when she finished her job late at night, all she wanted was a bed, a shower, and a little bit of food.

Going on a boat in Italy and assessing its value should be one of the assignments. The size and features of assets always exceeded her imagination, but as soon as she met the crew, she wanted to escape back to land. The boat she was looking at was actually the finest quality super yacht. She didn't recognise the flag, but she was excited when she met a captain, very professional and welcoming giving her assurance that she will be fine onboard and safe off shore. He seemed to be the boss of the boat, showing her pictures and artwork that she was interested in and allowed her to work in his office. Soon, the engine started, and the boat took off. Maria was a bit worried after an hour or so. It seemed that this was not only a short manoeuvre. She got up and immediately became lost. This was not her comfort zone, and there was no one around to show her the way to the captain. Instead, when she saw a man in front of her, she didn't know how to react.

'You? Here? Am I kidnapped? Did you set me up? Should I be afraid?'

'Normal people say "Hello" when they see each other. Do you agree?'

'Oh, hello. I am glad I saw you again. Now, let me go.'

'Yes, please. Here is the door. If you know how to swim, enjoy swimming back.'

'Am I being detained?'

'Oh, don't be so dramatic, Maria. You are too old for this drama.'

'This can't be a coincidence, Alexander. Right? Why am I here? Why are you here?'

'I own this yacht, and as far as I know, you are at work.'

'Yes, I am at work. I didn't know we would sail away. I have booked a hotel and would like to return there after I finish my work.'

'And this will happen when you finish your work, of course.'

'If I say, "I finished my work," would you ask the captain to go back to the port from which we sailed away?'

'I am afraid, I can't do that. We have cancelled the reservation for mooring the ship.'

'So only swimming is left...'

'Or flying, if you have wings.'

'I am in trouble!'

'Why do you think so?'

'Should I start praying?'

'Again, you are being overly dramatic.'

'What should I think, then?'

'Think this way. You came to work, and you are finishing your tasks. I came for a holiday, and I will return when I finish my vacation. I am the owner of this yacht, and I will instruct the captain to return to land once my holiday is over. Until then, you have to be my guest... or my crew... depending on which role you wish to play.'

'I have claustrophobia and aqua phobia. I have all possible phobias. This place is not good for me.'

'Wow, then you are in trouble. You can't be inside, and you can't be outside. Why did you accept this assignment? You knew you were coming on a boat...'

'Because of my stupid trust.'

'Ah, yes, trust can kill you.'

'Will you?'

'Do I look like a murderer, Maria?'

'Everybody thinks that the devil is ugly-looking, but actually, he has an angel's face. A true deceiver.'

'I completely agree with you. So you think I look like an angel, but actually, I am a devil?'

'No...no...no... Things are not going well.'

Alexander was looking at Maria. Her upright posture was bending as she realised she was helpless. He didn't want to scare her off or see the fear on her face, but he couldn't help himself from showing her place. He wanted to show her his strength and power, not make her fear. Maybe this was a result of him exerting his power over her. He didn't want to be a villain in her life story. He wanted to get to know her better. This is all he wanted, but he started doubting his reasons after she spoke.

'If I am a threat to you in any way, please know that you have all the power over me. I will not be a burden; I will not be a witness; I will not be an obstacle. I have no power over you whatsoever. My only guilt is that I was in the wrong place at the wrong time.'

'Yes, Maria, you have, but I hope you are talking about the current wrong place and time, not about the past. You look scared, and I don't want you to be afraid of me. Be my guest for a couple of days. Nothing wrong will happen to you. Please relax. I will ask a stewardess to show you to your room. We will sail across the Mediterranean Sea for a couple of days, and I hope you will enjoy this trip.'

Has her time come yet? Is she about to leave now? There is still a lot to do before her time comes. Her bucket list is still full. Should she trust a stranger who frightens her to the core? Her life was a real hell, but she still loves living. A lot of people hurt her, but she still loves to be around them. She never had any regrets, no matter what she had done or what was done to her. Will she regret stepping onto this boat? How could she have known that she shouldn't have come here? Has she missed something?

'I need my medication. I need to return to the hotel.'

'Your belongings have been taken from the hotel and are now in your room.'

'I also do not have summer clothes.'

'No worries, we will make arrangements.'

"He has answers to everything. He has already planned this."

'Is there anything you would like to eat tonight, Maria? Our chef has prepared a menu, but if you wish for something different, I am sure he will be flexible.'

'I am not picky.'

'Good then. I will leave you to rest unless you wish to join me in the swimming pool.'

"Swimming pool? And you are surrounded by beautiful, crystal-clear blue water." Should she tell him this? "Be careful with this man. You don't know how he will react to your words. You don't know him. You don't know why he kept you here. Actually, you know, but you don't know how important this is for him."

All the beauty in the room was not enough to cheer her up, and she was fond of beautiful interiors. She was completely helpless and didn't know how to defend herself. The only weapon she has is her brain. "If you wish to survive, this is the only weapon you should use," she heard her grandfather's voice. If these are her last moments of life, she will enjoy them. What a beautiful way to die. She will have a handsome man in front of her on a luxurious yacht surrounded by breath taking nature. What else can you ask for? She was always a grounded and down-to-earth person, constantly reflecting on what she had and what she could do. If she needs to leave this life, at least she will be surrounded by beauty.

Alexander was thinking about his life while sitting by the swimming pool. He always felt that something was missing in his life. His parents gave him a good life. He monetised this and established a secure future for himself and his family. He had a beautiful and supportive family. There were no arguments in his marriage, and his children were obedient. Everything was perfect. Nothing was missing. Still, despite lying to himself, something was missing, and he didn't know what. He was always searching, looking for new opportunities, meeting new people, and constantly involved in new projects. He met strange men who offered him spiritual and mental peace, but he was already at peace. Was he? Or maybe not? Has he done everything he wanted or should have done? Have all his decisions been correct? Has he missed something in his life? Are his friends true friends? Has he helped someone he should or shouldn't have? He has everything, done everything, been everywhere, so why is he feeling this way? Why now? Are these questions that all men ask themselves at a certain age? Was Maria causing this? This person was just a passer-by in his past. No one to think or worry about. But still, he cares about her. Was it a guilt, a tiny guilt that his sub consciousness carried throughout his life? Did he somehow connect his passive behaviour during the war and executions with everything that happened to his grandfather and great-grandfather? Despite what happened to his mother, she never had any hatred towards people from where she was from. On the contrary, despite carrying guilt and shame, she was always surrounded by people from Yugoslavia. She loved the culture, languages, and history. She never wanted to assimilate and become Swiss. She had a deep affection for her homeland, and she never passed on any feelings of hatred to her children. Alexander also never hated anyone from that region. He grew up listening to horrible war stories, hidden behind the sofa so he could hear the grown-ups talking. Maybe these secrets subconsciously made him passive towards what he was looking at during the war. Maybe this made him not react to the horrible scenes he was witnessing; it was so common and normal. His duty as a participant was to witness and monitor cruel situations, but he was not allowed to interfere in any situation. At that time, he behaved like a robot, obediently carrying out tasks assigned to him. But this was not correct. He didn't do anything to help anyone. Maria was the one who reminded him.

'I have a confession to make. I was in Bosnia during the war.'

"What, am I a priest for you to confess to me? I know you have been there. I remember you very well."

'Oh, really? Like a United Nations soldier?'

'No, I was an observer. I was a Swiss soldier working for the Vatican at that time.'

'At least, you haven't been Dutch.'

'No, I haven't been; otherwise, all the guilt would be on my shoulders.'

'Right! They are not guilty...How long have you been there?'

'I have been almost six years.'

'Do you speak the language?'

'Yes, a little bit.'

"Oh, how nice. You learned a few words. I bet these are beer, swearing, and money."

'That's nice.'

'I think I saw you somewhere over there. But I forgot the location.'

"You remembered me, you idiot, but you forgot the place. You are a very intelligent man!"

'Yes, it is indeed hard to remember all those places. I forgot them as well.'

'Do you ever go home?'

"Who should I go to? Evil people took everything from me."'

'Yes, I go sometimes.'

'Do you have a family there?'

"My family, who didn't want me, is dead to me. All of my deceased family members, whom I loved the most, are exposed up to now. There isn't even a grave to go to."

'Yes, I do.'

'I have a feeling that you are just being polite to me.'

'Oh no, you are wrong, Alexander. I am polite to everyone.'

'Stella told me that you have developed a special bond. She likes you very much.'

'Yes, she is a very nice girl. However, I wish she hadn't invited me that day.'

'I really do not understand why you regret that day.'

'I wouldn't feel guilty right now.'

'Okay, do you really want to know what happened that day?'

'No, no, I don't want to know.'

'These children and their teachers are survivors.'

'Ok. Survivors. That's fine.'

'I have a hobby. I collect broken people.'

'Oh, what a nice hobby.'

'Ok, now you are mocking me. Ask whatever you want, and I will tell you, but please stop mocking me.'

'I don't want to ask you. I don't even want to be here.'

'I have a feeling that you have the wrong perception of me and what you saw.'

'I saw a bunch of sick adults and children wandering around Pharmakos in bad weather, in a dark wood. I know that I shouldn't judge a book by its cover, but you are persistent in keeping me by your side. What should I think about the whole situation?'

'Pharmakos, how you assume, is to be a replica of a Greek temple. My brother bought the mansion with that place. You would have seen that it is a very old one. All the people you say are sick are actually wounded, not sick. I provide asylum for abused individuals, whether it is domestic abuse or any other form of abuse. I keep them safe in that place because their abusers wouldn't let them have peace and would continue harassing them until they complete the job. Adults are not children's prison guardians. They are people who were in the same situation as children currently are, and they know best what they are going through. They were scared when they saw you because they thought you had come to harm someone among them. There is no human hunting or sacrifice there, lady. Nothing like that.'

'Okay, nothing like that. I believe you. Can you please ask the captain to go back now?'

'No! You will go back when you start listening to me.'

'I listen to you. I do. And I believe you.'

'Ok, I forgot that your stubbornness is in your genes.'

'And stupidity and naivety, too, don't forget.'

'So, which one are you, Muyo or Haso?'

'Now, you are mocking me.' "Idiot!"

"Asylum!? Go and tell this to someone else, you idiot. Do you think I am stupid enough to believe your lies? Why would a rich man help a poor one? Why would anyone help these unfortunate little beings? Go and tell this to your mother if you dare!"

'So, how many boats do you have?'

'You tell me.'

'What do you mean? Do I know better than you?'

'You keep the list on your computer.'

'Oh no, you are one of our clients?'

'Which clients? I don't have clients. This fleet belongs to a trust portfolio.'

'Do I work for you?'

'Actually, you work for a company that takes care of the Trust. The company belongs to a group that is under my supervision.'

'You owe that group?'

'Yes, I do... Are you not going to ask anything?'

'Yes, I will... How much is enough? I have always wondered how much I should earn and owe in order to have the feeling that it is enough.'

'Wow! I didn't expect this question... I expected to be asked, how come I came to work for you?...How much is enough?'

'Well, this is a general question. I didn't have much in my life, and honestly, I was happy if I had something. But even if I didn't have anything, I would still feel fine. '

'If you dream big, you will achieve great things. If you dream small, you will achieve small things. Or nothing.'

'Yes, I have always wondered why some people are poor. Now, I have the answer: they dream small.'

'What did you dream about, and what did you achieve?'

'My grandparents owned half a mountain but still lived in a wooden hut. They couldn't afford a good solid house; it was made of wood and mud. I still own the land. Maybe I will return there when I get older. My parents dreamed big, but they hadn't achieved anything. Only broken homes. My grandmother died because my father built a large house. My mother dreamed of a good life. She was a cleaning lady who married an elderly German man. He gave her an ultimatum: she could be with him and give birth to German babies, but she would never see her Bosnian baby. My dad also dreamed big. He worked as a handyman in a car factory. He earned good money, in my opinion. He married a woman who had money and used her funds to open a garage. He did everything she asked, but forgot about a non-human child on a mountain. Their children are doing fine. All of them are educated, earn good money, and live nice lives in nice places. As for me, I forgot to dream...I still achieved something without dreaming.'

'Have you ever dared to dream?'

'Yeah, I wanted to be a nun!'

'A nun? Why? Was this the only option you had during your childhood?'

'Because the only future I had was milking sheep and making cheese. Not that I didn't like it.'

'I think you are doing very well now, considering that you are not a nun.'

'Yes, I am doing well. I am on this big boat with you. Playing Scheherazade.'

"Ah, it is pointless to speak to her. She won't open up. It is better to remain silent. As soon as we reach the first harbour, I will let her go!"

Maria was sitting at the large dining table, her nerves tense on the inside while appearing calm on the outside. She was wandering with her eyes across the room. If she didn't feel the swinging motion, she would have thought that this was a hotel. The interior exuded power and wealth. She wasn't able to admire the life of rich people. She always analysed everything and decided not to admire their lives, but she couldn't help herself wishing for an easier life. She didn't know the man opposite her, so she wasn't sure if this room was his imprint. She felt pity for anyone who had to polish wood and tables. It seemed spotless. The carpet on the floor exuded a sense of pristine whiteness, while silk curtains delicately adorned the room, concealing two beauties - one from the outside world and one within. If this were not her life, if this were a different situation, she might have enjoyed staying in such a magnificent room. Her fear dashed her hopes that this was real and that she couldn't enjoy it, not even for a moment.

The silence in the room was a bit unpleasant, but the music from the shores was very pleasant. It came to their ears in waves, just as the sea waves brought it to them with a purpose, offering both of them peace and relaxation. Maria opened the curtains, and a huge window appeared, allowing distant lights to come in. The magic of the night silenced their fears as well.

'The music is very beautiful. Don't you think so?'

'Yes, it is.'

'Would we be able to go to that place?'

'No. The yacht is too big for their harbour.'

'I could swim there. It is not too far.'

'It looks near, but actually, it is too far away.'

'I am a good swimmer.'

'I believe you are, but you cannot escape.'

'I don't want to escape. Besides, you are not a person who does not finish the job.'

'Why are you so scared of me? Why do you think I would harm you?'

'I don't think you would harm me…If I did something wrong, you wouldn't waste your time on me. Maybe you wish to know if I talked to someone or if I said something you didn't want me to say... But then, you would do that in a different way.'

'So, I have to make you talk?'

'Well, I am here for this, am I not?'

'Yes, I suppose you are.'

'I feel like Scheherazade now...'

"Woman, don't flatter yourself so much. You are not very attractive, and I am not very interested in you!"

'No, we are not going to spend one thousand and one night here. I am sorry... Besides, how did these thoughts come to your mind?'

'They just come; it is the Bosnian mind… All right, I will answer all of your questions. Sorry, I am ready. I haven't shared my friends' details, I swear. They don't know where the house is. They don't know Stella's name or yours...'

'Maria, this is not what I wanted to ask you.'

'Sorry, what did you want to ask me?'

'I wanted to ask you about the war in Bosnia.'

'It was such a long time ago. I really wanted to forget about it. The war ended, and I survived. I have other things on my mind. Who cares what happened there anyway.?'

'I care. I wanted to know how you survived.'

'Survival is an art of my people, my region, and my country. This is what humans do. We survive the most difficult situations, and we continue living. Yes, we are crippled, broken, injured, and shamed, but we still live. You have no choice but to keep on living. Some people embrace their guilt, someone's shame, and others their fear. We gather our pieces and create a new home. Some of us build even better homes.'

'Do you feel hate?'

'Hate?! Why would I feel that?'

'Has anyone hurt you during the war?'

'Man, everyone have hurt me. But none of them deserved my hatred. I feel pity for them because they were bewitched by war ideology and personal interest. All of them believed that they were being attacked and were defending themselves. All of them believed they were victims. At the same time, they did everything what that the first one did. It was a hate link. They forgot what was right and what was wrong. They were hypnotised by war media machinery. They were all ruthless killing machines, deriving pleasure from inflicting harm upon one another. Why would I reward them by thinking of them? Who are they to me that I have them on my mind for the rest of my life?'

'Obviously, nothing has happened to you, so this is how you think.'

'How do you think nothing happened to me?... Do you want a romantic war story or a true story? Because if I were to tell you the real story, you wouldn't want to hear it. It would be too much to hear. I already told you about the romantic side of the war, so we can part ways now.'

'The true story of the war?'

'Yeah. Maybe you should read the books that Miroslav Krleža wrote. When you read his books where he explains the war, you can almost smell the war. You could smell the stench of rotting flesh hidden under dirty bandages, hear the screams of dying soldiers and the whistling of bullets, and feel the pain as they tear through flesh. You should read it sometime. He explained it very well.'

'You don't need to explain me the physics of war guns. I don't expect you to give me details on the speed at which a bullet tears through human flesh or when the pain begins after the bullet hits the body. You don't have to explain to me when a human mind registers a sound. I already know that. I have been there, remember? I want to know how you survived the war. What happened on the day when you realised something terrible had occurred?'

'What happened, happened.'

'Have you been scared?'

'You accept aggression as a normal thing if it is not directed at you. Even today, when I think about those days, we accepted hell as a normal part of life. We didn't think we lacked freedom as long as we were free to walk. We adapted to the lack of electricity and heating, which were comforts that people had. We have found a way to survive. We heard every day about someone dying in a bizarre way, but we just nodded and forgot. It is not that we didn't have emotions, but we cried silently. We were helpless, but we continued to fight in any way we could. A human have a strong instinct for survival, and no matter the circumstances, they always find a way to survive.'

'Do you think you are lucky you are still alive?'

'Human psychology in war is a fascinating subject. There is no right or wrong. There is no "you shouldn't" or "you have to." It is ruled by a philosophy of stronger and faster. All human norms are dead in the war. The worst thing is that human life has no value there. They would feel more for a piece of gold that they haven't been able to collect than for a human life. They wouldn't care about you whether you were their childhood friend or a next-door neighbour. You are a target for elimination.'

'I always thought luck was the most important to survive the most dangerous situations.'

'You wanted to know what saved me in the war? It was a tattoo. I didn't want to get a tattoo. My great-grandmother had it. My mother had it. It was a tradition for women in my family to tattoo a cross on their bodies. It is an old tradition that comes from Ottoman times. The Ottomans used to kidnap our children, boys for the army and girls for the Harem. People needed to find a way to stop the Blood tax, so they used to mutilate boys and tattooing girls. The most beautiful girls had crosses tattooed all over their arms, faces, and bodies. Ottomans didn't touch these girls or take them to the Harem.'

'Is it a lucky charm to you? Do you think this is somehow connected to the power of God?'

'A cross is a symbol of Christianity. But also teaching what is right and wrong. For some reason, people act differently when they look at religious symbols. It has a great impact on their minds and behaviours. No matter how bad they may be, when they have this symbol in front of their eyes, they act peacefully. They stop doing wrong things. For us Bosnian Christians, Islamic symbols represent oppression, slavery, and death. This is what we experienced with the Ottomans, and it is very difficult to believe that their religion is tolerant of other beliefs. It took me some time to change my mind.'

'Why so?'

'Why? The uncle who saved me was a Muslim. He used to buy sheep from us. He became friends with my grandfather, and I was friends with her daughter at school. They were not religious, and I didn't have much choice. When we escaped the slaughter in the village, we were constantly moving from one place to another. Finally, we were forced to go to a Muslim village. He thought we would be safe there for a certain period of time. We lived in different places, but we ended up there. However, Mujahedins came to the village. They were foreigners, probably Arabs. They had long beards and wore white or dark dresses. They enforced their Sharia law on us. I lived in the village for a while. The host was telling me that it wasn't safe for me. But I didn't listen. The first person who saw me uncovered started yelling at me to cover myself up. He started pushing and pulling me, and I was trying to get away from him. He brought a piece of linen and covered me, but I took it off. I am not a Muslim, and I didn't want to cover myself up. My family fought against oppression in the past.

I didn't want to accept that; my family fought in the past so I can have freedom of choice as a woman. But he was so aggressive that he started beating me on the street in front of everyone. No one dared to step in and protect me. They had long knives and shouted in their languages. The more I defended myself, the more persistent they became in trying to cover me up. Suddenly, one of them ripped my clothes off, and my tattoo was revealed. He was paralysed when he saw the cross on my body. I think he didn't know that there were Christians hiding in the village. He swung his machete and almost beheaded me if I hadn't instinctively moved. Then, a young man from the village intervened and spoke to him in the Arab language, the only one who was courageous enough to step in. Mujahedin agreed. But then he asked young man to do something to me in front of everyone not having trust in locals. The young man refused. Some other local men told the young man to take me out of the village and kill me, giving signals to him to take me out to freedom. So, he took me by the arm, and we went out. We were walking, I don't know for how long, when he handed me over to another man. The man led me to a village where Serbians lived. I thought they would kill me, just as they had killed my fellow villagers. They hadn't been the happiest to see me, but they allowed me to board the bus, and I arrived at my next destination. Did my tattoo help me survive? I want to think that it helped me more than my own people.'

'What happened to the young man who helped you escape from the village? Wasn't he supposed to execute you?'

'He never wanted to kill me. He wanted to help me. Has he survived? I think this question is for you, Alexander.'

'What do you mean?'

'You were there. I was there...'

No matter how much he wanted to hear that she knew who he was, where they had seen each other for the first time when he heard her say that, he felt ashamed. Up until that moment, he hadn't realised that there was anything wrong with him being there in those moments. However, her voice shattered his pride and filled him with shame. His confidence, for the first time, left him on the ground, on his knees. He wanted her to know that he had been in her presence at times in their lives. He wanted to express that he understood what she had been through, but this feeling of understanding turned into shame. When she confessed that she remembered him, even though so many years had passed and their faces had changed, he knew that there was more to their connection. Nevertheless, she gave him a blow to his ego that caused him to question all his beliefs about himself. How can one casual look possibly be so important to someone who has never talked before that they remember it for the rest of their lives? How come this short meeting was so important in their lives that all their decisions were based on that moment? But was it only a moment that connected them?

'How did you know I was there? And where exactly have you seen me?'

'I recognised your posture. I have never seen a man standing so proud and calm in moments of human cataclysm. He was just like you sitting at this moment. You were on at the bus station, where we were gathered and where buses waited for us. You were not alone. Other foreign soldiers were also present. Journalist as well. All of you wanted to have a better view of the situation. All of you knew what would happen, and you all wanted to do your job. We were the subjects of your report. You were all war paparazzi. You profited from our suffering. You didn't care whether we were heading towards our ultimate destination or if it was just a transition to another life.'

'How did you remember me out of all the people there? Was it a uniform? Did I do something?'

'You were wearing mirrored sunglasses. I couldn't see your eyes. I noticed your posture. Your uniform was black. You resembled a German officer in war films, standing on a platform with your hands behind your back, observing Jews being transported in wagons to their ultimate destination. This time were not Jews, but Bosnians. I felt this way. I knew as I saw you this was it; there was no hope for me… But here I am, still kicking… Most of those whom I saw on my side didn't have a chance to see your face, silent witnesses of that time, and tell them that you were as guilty as our executors.'

'Do you think I was able to change anything? If I said one wrong word, I would accompany you on your side.'

'All of you thought so. This was just an excuse for all of you. You all earned a lot from us. You all stole our national treasure, our pride, and our future. Maybe you thought, "Oh well, one nation less, let's go further." But, you see, we are still alive. You probably said, "Let the fools fight," and we fought. We didn't know that someone among you had planned that. We were just bloody fools, thinking we were de-fending ourselves. You bombarded us with your propaganda, and we finally believed. We fought, and while we were fighting, you stole everything you could from us.'

'I am really sorry for everything that happened to you. I went to Croatia first and then was sent to Bosnia. I stopped there. I couldn't see what was going on there. Am I guilty of being a witness? If this is a crime, then yes, I am guilty.'

'No! You are not guilty of being a witness. You are guilty of remaining silent about what your colleagues did to us. And you too.'

'What did they do to you?'

'Tell me you don't know that journalists were kidnapping our children and selling them on the Western black market. Or buying women who have been captured and selling them as prostitutes to politicians in the Western world. Or stealing our statues, pictures, gold, and whatever brought money to you. Tell me you don't know anything about ritual killings. What about doctors? So, generous doctors who came for organ harvesting. War was halted while some Westerners underwent kidney transplants in temporary theatres on the battlefield. Have you ever reported this to anyone?'

'… Yes, I know that… No, I haven't. No one wanted to listen. No one wanted this information.'

'Do you think they would have listened now?'

'Of course not. The war is over. You are alive.'

'Yes, I am indeed. And I wouldn't think of war if one person didn't want to remember me. Why were you so eager to understand what happened to me during the war?'

'Maybe subconsciously, I wanted to know if you were alive. Maybe without a logical explanation, I became curious about what happened to you after I met you. I didn't know you were the person I was thinking about for so many years.'

'Really?! Who would have said that a simple, inconspicuous, peasant girl would have had a privilege to be remembered by a high class person?'

Alexander's thoughts were swirling around his war experience. He was utterly confused. It was late at night, and one thing he knew was not to speak while it was dark. The night was never a clever period of the day, so he didn't want to say something he might regret in the morning. He excused himself without providing any explanation and left her alone on the deck to contemplate. He noticed that she stayed there for the next couple of hours, gazing at the stars. He wanted to sleep and forget about what he had just heard. He wanted to swipe words Maria told him. For someone who hadn't experienced violence and war, these words didn't hold any meaning. However, for Alexander, who was, as Maria said, a silent witness, it meant guilt. Images flooded his mind. Bloody pictures. For all these years, he didn't feel remorse. He never blamed himself for witnessing such horrific situations and taking no action. He knew that he wanted to understand what war was because his background was connected to the war. He wanted to know what it was like to be a soldier in a bloody war. He wanted to hear these voices of horror and challenge his emotions. While he was a witness, he didn't have any emotions. He didn't experience fear, or sadness, or joy. His body was present, his mind was present, but he acted as rationally as possible. He thought that a soldier should not have any emotions. As a good soldier, he pushed away any thoughts that made him feel emotional. Now, as Maria clearly stated, he was actually blaming people who were in conflict with each other. He always thought that this area was a powder keg, but it was indeed an outsider who lit the match. Was he one of the outsiders? He was communicating with everyone, and he didn't care about what he was saying. His colleagues did the same. Sometimes, his colleagues would split up, monitoring the situation from different angles and then re-convene to discuss any weaknesses they had identified, selling information to opposite sides so they would fight while they would laugh. They felt the power of waging war. They didn't care that someone would die in that moment. All they cared about was the power they had in that moment. Was he one of them? Did he say something that could have caused someone's death? Was he really as innocent as he thought? Yes, things happened. His colleagues haven't been the best people, but what about him? He wanted to know what had happened to her after he saw her, but now, as he heard her story, he wished he hadn't heard it. Deep down in his soul, he wondered if she was alive and quickly concluded that she wasn't. However, to his surprise, she was very much alive. Nevertheless, he feels guilt like he has never felt before. And this feeling of guilt, of knowing what had happened, was something new to him. He understood what it means to be weak, to not be able to defend himself. He was saying to himself that war machinery was so powerful that he couldn't do anything to change the course of the situation. Yes, exactly what it was. He was powerless against the war machinery.

'Maria, I was thinking, if you wish to go home, we can stop at a harbour and help you find a way to get back.' - He said the next day to her.

'Why so, Alexander? Have I been a burden to you?'

'No, of course not. I thought you didn't want to be here, and maybe it wasn't the best way to invite you. I scared you, and I wasn't the best host. I apologise for that.'

'Oh, Alexander, everything is fine with me. If I am not a burden, I would like to extend my stay for one more day. Maybe we could stop somewhere to see a town.'

'...We can stop, of course. I thought I crossed the line by bringing you here.'

'No, I am fine.' "You brought me here without explaining why, and you think I will let you go so easily? It's my turn now!"

Malta was on Maria's bucket list, and she had always wanted to see the island. She was a bit surprised when Alexander agreed to stop there. Maybe he wanted to get rid of her, but this time, she didn't want to let him go. She knew that if she didn't get an answer from him, this would be her last chance to do so. He will return to his own life, and she will not be able to locate him or approach him. Their worlds have not been equal, and it wouldn't be possible to find him in any other way. This was the only opportunity to get the truth from him.

Alexander noticed that Maria's clothes were not appropriate for the weather or the town. She wore business clothes, which made her look out of place among tourists. He offered to go inside a clothing shop and buy her a dress. She was visibly surprised and felt humiliated. She suggested that there was nothing for her there. Her surprise made Alexander feeling awkward because no girl had ever refused him to pay for her clothes. He was a walking bank to all his companions.

'Maria, I apologise if I have done or said something wrong. Have I done something wrong?'

'It is inappropriate for a married man to offer to buy clothes for a single woman. Especially if they are not in a relationship a man shouldn't buy clothes to a woman.'

'I am sorry for offending you. I didn't realise that this was inappropriate. Besides, the shop appeared to be very expensive.'

'Yes, the clothes were very expensive indeed. I will choose the shop and pay for it myself. But you can buy ice cream. I don't mind. I will pay for lunch.'

'Oh, is this how it is in your culture?'

'Of course, no pressure.'

It was a very hot day, strolling through the ancient streets of historic sites, absorbing the essence of the past in the present time. Millions walked the same streets, leaving their footprints on the cobblestones. If those stones could speak, they would tell millions of tragic events, happy thoughts, hopes, and prayers. Alexander and Maria were one of millions of couples in the present time who future generations will think about. Each brick of the wall could sing a song of its creator, and each window could show you a picture of past inhabitants. Nothing has changed in the place except for the fashion of a traveller. Like everyone in the past, these people today could tell the same tragic life stories, hope for a better future, and admiration and wonderment at the intelligence of ancient people. When walking through the gate, their lives blended with the lives of the people who were there before them. All their energy was infused into the stones of the streets, absorbing their power and generating a universal time machine. What makes past humans different from present ones? Some are not alive, while others are. While generations came and went, the island remained in all its glory, serving as a testament to the stories of the past for future generations. Every generation leaves a mark; whether it is good or bad, it still is a mark. A sharp eye would notice a message left for them to learn something valuable. The lesson should be passed on to someone else, someone who doesn't see or hear.

'I have been fascinated with this island for a long, long time. I have been reading about their history in the past. This visit is only confirming what I read.'

'Did you enjoy reading when you were young?'

'Oh yes. This shepherd girl was reading books every chance she got. My grandmother used to go to the town library and take books for me. They never minded if I returned books late. This was the only window to the world.'

Alexander was walking beside a woman who, when she changed into brighter and more casual clothing, looked like a true lady. She was walking so gracefully while her short hair was covered under a summer straw hat. Alexander had doubts about every word she spoke regarding her being a peasant girl. He remembered how she looked the first time he laid his eyes on her. She looked like a teenage boy, very skinny and inconspicuous. She wouldn't attract any men looking like that. This lady made him look in her direction without blinking. He was constantly surrounded by beautiful and intelligent women. Some of them attracted him, while others made him regret ever meeting them. Maria made him wonder who she was. No woman made him wonder about this. He met them, he was attracted to what he saw and heard, and that was it. There was no mystery. There was no desire to discover the soul of that person. But he wanted to know more about her. She surprised him. She was changing his opinion of her. He had an opinion about her some months ago, and as he could easily read people, he noticed that this lady was very keen on maintaining an air of mystery. He was surprised by her extensive general knowledge and ability to connect information. Her logic was sharp and distinctive, and she questioned every piece of information she heard. Yet, she presented herself in such a shy and humble way.

'What is the colour of my eyes?' Maria, who was wearing sunglasses, interrupted his thoughts.

'Light green. Why are you asking?'

'What is the colour of Stella's eyes?'

'Ah... Blue... What is this?'

'What is the colour of your children's eyes?'

'Oh... I was supposed to know that... Blue. Wait, I don't have blue eyes, and my wife has brown eyes... Oh, what a shame... Brown. Yes, brown. They definitely have brown eyes.'

'What is the colour of my hair?'

'Your original colour was light brown, almost blond. You dyed your hair dark brown now.'

'What is the colour of Stella's hair, the hair of your children, and your wife's hair?'

'What is this? Why are you questioning me?... I don't know, Stella's hair is like yours, my children's, both light brown, and my wife's. Oh God, I don't know. She is dyeing her hair every little while, so I don't know her original colour. Why are you asking those questions? What is the purpose of this?'

'A woman asks a man if he is happy in his marriage. I ask this question.'

'I am happy. I am a very happily married man.'

'Yet, you don't know the most important thing about them.'

'You want me to think about what a bad parent I am?'

'No. I want to ask you, how does it feel to be in a convenient marriage? Men like you never settle down but always choose someone to portray themselves as a married man. In fact, they never marry a person, but a presenter.'

'Wow! How could you possibly know that? Why did you marry your husband? Was this for convenience's sake?'

'I loved my husband. He was my first and only love. I had never been with anyone before or after him.'

'Of course. You are a Virgin Mary.'

'You see, when you truly love someone, you don't need anyone else but that person. Even if that relationship doesn't last, love lasts forever, and your soul is full. You don't need to fill it up again.'

'Do you still love him?'

'Yes, I do.'

'He hurt you badly. How can you love him?'

'He filled my heart with love. I know how it feels to have this emotion in my heart. He became my world, my everything. It is the best feeling knowing that someone resides in your heart.'

'You still love him even though he hurt you badly? What is wrong with women?'

'I am grateful for being given this opportunity to learn how it feels. I met thousands of men who may be better than he is. Thousands of them could provide me with the future I desired, but none of them could grant me the gift of love. This is a heavenly gift. You have never experienced love, so you don't understand this.'

'What makes you think I don't love my wife? Maybe I haven't been completely faithful or honest with her, but I truly loved her. I chose to spend my life with her.'

'Yet, she is not with you at this moment.'

'I am here with you for a different purpose.'

'What is the purpose that made you leave her alone and wander across the sea with someone else.'

"...No... you almost got me...No. It is too early to tell you everything. I need to be sure that you are the one. I need to understand that you are the reason for my faith and existence. It would be a mistake to reveal myself. She is good; she almost got me."

Maria was disappointed in her ability to make him talk. She was never good at manipulating men's minds. She admired women who could do that. She couldn't judge them; they had mastered their arts. This was an art she could never learn. No one passed on the knowledge to her. Why should she try to manipulate this man? He was beyond her reach. He showed interest in her, not as a woman, but as a subject. Not even to a human, but to someone who can give him what he wants. But what is it that he wants from her?

It was very late at night when they returned to the yacht. The crew was waiting for them. Maria was pleased with how she was treated. "This is what I want. I want to be treated with respect by other people. Do I need to be wealthy in order to be respected in this way?" The day was very long, and all she needed was a bed. She had a million unanswered questions. She had a million doubts in her mind. But her body had limits, and all of them could wait.

Alexander was also in his thoughts. He went to sleep, knowing that he will stay awake the whole night. This woman shook his ego once again. He knew the colour of her eyes, yet he didn't know the colour of his children's eyes. He knew what her hair colour was, but not his wife's. He thought he was happily married and had a stable relationship, yet she knew he was not completely honest with her. He chose his wife for her intelligence, humble character, soothing voice, and the love and respect she showed him. She knew about his affairs but never confronted him. He loved her even more because of this. He loved his children. They were good children - obedient, quiet, and respectful. What else do you wish for your children? However, he never went on vacation with his family. His wife has spent holidays with either her parents or her friends. His children used to spend their holidays with their friends or grandparents. At the same time, he used to spend his holidays with his family, friends, or mistresses. Is this happiness? Is this a happy relationship? Or maybe this was really a marriage of convenience. He was rich. She was rich. They combined two empires and created an even larger empire. He was a master of their finances, and she was a mistress who enjoyed the benefits of their wealth. She never wanted to get to know him better. She doesn't know anything about his childhood, his nightmares, his fears, his dreams, his worries, or his hopes. He doesn't know anything about her either. The worst part is that he doesn't know anything about his children either. They are almost grown up. They don't need him any more. They have their own lives now. He knows only important information about them - their whereabouts, activities, and desires. Nothing else. How did this happen? Why did he need someone to tell him this to his face in order to understand that he was doing something wrong? Why didn't he know this earlier? Why didn't he think about this years ago?

Days have passed in small talk and discovering Malta. There was no pressure for Alexander to offend Maria in any way and for her to escape. Sometimes, he criticised himself for being too open and direct. However, knowing that Maria does not judge him or take offence at his words gave him the confidence to ask direct questions. He felt remorse for assuming that she was merely a simple, primitive, illiterate woman. She was nothing like that. She was a very confident person, and she knew how to behave and understand boundaries. He thought he had the skills to recognise personalities, but he was wrong. He also thought he would be bored with her, but he understood that her way of communication was unique. She could tell you to your face that you are worthless without understanding this. She could convey that you are a good person without explicitly stating it. It had been a long time since he had communicated with people from the East, whom Westerners used to refer to as anyone who was not on their list of chosen ones. But Maria proved to him that every west has its own east, and every east has its own west, no matter where it is on the globe.

People from Eastern Europe were glorifying the West without any valid reason while simultaneously belittling people living in the East, despite being aware that this is merely a stereotype. People in the West, no matter where "west" was, always criticised people in the East, forgetting that they were someone's East. Calling them stupid, ignorant, unorganised, and dirty actually demonstrates that these labels should not be stereotyped or exclusively assigned to any specific group of people. Maria was telling stories about the past inhabitants, highlighting their skills learned in the east, wherever that may be. She pointed out that people in the west were consuming knowledge from the east without giving them credit for it.

'Why are you always pointing this out, Maria. East and West. What do you want to tell me?'

'You see, I was born in Bosnia. On the west was Croatia, and on the east were Serbia and Montenegro. All Croats were looking at us as if we were feeble-minded. And all Bosnians thought that people from the east were like that. I have been mistreated all my life because of this stereotype. No one thought I was equal to them, that I am capable of doing the same things as they did. I left the Balkans, thinking that maybe Westerners would be different, but I encountered the same stereotyping. Nevertheless, I was treated even worse. How can I show Westerners that I am not inferior? I am being denied basic human rights, the opportunity to contribute to humanity, and the ability to pass on knowledge that they do not possess. How can I change that? Look, Malta is proof that Eastern knowledge has been implemented in Western societies. Isn't this architecture beautiful? It is sustainable. It is practical. Why don't they get credit for this?'

'I don't know Maria. I can't change the world. How can I possibly change humanity? People will always divide each other anyway. This is what humans do. In order to glorify themselves, they have to belittle someone else. This is the source of every conflict. But this is not the only thing. Humans are easily manipulated when a group is divided, and benefits are given to them. There is always an elite who manipulates the broad masses. I was so naive to think that there were ethnic wars going on in the Balkans until I saw the truth. Elite made you fight, manipulating and ensnaring you into their web. It wasn't so hard to do. In this contest I can say, Easterners are inferior to Westerners political manipulation. Why Easterners do not manipulate Westerners if they are not inferior?'

He was confident in his world. Whatever he did, it brought him pride and satisfaction. When he speaks with Maria, she blows his mind like a sack of potatoes. He always thought he was a very strong person, but when talking to her, he experiences fear. In a short period of time, she made him feel small and vulnerable. His straight posture suddenly started to slump. But he was a fighter; she will not win.

'Maria, what happened that you lost your child? Stella was speaking about this.'

'What did she say to you?'

'Something I have doubts in.'

'Well, it is a long story, but I think I made the wrong choices. My ex-husband's current wife told me what happened. She said that my husband's previous girlfriend told him that she would no longer be with him. He told her that in this situation, he would marry the first girl he saw. She pointed at me, and he said, "Alright, I'll marry her."

He decided to make her angry by marrying me. I wanted a church wedding and didn't want to engage in premarital relations before the ceremony. He agreed because he wanted to provoke his girlfriend's anger. Instead of making her angry, she married a foreign guy and left the country. He stayed with me, but he didn't want the baby. I annoyed him because I was uneducated and primitive. I felt ugly and didn't know how to behave. He didn't have a future with me because I couldn't provide for him and our baby. I was just a cleaner. Then he met a girl who could give him everything he wanted, and he left me. He had connections in the church and asked if we could easily get a divorce. We divorced very quickly. However, the baby was a nuisance to him; he asked the nuns if they could get rid of her. He was very persuasive and a smooth talker. He received some money from nuns, and the baby was handed over to a "child collector".'

'A child collector?'

'Yes, a child collector. Nuns thought I was disrespecting Christianity and that I was an immoral woman who had lost her chastity and dignity. That I wasn't a good person and I should be punished by eliminating my genes. There was a couple who collected children in order to give them up for adoption in foreign countries. They didn't want to keep the children, but they were only intermediaries in the adoption process. That was something I didn't want to hear. They probably gave my baby to a paedophile or some sick individuals who killed my baby...'

'…What did you do to this woman after she told you that?'

'...Nothing...I put medication in her coffee...'

'What kind of medication? Did you kill her?'

'Oh, no. I wouldn't kill her. I let God do this to her and to my husband... She spent a day on the toilet and later had to go to the emergency room to have her stomach pumped. Oh no, I wouldn't kill her. It would be too easy. She will be afraid of me for the rest of her life because she will think I might harm her offspring. The biggest punishment for these kinds of people is fear. Fear will do the rest. Fear will be God's punishment.'

'...You are indeed a truly strange person...'

'Why so? Because I didn't harm her. Or my husband? Would it be better if I killed them first and then myself? Or end up in jail? What would I do? No, I want to see their punishment first. In the same way, I witnessed my parents' punishment.'

'What happened to them?'

'My mum asked her children to find me on Facebook. They found me. They contacted me and asked if I wanted to see my mum. I went to Austria. She had a stroke. She was in a house with strangers. Her children visited her once or twice per month. They had their own lives. She felt remorse, so she wanted to apologise. I asked her why she wanted to do so. Was it for the sake of her soul or for the sake of my soul? She didn't know the answer.'

'What about your father? Did you ever see him?'

'Oh yes. He heard about me, and he was very proud of me. He came with his children and wife to my dissertation. I didn't recognise him. I was honestly surprised to see him. He was so happy that he bought me a Mercedes as a gift. He told his children that they should have done the same, but since I don't speak German, I don't think they understood what I told them.'

'What did you tell them?'

'I told them that they should have experienced life on the streets, feeling hungry and humiliated, without parents or money. They should have been beaten from all sides of the earth. They should have been left alone, without any help. This was my secret to success. If they wish to succeed in life, they should avoid these ungrateful, God's mistaken beings. I told him to move the car out of my sight, or I will light a match. He didn't expect this I guess. He told me that I am un-grateful, just like my mother. I returned and said, "A real man never blames a woman for his choices and the mistakes he has made. She didn't rape you; you slept with her and made me. I am paying for the mistakes you made in life. Your mother paid for this as well. I have witnessed first-hand what happened to her."''

'He didn't expect that.'

'Oh no. I even told him the name of his mother's killer. He went to Serbia with the intention of killing the man, but instead he was handed over to the police because he was threatening the family of a man who killed his mother. He ended up in jail. So, he didn't do much. He was humiliated to the core.'

'Was this to your satisfaction?'

'No. This was not important to me.'

'What is important to you?'

'I want to find the grave of my daughter. I want to have a place to burn a candle if such a place exists. This is all I wanted.'

Alexander was thinking day and night. There are no coincidences in this life. Everything happens for a reason with mathematical precision. Their lives crossed paths for a reason. They have been so different, with different lifestyles and destinies, yet something connected them. There have been too many things that he needed answers for. He asked for a DNA test to be done, and when he received the results, he was not surprised at all. He was thinking about what he should do. He needed answers, too, so he decided to speak with Stella first. He was still on the yacht making a video call.

'Stella, where did you meet Maria?'

'Oh, I met her in at one an accounting practise, in the UK.'

'Since when do we outsource?'

'I just wanted to give it a try. It is not a big deal, Uncle.'

'I think I need to have a serious conversation with you, and I don't believe what I'm about to say will make you happy. I just hope you will act like an adult and consider what I have to say. OK?'

'You sound very serious.'

'I haven't been honest with you, and I believe none of us have been honest with you. But I am the guilty one. I want you to know that your mother is not my sister…We adopted you…'

'Oh, Uncle... I already knew that. This is not news to me. I was just waiting to see how long you would keep it a secret. There must have been a reason for this, I guess. Mum knows that I know, too.'

'How do you know that? How long have you known that?'

'I have known that for many years now. I always had suspicions, but when I went to the hospital and had a blood test, I discovered that my mother couldn't be my biological mother. At first, I thought my father had another woman and that I was her child. However, when I confronted them, they told me everything. They have been afraid of your reaction, so we kept the secret.'

'So, you won't be angry with me if you know the whole truth?'

'I understand that you didn't want me to lose or disturb my peace. If I had known this before, when I was younger, I would probably have reacted differently. However, now that I see things from an adult perspective, I am not angry with you. All I want to know is how did you decide to take me in?'

'It was just an impulse. If I hadn't taken action, I suppose you wouldn't be alive. It was not planned for you to be adopted. I just saw your eyes, your beautiful blue eyes, and fell in love with you. I wanted to rescue you and give you another chance. But the family came in, took you in, and treated you as one of us.'

'I am very grateful for this uncle. And this is why I would never be angry with you. But maybe you will be with me. I brought Maria into our lives for a reason. I wanted to get to know her better and understand her.'

'I took a DNA test, and it turns out that she is your biological mother.'

'I know that, Uncle.'

'How did you figure this out?'

'Well, you know those websites on the internet where you can find information about your ancestors and trace your family history using DNA? I found some relatives in Austria and Germany. I asked them about their lives and if any of them could have been my parent. They gave me the addresses of two people who I believe were my grandparents. The grandparents were afraid that one of their children gave birth without their knowledge. But in the end, we discovered that there is someone whom they do not consider to be exactly one of theirs. And this was Maria. She worked for one of our consultants, and I asked a recruiter to offer her a job here in the UK. She accepted, but she was not very happy about working there. Anyway, I had to find a way to conduct a DNA test, so I invited her to come over for lunch. And if you remember, everything went wrong, but at least I got my result. She is my biological mother. I never had the opportunity to get to know her better or to tell her that.'

'Who would've known that you are so clever, lady? Now, when I have a chance to meet Maria, I know that you inherited it from her.'

'She is a special, isn't she? She always speaks from her heart, not much from her mind.'

'She believes that you are not alive. The worst part is that I don't know how to tell her what happened when she lost you. If I tell her that I bought you, she will kill me. She will not show mercy to me. She will not understand that I just wanted to help you.'

'...Uncle... I wouldn't tell her now. Let's meet and get to know each other. We'll make something up eventually.'

Days passed by with small talk and the exchange of opinions. Alexander found it very hard to follow Maria, mostly because he didn't know if she was being serious in her statements or if she was mocking him. She always made her point by giving him examples of life situations that he knew very little about. He realised how little he knows about real life and what causes certain difficulties in the lives of the general population. Two different lifestyles, two different understandings, and two different views on life. Maria had the opinion that all the difficulties humans face are caused by the greed of certain groups of people or those who are at the top of interest groups. Alexander's view was that humans are not interested in hard work and are not innovative, so they couldn't find a solution to their issues. Being at the top of this elite group, as she pointed out, it was unthinkable for him to experience, for the first time in his life, that his opinion was not accepted unconditionally and was being questioned. But again, being a very intelligent man and appreciating other opinions, he let Maria tell him that his opinion is not set in stone and may not be the most correct. People in his surroundings always left him thinking that he knew best, but this lady didn't let him think so. It was a blow to his ego, but once he realised that he had to fight to be right, he had to reconsider what he was saying. "Being right or being happy" made him understand this, but he said to himself, "She is not my wife, and this only applies to married couples."

Little did he know that Maria didn't care about being right or wrong; this was the only way to confirm her suspicions. She was way ahead of him, and once she got everything she wanted from him, her dreams began. At first, she thought it was because she had drunk wine before sleeping, or maybe she had eaten something her body didn't agree with. But as she changed everything she thought could be causing her dreams, and the dreams didn't stop, she realised they were conveying messages. She recognised places from who knows where, faces she couldn't place, and situations that seemed familiar but she couldn't remember when they occurred. However, they were so vivid that even after she opened her eyes, she couldn't shake the feeling that these dreams were real. She understood what she was doing in this life, why she faced all these challenges, and what she was supposed to do, as this was the most important thing.

'Maria, do you think that your daughter might still be alive? Have you ever considered other possibilities?'

'Even if she is alive, I still feel remorse. Would it change anything if I knew whether she is was alive?'

'Maybe. You never know.'

'What would I say to her if I met her; I am sorry for not being able to take care of you; others are guilty, not me, of your miserable life?'

'Every child, whether adopted or not raised by their biological parents, would like some answers from their parents in order to move on with their lives.'

'Well, this makes sense maybe to them, but not to parents. You know, my mother never thought it would be beneficial for me to learn about her character. For her, the most important things were: Was I fed? Had I grown up? Did I have a roof over my head? Did I have enough food and clothing for myself? It may sound selfish, but parents only care about this. Did your parents find out about the person inside you? Did they care about the reasons why you were rebellious? Did they ask you about the reasons behind your decisions? Have they cared about what kind of person you will become when you grow up? Have they taken the time to teach you lessons that will help you become a good person? No. It was most important for them to provide you with food and shelter, and to help you become productive and learn how to find a job so that you would not starve. It is quite animalistic, don't you think? So, what did you do? You grew up by copying the character of your parents and the people in your surroundings.'

'Maybe your daughter would like to learn about your character so that she can better understand herself.'

'Maybe. But how important is a genetic inheritance for your behaviour if you have the free will to change what is not good? How much of your character is just learning behaviours taught by society, media, and school? … Do you know who you are?'

'Do you?'

'Yes, I do! I understood who I was many years ago. When I was down on my knees, beaten by everyone. I was crying my heart out. I wanted to please others so that they would love me. If they had loved me, maybe I could have had an easier life. But, no! I was not one of them. They didn't want me. So I asked myself, "Who is in there?" "Who is in front of you? This is you!" - was the answer. I grew up in an area that everyone mocked as being the most primitive in Europe.

Why? Because I didn't have electricity. Was I less human if I didn't wear mini skirts and paint my face? Am I now a more acceptable, evolved human if I do it now? Maybe I was stupid for not having a piece of paper to prove my high intelligence. Am I acceptable now? I did this because I had a predisposition. It was very easy. Do you want to know what wasn't easy? To forgive them for all that they did to me. This was very difficult.'

'Have you really forgiven everyone? Have you never had a need for revenge?'

'I had! Of course, I had! Would it make a difference if I killed someone, if I caused someone the same pain I once experienced? There is a difference between me and others. I knew I would not be able to do that in the way they deserved. I knew that if I raised my hand against someone, I might end up hurting an innocent person, just like I was. What would I do? Continue with the vicious cycle. I knew I was a person from heaven and had to act like one. Heaven, not like someone from Earth.'

'So, what do you gain if you seek revenge from heaven?'

'I didn't want to be someone's teacher. I wanted to be my own teacher and student. You asked me if I know who I am? I am a light-worker. I am a person who is breaking vicious cycles. I am a person who is capable of doing everything correctly, in the way it should be done. And if you wrong me, my light will change this in the way so you will become your own teacher.'

'You are now so confident in yourself that you think everything you are doing is right. Don't you think this is a bit arrogant? Not a single person knows what is right and what is wrong.'

'You will know if you listen to yourself? If you let your ego lead you, maybe you will end up in hell or maybe in paradise. However, if you control your ego, your soul will guide you, and you will discern what is right and what is wrong. Have you ever controlled your ego? Your ego is not your soul.'

How can he counter her arguments? Not possible. "I can only hurt her if I continue." Maybe she will stop talking. She always has to be right, making me wrong. It is ridiculous. I just have to bring Stella. I will see how she will behave then.

'What are your thoughts on Venice? We will be going to Venice for a couple of days. Have you ever been there?'

'Venice is my neighbourhood. Of course, I have been there. It is the most romantic place on Earth. Maybe there are more interesting places on Earth, but Venice reminds me of the small world. If stones could speak, what would they tell you?'

'So, you will be enjoying a visit to Venice tomorrow. Stella is coming to your Centre of Universe.'

'Oh, how lovely. I know she will appreciate all the art and craft created by ancient craftsmen. I know she will appreciate the beauty and the romantic souls of the past inhabitants that they left for us to enjoy.'

'Okay, so I am not sophisticated enough to fully appreciate the beauty and intellect of the town builders from the past. Only women can understand this. Men have not yet evolved.'

Alexander loved having Stella around him, sometimes even more than his family. She was like Maria; she never closed her mouth, throwing words without thinking, constantly challenging his intellect. Interestingly, he was never bored or tired of what she was saying. Maybe Maria thinks that he is suffering from listening to all her babbling and brainstorming, but actually, he can listen and relax without saying a word. He let his mind flow in the direction of the words coming out of her mouth without making an effort to engage his brain cells. Tomorrow, he will have two of these, so he will be merely their shadow, walking behind them, acting as their silent lackey. He will be just the spirit of the town's past. He will need a mask. Perhaps he should buy one along with a tricorn or gondolier hat, depending on the role he will have.

The yacht arrived at the marina at the same time Stella arrived at the train station. They didn't want to waste their time relaxing, so Alexander, as he had predicted, had to accommodate both ladies and fulfil their wishes. Two giggling women, after hugging like two ducks, hand in hand towards the canal, leaving Alexander to chase after them like a young boy. "What is this? This is even worse than I thought."

'Ladies, if you want, I can let you go by yourselves in the town. Obviously, you don't need me to accompany you.'

'No, Uncle, I am sorry. Poor man. We are really horrible. Come to the middle we'll hold your hands.'

'So, you will not lose us. - added Maria, laughing at his confusion when she touched his hand.

"Why is she touching my hand? She is not my wife, and I am not attracted to her. Is she flirting with me? How should I act? Cold. I will not give much attention to it." He was usually calm and well-behaved, but he was losing his peace when they entered each shop along the way.'

'The same! All of the products are the same, girls. Why do you have to go into every shop along the way? I thought you would like to visit museums and churches. Didn't you say, Maria, that you wished to see and appreciate art?'

'Yes, today we are going shopping, and tomorrow we will visit museums. And churches... Are you losing your nerve with us, Alexander?'

'Women! All of you are the same, just variations... Okay, this is the last shop we are going to. You have internet, so please shop there.'

"So, this is the cross she was talking about!"? His heart stopped, and his mind drifted somewhere else. Maria's tattoo was revealed when she changed into the dress she had just bought at the shop. She didn't want to be indecent in front of a man who meant nothing to her. It wasn't tattoo only she didn't want to be seen, bullet mark as well. It was a mark of a devil as she was saying to herself. Alexander couldn't stop staring at the tattoo on her lower back. It was a very artistic cross, wrapped with thorny red roses and adorned with bloody tears. All that she had been telling him lately kept crossing his mind as he tried to find his answers. Didn't she say that she got the cross tattooed just before the war after her grandmother passed away? She knew something was coming that she would need to protect herself from, just as her female ancestors had protected themselves. Was this just a coincidence? But Maria didn't believe in coincidences.

Maria was looking at Alexander in the mirror in front of her. He looked straight at her tattoo and appeared puzzled. His arms crossed on his chest like he was trying to protect himself showing that he wasn't very happy to see this. His vision appeared, bringing him back to another place and time.

Just in a second, his mind was absent, but it looked as long as three days of struggle he buried somewhere in the back of his memory. His mind, triggered by the tattoo he was revelled to, brought him to a place he didn't want to be ever again, not even in his thoughts. But here he was, hearing his name being called out as he was pointed to join a group of heavily armed soldiers. Together with another observer, he hopped on a truck full of soldiers, being driven to an unfamiliar place without knowing the reason for his call. When the truck stopped and they jumped out, he was fully aware of what would happen minutes after. Men of all ages have been lined up on one side while his companions from the truck were on the other side. The command fell, "shoot." Adrenaline wiped away his emotions, and time seemed to stop as the deafening sound of gunfire filled the air. Captives were falling to the ground as if it were a game. His mind, just for a brief moment, thought that this was really just a game. But it wasn't. Blood was flowing out of bodies, causing tremors and revealing within organs. Some of the captives attempted to escape in front of the soldiers but were gunned down, falling in slow motion onto the tall grass, concealing their final moments. He was not aware of his thoughts or actions until some soldiers brought him back to reality by swearing and shouting at him. "Take a gun and help us finish our job. We don't have time. Help us out, you worthless idiot! Why are you standing, you little girl? Shoot, or I will shoot you! Here, take one and finish him!!" A young boy with short hair and his hand behind his back was thrown under his feet. "Shoot, you pussy! If you can't kill a man, here is the boy. Be a man and finish him! What, you don't want to? Shoot, or I will shoot you!" He felt the cold metal against his warm, sweaty forehead. His mind ceased rational thinking. Instead, he remembered his mother's books, a hanging skeleton in her room. He heard a shot come out of his hand. The body fell. "This is how it should be done! Bravo! Now, shoot in that direction!!"His soul returned to his body after a couple of hours. It was as if the soul was ashamed of the body that had done that shameful thing. He sat down on the grass, head down, looking at the blood he sat in. Not far from him, his first victim showed signs of life. He looked on in horror as soldiers brutally finished off still-living bodies with cold weapons. He needed to save at least one life. One life is enough to seek forgiveness for choosing his own life over others.

'No, not that one. This one is mine. I need a souvenir.'

'Ah, Okay. As you wish. Do whatever you want. It is dead, anyway. I am tired. I will go for a drink. Are you coming?'

While pretending to drink and take drugs, he was thinking about how to return to the field and try to help the young boy. A command came to go back while it was night and collect some bodies and displace them to other locations. He was taken without too many questions, and this was his resolution. Powerful searchlights lit up the field, helping soldiers to select bodies. Alexander found the body of the young boy and, instead of placing it on a stack in a truck, he cunningly deceived the soldiers and put it in the car. In the early morning, he secretly transported the body to a hospital located miles away from the field. He handed it over to a male nurse who immediately called the doctor, and within seconds, the process of reviving took place.

'You! Come over! Let's smoke a cigarette outside.' – the on-duty doctor called Alexander outside of the hospital in private while looking at him directly in Alexander's eyes like he already knew all the answers. However, after a couple of minutes, he decided that it would be better to go inside to his office.

'Where did you find this girl?'

'A girl? I thought it was a boy.'

'Obviously, your mother didn't teach you the basics of human anatomy. It is a girl, man, a girl!'

'I found her in the backyard of a house in a village.'

'Which village?'

'I don't know. I don't know this place. Does it matter?'

'It matters, of course. I look at you, and I have all my answers. My people are dying everywhere, and I am aiding an enemy. But how can I stop being human? Look, has anyone seen you coming here tonight? If someone sees you, we will both be dead.'

'I don't know. I was cautious, but I'm unsure if anyone noticed me entering.'

'I suggest you go somewhere where you will not be seen or heard. I will take care of the girl for three days, and on the third day, I will leave you a message indicating where to come and pick her up. I hope it will be worth betraying my nation. I can't believe I'm doing this, but I am a doctor. I swore to help anyone in need. You should go to the coffee shop near the park and request a doctor's tonic.'

Three long sleepless days, vomiting and screaming silently, without food or drink, slowly losing sanity. However, he knew that what had been done belonged to the past. He couldn't go back and retract his decisions. Regrets didn't have any meaning. Hope that the doctor will save at least one soul was very small. But this is all he had. No matter how small it was, there was still hope. He showed up at the agreed time and place, and at the bottom of the glass, there was a piece of paper with the time and place written on it. Early in the morning, while it was still dark, he discovered the body of his first victim amidst other dead bodies, waiting to be collected in the hospital's backyard. He had to be there before the military truck arrived to collect and bury the bodies. He noticed the marks on her toes and fingers. He lifted the white sheet, and, for the first time, he saw the face. It was the face of the girl who had given him a strange look in the refugee convoy. He picked her up and put her in the car trunk. It took him almost the whole day, passing from one point to another, until he reached the border of Croatia. While he was driving, all his thoughts were in the back of the car. When he arrived in front of the hospital, which was still in a military zone, he prayed that she was still alive. He opened the car boot, and this was the time he saw her tattoo. A cross emerges from the centre of a rose, surrounded by tears. A nurse and a soldier approached him, bringing a chair and helping her out of the boot. They shouted at him to follow them and provide information about her, but he didn't, even though he had promised. He was completely shattered, and all he needed was a moment of tranquillity. A grenade fell nearby, causing soldiers and police to shout at civilians to run away. He got in his car and ran toward the Capitol.

It took him a couple of months to breathe again without remorse and guilt. His mind stored the memory somewhere in the back of his mind, as it was the only thing he could do. He was not allowed to tell anyone where he was, what he had done, and what he had seen. He was scared not only that he would have to face legal consequences, or moral, but also because he knew it was his ultimate failure as a human being. He was playing God, taking someone's life out of fear for his own.

Maria stood calmly, waiting for him to finish his contemplation and come back to reality, which he did after he noticed that she had allowed him to see this. She patiently waited for him as she wanted to see his reaction; as she knew all.

'It is the same as mine. It looks very old. You said you made it just before the war.'

'Yes, this is the first thing I have done after my grandmother passed away. I went into the city and found the best tattoo artist available. I told him what I wanted, and he made it even more beautiful. He didn't take a picture of it. How did you know what you wanted? I saw it on your chest.'

'I had been dreaming about this for many years. I just had to do it. I don't have any more tattoos, just that one. I thought it meant something. But now, I don't know.'

'It means all my life. All of my struggles, all of my pain, all of my tears. Cross means more to me, like a destiny, something I had to endure, and roses are a symbol of my soul. I didn't know at that time what it meant, but now I know.'

'Uncle, stop dreaming. Wake up. Let's go further.'

A day passed, struggling to understand what had happened to them. All they said to each other, all the things that happened to them, made them think whether there is something greater than themselves, beyond their will and comprehension, that is crucial for them to understand. A few more days passed, enjoying the charm of the old town and exploring every corner of its rich history. Stella was the only one who spoke, trying to entertain them. However, she also sensed that something was amiss with those two. They have been lost in their thoughts, silent and absent-minded, yet physically present. "Did they fight? I would have heard something. They were fine when I arrived. Have I caused something? I don't want them to fight. I want both of them in my life. If they fight, I have to choose a side, and this is what I want to avoid."

'Stella and Alexander, I have to thank you for these past couple of weeks together. I had a wonderful time, and you have been great hosts. Thank you from the bottom of my heart. But now, the time has arrived for everyone to go their separate ways. I want both of you to know that if the situation was different, I would love you both from the bottom of my heart. But this is not possible. You don't belong to me.'

'Maria, before you proceed, I need to know something.'

'What do I need to know, my love? I know it all.'

'Maybe you don't know Maria. You should listen to what Stella has to tell you first.'

'I don't want to hear what I already know. And this is what I want to say: you don't belong to me. You are here in this life, not for myself, but for the sake of your uncle... I lost you, not because I have been a bad mother or couldn't give you the life you deserved. I have just been a life bringer, your life bringer. I loved you so much; only a mother understands that. I tried to keep you, but you were taken away from me. Maybe this was caused by the evil in those people who took you away. I don't want to judge, but I prefer to believe that this was caused by fate. It took me a long time to understand that you were given to me for a reason and taken away for a reason. Now, these days, I understand why. You healed my soul and my heart.'

'So you know about me, Mum.'

'Stella, my dear, my heart, my light, I gave birth to you. Yes, I know that you are the child I gave birth to, but I am not your mum. Your mother is the woman who raised you to be such a good person. She was above your head when you cried. She was the one who offered her hand when you fell and bled. She is the one who taught you how to sing, talk, dance, and laugh. I haven't been able to do that. Your dad protected you when you were threatened. He taught you maths when you couldn't do your assignment. He was the one who made you proud of him. I wasn't that. If you stayed with me, you would suffer. I was working as a cleaning lady at that time, trying to make ends meet. I wouldn't be able to buy food for you. I wouldn't be able to buy you clothes. I wouldn't be able to provide you with shelter. You could become a victim of sick and vicious people. You would probably be caught in the middle of your father and me, listening to us fighting every day. You would probably hate me very much, wishing I had never brought you into this world. But that was not the purpose of your life. You found your uncle and went to live with him.'

'I guess you know everything that happened during the days when you lost Stella.'

'I don't, Alexander, but this is not important at all. I thank you for saving the life of a human being. I don't care if you gave money to get her. I don't care if you were the one who took her from the church. I don't care if you took her for different purposes. I don't care!!! All I care about is that she is alive and that you have given her a life that I would never be able to provide. I thank your sister for taking on the role of Stella's mother. Even more, your brother-in-law gave me hope that humanity will survive by taking an orphan under his protection and loving her as if she were his own, despite not knowing anything about the baby. Maybe all of you had other intentions that were not as noble as I would like to believe, but in the end, Stella is happy with all of you. You gave her what I wouldn't have given her if she had stayed with me.'

'I really didn't want to disturb your peace, Mum, Maria... - she said, tears streaming down her face.'

'Stella, I knew you were coming to meet me when you sent the message to my nephews. One of them found me and told me about you. I never spoke to my siblings, but again, you can't stop being human. My siblings gave you some directions on how to find me. I know you came to the company where I worked in Croatia. My colleagues informed me that my daughter had come to visit me. I knew it was you. I didn't have any contact information or name to find you. You hired a recruiter from the UK to offer me a job, which I accepted. Too many coincidences, don't you think so? Finally, you came to the practice where I met you and offered me a job. You are the spitting image of my grandmother. She looked the same when she was your age. I didn't want to disturb your peace, my love… I let you play this role until today, but today, I have to stop everything.'

'What makes a difference, one day or another day? Why today?'

'I understood many things today. Most of them are important to me, perhaps not as much to you.'

'What did I do to make you reject me? Why don't you want to stay with me? I want to get to know you better...'

'Stella, all you need to know about me is already in you. Yes, I gave birth to you, and I love you with all my heart. However, please try to understand that you are not here solely for me. You are here for your uncle. I don't know how else to explain it to you.'

'I know he took me away from you. I apologise for that. I am really sorry.'

'Stella, please, behave yourself. Stop crying and begging. If Maria doesn't want to have anything to do with you, let her go. You will survive. I wanted to give you some answers, some peace of mind... but this depends on Maria. Let time work for all of us. Maybe we'll get answers in the future.'

'Alexander, all the answers are within you as well. You cannot find peace, and you don't know why. I am not your answer. But as you said, when the time comes, you will get all your answers in the same way that I obtained mine.'

'Would you like to share your discovery with us, Maria?'

'No, not today. One day, perhaps, but for now, I need to continue on my way.'

A storm came, changing the monotony for these three people. Peace arrived the next morning when they separated from each other. All lost in their thoughts, consumed by sadness, and trapped in their own mental bubbles, they went their separate ways and led separate lives.

***

After three decades of wandering, Maria decided to return to Bosnia. With her education and experience, it wasn't difficult for her to find a job as a professor at the university. A humble peasant from a lofty mountain finally received the respect worth of a human being. No one could find a word to belittle her. She found the strength to leave her past behind and forgive her people. She wanted to hate them, but she decided to forgive them. They were all tricked. They were all victims of their foolishness and ambitions. Even those who gained material wealth lost their peace of mind. The true freedom is in being fearless. If you don't feel fear, no one can break you apart, enslave you, or hurt you. Maria was there. She never felt fear, even when she thought her days were coming to an end. She survived despite the difficulties. Not that she survived, but she lived her life to the fullest, embracing the destiny that was given to her. She met unique individuals, like herself, who supported her in her personal development. She understood that she could contribute a lot to young people who are embarking on life with dreams of healing the earth and surpassing their parents' achievements. The knowledge is not hard to obtain, whether it be from a university or the streets. The hard part is what you will do with the knowledge you have acquired.

After many months, Maria decided to return to the mountains to seek forgiveness and heal her emotional wounds. Nothing was the same as it had been in her mind. There was no road to walk on when she went to school. Now, there was a gravel road leading towards the mountain peak. Houses in the village were unrecognizable. There was a new school for the younger generation, who were preoccupied only with their childish problems. They don't know about the dramas that took place on their playgrounds. They are now playing football with plastic balls. They didn't know that sometimes children played football with actual human heads. It is better for them not to know that. She was looking at them, thinking about what kind of people they would become in a couple of years. Will they take guns again and fight each other? Will they become the worst enemies if politicians manipulate their minds? Will they be smart enough to recognise who their real enemy is? Will they be smarter than previous generations? Will they be strong enough to overcome their weaknesses, or are they weaker than previous generations?

The forest she used to know has changed a lot. It looked like she was going to a park. No animals on the horizon. She barely heard birds chirping. She looked at her legs. She wore expensive hiking boots and clothes. She was grateful for the rubber boots she wore with woollen socks when she was little. She didn't have a waterproof jacket while walking in snow higher than her size. Her woollen, handmade coat was all wet, opening a path through the snow. But all children have been like her. She was not different from them. They didn't know for better. Most of them lived with their grandparents while their parents worked abroad. They ate bread and fresh cheese on their way to school. She was sad because she didn't have parents and because she didn't live in the village. She was not alone in her sadness; there were many children experiencing the same emotions. They didn't understand the purpose of their lives. If they knew what would happen to them in a few years, they would enjoy their lives more. They wouldn't mind any difficulties they might face. The entire generations of people were destroyed due to the greed of politicians. Next time, they should sacrifice their children first to satisfy their greed and ambition. Next time, parents should be smarter and prevent their children from participating in the madness of politicians. Next time, humans should recognise the madness aimed at them. Next time, humans should be smarter in recognizing mad leaders. They should hold them accountable for their leadership. There shouldn't be a next time if humans are smart. They should stop crazy ideas in their minds. Humans should evolve to a higher level.

Maria reached the top of the mountain, searching for her village, but there was not a single trace of houses that existed in that place. Nature has taken over human work and wiped out the history of human existence. How many generations have lived in that place? How many human tragedies does this mountain keep hiding? Snow falls every season, covering the traces of humans walking on the mountain soil. Every spring, when the snow melts away, the mountain reveals its vibrant colours, bringing new life and meaning. Seasons are changing. This is how it has been for the past three decades, showing the true power of life on Earth. Nature is the true owner of this planet; humans are seasonal intruders, and their stories hold little significance on a higher level. As humans look down on ants while walking on them, this is how nature looks down on humans. Maria's life story was not recognised by her mountain, forest, or wild animals. She was not important. She was just a seasonal intruder like many before her. She loved her mountain. For some reason, she wanted to believe that the mountain loved her in return. However, upon realising the absence of any signs of human presence, such as houses, she came to understand that humans are merely visitors on Earth and should not attach such significance to themselves. They cannot be nature saviours. Nature can heal itself without human intervention. "Know your place!!"- she heard the whisper of the mountain. No matter what, she felt a connection with the place. It is the place where she belonged.

Coming back to her work, she was thinking, would it be possible to revive the place if she had a good project. Will she find an investor who will help her bring life to the mountain? Unfortunately, the project was not good enough for foreign banks to grant her a loan. She turned to local authorities, but they thought she was crazy. Who would want to live in a rough environment? "People live in the North Pole, why wouldn't we try?" she screamed back at them. But, no results. She should use her students to generate ideas on how to attract investors.

A year has almost passed since she was on the yacht with Alexander. She found peace in her soul. She immersed herself in various activities just to distract herself from thinking about him. The project on her mountain started a couple of months ago when she received donations that her students initiated on social media. In rare moments of peace, she waited for him or Stella to find her. She missed both of them, but there was no sound of their presence. One night she was looking at her pictures on her phone and came across a photo that had been taken of him secretly. She sighed and quietly said, "If you're still struggling to find your answers, come to me, and I will tell you everything about yourself and me."

Maria was sitting by the fire that her students had lit. All of them had been city children, disconnected from nature, so they had a different vision of being in nature than she did. They thought it would be romantic to roast corn on a campfire, so she let them do it. She stayed looking at the campfire, fearing her students will cause a disaster with their romance, looking at the stars and contemplating. Suddenly, she felt a strange energy nearby. She understood that Alexander was behind her.

'Come sit by the fire. The stars are very clear tonight. You can read your future if you wish... I haven't heard your car.'

'I didn't come with a car on the top. I came on foot. I remember very well these mountains.'

'You could have escaped from here more quickly if you had been in a car.'

'I don't want to escape. I am ready to face the truth.'

'You can't find bears any more. All of them are dancing for Europeans. You can find very rare wolves, but they are so well-educated and well-behaved that they will not steal to survive. So, it's only me who can make you scared.'

"He didn't even smile. He was very determined to come here. And he lost a significant amount of weight. How tired he looks..."

'I came here for a reason. For the truth.'

'Is everything alright with you?'

'Nothing is alright with me. I don't know what is going on with me. Maybe midlife crisis. I don't know. My whole life turned upside down. I can't find anything that motivates me to move forward. I have strange nightmares. I don't understand why. I heard your voice calling me, so I thought maybe you were in trouble. This is why I came.'

'Yes, I called you. I called you to tell you the truth.'

'Ok.'

"How can I tell him? Will he believe? Will he think I'm crazy? He is too focused on the material world. He will never believe me if I tell him the truth. I have to tell him, even though he will not believe it."

Farewell, Farewell

Till we meet again

Sparks in our eyes

Will tell secrets

Of our past lives.

I will find you in the depths of hell

And I will give you my hand

You will show me the beauty of paradise

While healing my earthly wounds.

We came as soldiers of the universe

Divided into two parts

We promised each other to hold our hands

For eternity, until we become one.

Farewell, farewell

My dearest friend in the universe

My other part of my soul

My sorrow and my joy

Remember, while I am gone

You are never alone.

I am waiting for you to come

In the world where I dwell

Waiting for you to meet us again.

'It sounds so beautiful hearing you are singing this song. How do you know it? I thought, this was my song.' – He joined, singing it while she was on the half of the song.

'It wasn't only yours. It was ours. It is hard to believe in these things, but there is something above us, above our earthly understanding.'

'I think I am prepared to listen to you if you wish to enlighten me, Urruh.'

'Two entities were sent to Earth,: two souls, one white and one black. The one was called Urruh, and the other was Arahdahl. One carried positive energy, while the other carried negative energy. The white soul had to know only what was good and positive, while the black soul only knew what was bad and negative. In the beginning, neither of them could solve any of the tasks given to them because the white soul did not understand what was good, and the black soul did not understand what was bad. Urruh was a soldier of light, while Arahdahl was a soldier of darkness. Those two souls fell in love with each other. They couldn't live without each other. They tried to separate, but they couldn't. They thought that if they separated from each other, they would be able to do their jobs better. However, they soon realised that it would be more beneficial for them to unite. The souls realised that they had to unite and combine their efforts in order to discern between what is good and what is bad. Working together, their emotions overflowed. They were in love with each other. However, being of different kinds, they experienced love and hate simultaneously. Teachers from both entities were dissatisfied because they were unable to obtain any results from them, and both soldiers failed to carry out their assigned tasks. So, the teachers came up with a plan. They were told that both entities would only return home if they overcame all earthly hardships and completed all the tasks assigned to them. Urruh and Arahdahl realised that they would only achieve this if they united, setting aside their love and hate, and worked together instead of fighting or loving each other. They decided to merge their worlds and experience the same things together by following instructions. Urruh, experiencing bad things in the world of Arahdahl, understood the concept of goodness, while Arahdahl, in the realm of light, discovered the true meaning of evil. The reward for learning was a ticket home, so Urruh, who was not afraid of the bad, solved tasks faster than Arahdahl. Arahdahl did not develop well without the guidance and help of Urruh, so he lagged behind in progress. One day, Urruh completed all the tasks she was assigned and was allowed to go home. Arahdahl, realizing that he was not progressing as quickly without Urruh, became consumed by jealousy and replaced his love for her with hatred. He despised Urruh so much that he slandered her in front of the teachers just to bring her down to his level. The teachers, understanding the situation, gave Urruh an ultimatum: either she would rise to their level, or she would be sent back down to earth, never to return, even though she didn't belong there. But Urruh, made of light and love, didn't want Arahdahl to suffer any more. She was a skilled negotiator, and she successfully persuaded the teachers to grant her a little more time to complete everything she had on her mind. She returned to Earth under the condition that the Arahdahl recognised her. If he recognises her, she will entrust her fate to him. However, Arahdahl did not recognise her on Earth. She was free to return home and become a teacher, but Arahdahl would stay on Earth forever. She loved him so much that, despite the ultimatum, she exercised her right to choose. Therefore, she decided to stay with Arahdahl on Earth until he also reached the same level as Urruh. She decided to disregard the guidance of her teachers and made the decision that they would both return home together as one unit.'

"Wait, did he just call me Urruh?"

'Nice to meet you again Urruh. My name is Arahdahl. You gave me a hard time to find you, indeed. But here I am. How did you manage to organise our meeting, I wonder?'

'How did I manage to organise everything without you being suspicious? I used Tarah. I used the geographical position on Earth that you might be interested in and the body that you might not be interested in.'

'Sorry, darling. I knew you were Urruh all along, but I let you play your role. I recognised the tattoo that moment I saw it, on the field. I almost failed, badly. I realised that I couldn't bring myself to hurt you, fearing that it would alter my destiny and my existence. But it wasn't fear only in question. It was self-doubt. I didn't trust myself. I was very confused.'

'Ah yes, that place. This assignment was my choice of challenging you. It was my test given to you. I wanted to know if there is a chance to change you. You haven't failed. On the contrary, you gave me the indication that I was right to trust you.'

'Tell me, how did you involve Tarah in this?'

'I had an agreement with her: if I manage to bring you home forever, I would let both you and her live in peace. She was greedy. For someone who is a priestess, she should have known better. I needed an intermediary to accomplish what I had planned. I didn't want to be too close to you, making the same mistakes, or too far away that I couldn't find you. I needed her because of her love for you. I connected my energy to hers. I told her secrets on how to be your light in the darkness and your guide in hard times. She didn't know much about it, and she thought that what I told her would be enough to keep you on her side forever. She severed ties with me, thinking she could deceive me and come to you. This was not possible, was it? Love is not enough to keep someone by, isn't it? When she realised that she was losing you once again and she wouldn't be able to keep you, at least not in the way she had hoped for, she made the decision to connect me with you.'

'I believe she now understands the meaning of soul attraction. I was kind of happy when she told me that she is was getting married. She said she had found her soulmate. Maybe she will find peace after all.'

'I hope you will understand your assignment as well, Alexander.'

'I don't understand how did you survive the terror… How did you survive? This nightmare is not leaving me the peace. How?'

'When you shot me, I found myself in front of luminous beings, in a certain council and heard them say, "They failed again. I knew that giving them one last chance was a waste of time. Look at what his representative did to our being." "You are absolutely right,; they were never trustworthy." "We shouldn't waste our time with them." "I share the same opinion." "We were very clear that if their representative doesn't change their actions, we will eliminate the entire nation." " They mocked us, again!" "It is time for our action." "They failed to change." "No more mercy for them." '

'Honourable members of the Council. You listened to me the first time. I beg you to listen to me again.'

'Urruh, you should be on our side. You played the most significant role in the entire action. Don't you think they will never change? Look what Arahdahl did to you. It is time to step aside and let us finish with them.'

'Please, let me speak first, and then you can make the decision.'

'Go ahead! Speak!'

'Every nation sent representatives to achieve what it wanted. You decided to send me to learn. I failed. Over and over. You haven't been satisfied with the results I have brought you, just as you haven't been satisfied with my predecessors. You blamed me for not being able to fully utilise my potential. And I couldn't, indeed. But I met Arahdahl, who was in the same situation. We joined forces and achieved something. We brought results that you were satisfied with. You asked which energy we should be a part of. You decided that we should harness the power of light and positive energy at a specific frequency. This happened only thanks to the Arahdahl nation. They helped, and you discovered that positive energy is lighter and more productive, but without negative, we were not moving in the right direction. You have decided that the experience I brought you is satisfying and educational. It is beneficial for our nation. All of your decisions were made based on the experience I had together with Arahdahl. You decided that the level I reached was good enough to finalise my cycle. You examined my spiritual evolution and marked it as the highest. But what you have to understand is that negative energy is stronger, heavier, and harder to evolve or move to a higher level. This has nothing to do with intelligence; both positive and negative energy carry equal intelligence. It is you who said that positive energy is connected with spirituality and negative energy is connected with the physical realm. Are you sure this is bad enough to condemn the entire nation? Arahdahl and his nation are making efforts to balance the spiritual and physical realms, unlike us, who only desire the spiritual. It would be extremely ungrateful to destroy someone who helped you reach the stage you aspire to be, by isolating and rejecting your benefactor. It is we who left Arahdahl at a lower level. It is we who took advantage of them. We never gave them credit for what they did for us.'

'We gave them too much credit. Too many opportunities. They played victims while they were oppressors. All the evil comes from them. So many nations suffered from them while they were pretending to be victims. We were all watching, not knowing or willing to find out who to blame. We were weak and ineffective in protecting others.'

'By eliminating one nation, we will not become stronger. We will demonstrate the power of leadership by showing them their rightful place. Their place is among us, not behind us, not above or below us. They have incredible potential, but we need to help them achieve it. It will be beneficial for us to show them that they are equally as good as we are. They will teach us to become even stronger, utilizing their knowledge and strategies of offence and defence. If you wish to defeat an enemy, you should use their strategy. How can you learn this if you eliminate them?'

'So you are not their friend after all, but you use them for learning?'

'Isn't this the point of life? To learn, so you can avoid repeating the same mistakes.'

'But they are making the same mistakes. It seems they are not able to overcome their weakness. Or maybe they provoke us to learn about our weaknesses?'

'If they find someone better than themselves, they will learn from them. They will realise their mistakes and improve their actions. If you threaten them, they may alter their strategy to survive, but they will not evolve or recognise the mistakes they are consistently making. If they feel threatened, they will attempt to defeat anyone who is their enemy, and their enemies are anyone who does not support their illusions. Eventually, they will defeat everyone through fear. Everyone will defend their mistakes only because they are afraid of facing them. Our fear and inability to comprehend their actions will be our downfall. But not ours only. It will be theirs as well. They are trying to gain knowledge by probing our strategies and weaknesses. Do we know what our weakness is?'

'What you're trying to say is that we need them in order to learn more? Are we not omniscient beings? Do we need them to be stronger? Are we not the strongest?'

'If we were the strongest and omniscient, we wouldn't be here now discussing the future of their nation, but also our own future.'

'Urruh is right. We need to learn in order to preserve our freedom and secure our future. Unfortunately, we need Arahdahl and Asbu nation. I have to admit that his nation is very brave, and he is as well. Urruh convinced me that in order for us to be strong, we need to act weaker, leaving the brave ones to reveal problems and solutions that we are not yet aware of. Arrahdahl is really a courageous leader and explorer, showing us the real power and strength. I admit that we wouldn't be able to face challenges he is facing and overcome all of it by continuing with life.'

'What does this mean for us? Should we allow this wrong doing nation to harass us until we disappear?'

'No, they should be aware that we are monitoring and learning from them. If they become aware that we know their weakness, they will behave.'

'If we eliminate them, we wouldn't have to worry any more.'

'A strong leader doesn't bring easy solutions. He brings clever solutions. Eliminating an entire nation is a sign of weakness and low intelligence because it shows a tendency towards seeking bad solutions. What will be the future of our leaders and nations after that?

Victor and the victim will be equal. Positive and negative will be equalised but not harmonised. Who will be the teacher, and who will be the student? You gave his nation the right to choose, so they had a chance to choose, but you took this from us. We had never had a choice. Instead, you gave us compassion and understanding. I ask for equal opportunity.'

'Urruh, we need a quick solution, not necessarily easy.'

'Maybe you should give our nation the right to choose and his nation compassion and understanding. Allow me to go back and show the solution to Arahdahl. I realised that his nation had developed consciousness and remorse. I hope they will have the willpower to accept their actions as something that should be changed for their benefit. They cannot enslave or eliminate other nations; if they continue doing that, they will disappear trying to do so.'

'Alright, Urruh, go back and try to do that! We are leaving their destiny into your hands. - They sent me back to the same body to finish my work.'

After a long silence, Maria was thinking while looking at his serious face whether he believed her. He didn't show emotions on his face, but he looked engaged in deep contemplation. Or perhaps they were using each other again in their game. He recognised Urruh after he had seen her, but also he raised his hand at her.

'I don't believe they would have brought a decision to eliminate us. I don't think they had the courage to make such a drastic decision. We are the strongest!'

'You exist only because we give you that choice. Darkness is only a result of a lack of light. Not the opposite. We allow you to exist, to live. There is no life without a light. In a pure darkness, nothing can grow, nothing can rise, nothing happens. You thought you were the masters of the Universe, but we are the ones that own you. We gave you the right to experience the "benefits" of darkness, but you were the one who was escaping into the light, desiring both pleasure of flash and peace of holiness. You were the one who couldn't choose so you flirt with both sides. You still chose the dark because you were not strong enough to reach all the challenges of existence, lying to yourself that you are happy, but you don't know that happiness belongs to us. Happiness is not a feeling that people living in darkness can experience; this is a lie taken from the time when you lived in light. It is you who believed there was an easier and quicker way of shifting in the realm, but actually, you made one step forward and two backwards. You can't lie to the Universe. They created us. They are our programmers. There are no Masters of the Universe. You believe you are the strongest if you take someone's right to live or show mercy to continue living. You are poor beings! You are shape-shifters with a blessing to grow and choose. So choose. If you want to live, you have to come out to the light because life belongs to the light. Without a life and light, darkness doesn't have the power to exist.'

'Are we going to be weak if we shape our current existence? We'll be in a huge pain from what we might see.'

'Weak? No. The knowledge and truth belong to the strongest one. How can you be weak if you possess all the knowledge of how to defeat weaknesses.'

'We will feel the pain of flesh if we will do not have enough knowledge to protect ourselves.'

'Yes, you will feel the pain of the flesh. If you have had to choose the shorter material pain and longer spiritual pain, what would you choose?'

'I would've felt defeated if I saw that my executor didn't experience the same pain as I had to go through.'

'I am looking at my executor right now! I have no feelings whatsoever for him. No wishes to see your pain, no remorse, no gratitude, no hate, no love, nothing. I don't need your sorrow, no excuses, no explanation. I don't need anything from you. You punished yourself already by choosing yourself. You chose to live with remorse and fear that someone might retaliate against you. Maybe your family will understand what you did, the people you love. Maybe you will be stripped of the earthly privileges you have. I understand that you will justify yourself by not having the power of choice because your life depended on someone's power, so you chose yourself. Maybe the one who pressured you to shoot at me was pressured as well. He has chosen his life over yours, and you chose your life over mine. But here we are. Do you have power over your life now by looking at my eyes? What do you choose right now, darkness or light?'

'I need light. I am tired of darkness in my soul. Indeed, I have a life; I live, but truly, I am dead; I live in darkness. Every day I wake up with hope someone will give me a hand and pull me out of this state. Tell me what I should do now.'

'Now? You belong now to me. We will continue our learning. This time, you will be my student, and I will examine you and punish you if necessary. I will give you a hand to understand what your decisions are causing. I suggest you listen to my teaching as there are no other choices. I can be as bad as you are if necessary, and trust me, Light can be a much stronger executor if it has to be the one. I need you to find your potential and balance your nature. I don't want to change your nature, rather to direct you because light cannot fight against the dark in the same way. Darkness used the light to fight against the light, but now I will ask the darkness to fight against darkness in the same way you made us fight. Both light and dark will unite to reach the same goal and that is to balance the Universe. At the end I need to take you home, Arahdahl, as I need to go home, too. We will go together as one unit. We promised each other, each life, that we would come back to take one another home, as this is what I am doing now.'

***